Friend or Foe

MISSION POINT PRESS

Readers are encouraged to go to www.MissionPointPress.
com to contact the author or to find information on how to
buy this book in bulk at a discounted rate.

Published by Mission Point Press
2554 Chandler Rd.
Traverse City, MI 49696
(231) 421-9513
www.MissionPointPress.com

ISBN: 978-1-950659-16-6
Library of Congress Control Number
available upon request

Printed in the United States of America

Friend or Foe

J.R. Seeger

book 2 in the   MIKE4 series

MISSION POINT PRESS

This book is dedicated to the men and women who work in the shadows, fight in the night, and keep us safe.

> *I keep six honest serving men,*
> *(they taught me all I knew);*
> *Their names are What and Why*
> *And How and Where and Who.*
>
> *I send them over land and sea,*
> *I send them East and West;*
> *But after they have worked for me,*
> *I give them all a rest.*
>
> *I let them rest from nine 'til five.*
> *For I am busy then*
> *As well as breakfast, lunch, and tea.*
> *For they are hungry men.*
> *But different folk have different views;*
> *I know a person small,*
> *She keeps ten million serving-men.*
> *Who get no rest at all!*
>
> *She sends 'em abroad on her own affairs,*
> *From the second she opens her eyes,*
> *One million Hows, two million Wheres,*
> *And seven million Whys!*
>
> *—Rudyard Kipling*

CONTENTS

AAR: after action report

Alpha: Surveillance terminology for a target location of interest.

Bravo: Surveillance terminology for a person of interest.

BTK: Acronym for below the knee amputation.

Charlie: Surveillance terminology for a vehicle of interest.

COS: Chief of Station. The senior CIA officer in a field station.

CPU: car pickup

CQB: Close quarters battle aka urban assault operations.

CSM: Command Sergeant Major. The senior non-commissioned rank in the US Army.

CWO: Chief Warrant Officer. A military rank with ratings from CWO1 to CWO5

DCOS: Deputy Chief of Station. The number two officer in a CIA station.

Downrange: A generic term applied to any combat tour.

FOB: forward operating base

Foxtrot: Surveillance term for walking surveillance, in contrast to vehicle surveillance.

FWD: forward. When a command is split in multiple locations, each of the locations outside the main headquarters are listed as "fwd." In this story, both Balad airbase and Bagram airbase have a SOF(FWD) contingent.

Glock: An Austrian pistol manufacturer. Glock pistols in this book are Glock19 (a compact pistol) and Glock26 (a subcompact pistol). Both are chambered in 9mm.

Green eyes: Night vision goggles, aka NVG.

Head of station: UK term for the head of the British intelligence in a field station. Also, "station commander."

HF: high frequency radio transmission.

HOA: Horn of Africa

HUMINT: human intelligence

Klingon: Military terminology for intelligence collectors, especially CIA operators in the field (see also OGA).

Makarov: a small, Russian officer's pistol. Similar to the Walther PP in design, it is chambered in a 9mm x 18mm cartridge

M4: US Army military rifle with a collapsible stock and short barrel chambered in 5.56mm.

MP5: A short-barreled submachine gun chambered in 9mm.

NAVSPECWAR: US Navy Special Warfare Command

NVG: Night vision goggles

OP: Observation point

OGA: "Other government agency" — a military term for the CIA.

One up: Surveillance term for working in a vehicle without a partner.

PCS: Permanent change of station — a long term assignment.

QRF: Quick reaction force. A military unit on standby to support a smaller force if necessary.

Red Gun: A non-functioning plastic training weapon with approximately the same weight as the real gun. Originally, all training weapons were colored red. They come in other colors as well, but are still called "red guns."

RTU: "return to unit." If a SOF operator does not meet the necessary requirements, he or she can be returned to their parent unit in the conventional forces.

SAP: "Special access program" — a program which has a limited and classified audience.

SAS: Special Air Service — a UK Special Operations unit.

SBS: Special Boat Service — a UK Special Operations unit.

Selection: A formal training program used by special operations units to select candidates.

Serial: A surveillance term used for a single, continuous shift following a target or observing a location.

SF: US Special Forces, aka Green Berets.

Shooters: Special Operations teams specifically trained to conduct raids.

SIGINT: signals intelligence

Six: The call sign for any commander of any military unit. Therefore, if the overall call sign for a unit is Mike, then Mike6 is the commander of that unit.

SMG: Submachine gun

SOF: Special Operations Forces

Squint: A less than positive name for analysts focused on imagery intelligence.

Standby: A surveillance communication term implying new information.

S&R: Surveillance and Reconnaissance — a fictitious US special operations unit.

SVTC: Secure Video Teleconference

Tag: An electronic tracking device.

TDY: Temporary Duty. A short-term assignment.

TF160: A unit from the US Army Special Operations Aviation Regiment. In this novel, they fly MH60 "Blackhawk" or MH8 "Little Bird" helicopters

TOC: Tactical Operations Center

Two up: Surveillance term for working in a vehicle with a partner.

Victor: Vehicle

VSO: village stability operations, a Special Forces counterinsurgency mission

Zero: The call sign for the team leader on a surveillance team.

ZULU: Greenwich Mean Time. When operations are conducted across multiple theatres, they are all linked to Zulu time so there is no confusion on what time they are starting.

WHO IS THAT MAN?

G inger had been waiting in the cafe for a half hour for the Syrian. He arrived five minutes before the scheduled meeting time and figured he would give the Syrian a full thirty minutes before he left the café and returned to base. Since his assignment with 171, Ginger had been working out of a SOF safe house in Dohuk in Northern Iraq. Zakho was a smaller version of Dohuk . It was not Iraq anymore. It was Kurdistan. The Kurdish flag flew in the town square and the police were former peshmerga fighters who had fought Saddam since 1990. There was little to show that the government in Baghdad had any influence in the village. It didn't matter much to Ginger or to the S&R team or to the small raid force working inside the compound. All they cared about was hunting Zarqawi's organization known simply as Al Qaida in Iraq or AQI although AQI worked as much in Syria as Iraq.

Abu Musab al-Zarqawi started life as a small time criminal. Drug user, drug smuggler, extortionist and murderer. He decided to become a supporter of al-Qaida in Iraq, Syria and Jordan and established his own gang of terrorists operating in Western Iraq, Eastern Syria, and Northeastern Jordan. No one knew for sure if this was simply Zarqawi's way of expanding his criminal enterprise, building a fiefdom in the Sunni regions of the Levant or whether he believed in the Islamic extremist rhetoric. It really didn't matter on the ground. Zarqawi's foot-soldiers were known for extreme violence. So extreme, that al-Qaida tried first to send moderators into the mix and eventually decided to isolate this group that was making the AQ brand less than acceptable to others in the region. Zarqawi was undeterred and decided to mix international terrorism with international media. He became his own "brand" of Islamic extremist and started selling that brand on the internet.

What he probably hadn't counted on was that this sort of showmanship brought him to the direct attention of the best terrorist man hunters in the world. Now, Ginger and the rest of the team were in Kurdistan focusing their attention on building a network that would find Zarqawi, fix him in place, and finish him once and for all. This might mean a capture operation or, more likely, "kinetic resolution" which was the preferred option discussed in SOF's team rooms in Dohuk. Ginger graduated from the US intelligence school known as the Farm in December and he was now working for the SOF human intelligence outfit known simply as 171, the address of the warehouse that they used at Ft. Bragg, NC. Ginger had less than a month in 171 before they dispatched him to Northern Iraq. It wasn't the first time he had served in Iraq and, he expected, it wouldn't be the last. Ginger had been in SOF for six years as a member of one of the raid units specializing in "kinetic resolution." Now, he was working on his own, building the intelligence packages, situational awareness or SA as the SOF seniors called it, to be used by his former teammates when Commander/SOF gave them the go order.

Ginger's current source in Zakho was a Syrian, known as Source 302 in his file. The Syrian was a smuggler. He was a Christian who lived in a mixed community in al Malikiyaah. Completely apolitical, he was willing to bribe anyone to keep his business and his family alive and well. In one of the periodic roundups that the Peshmerga conducted, he was captured, interrogated and released with the understanding that he would always report back to the local police when/if he returned. His business had grown progressively more lucrative in the new Iraqi Kurdistan with the help of the local Peshmerga, so he had lived up to his end of the bargain. Sometime in the last year, the Peshmerga had told their CIA contacts, "OGA" in SOF parlance standing for the "other government agency," about this smuggler and after they met him for about six months, they turned him over to 171 as an asset for the ongoing hunt for Zarqawi. 302 was Ginger's case.

One thing that you could always count on with a smuggler was his ability to pay attention to new groups trying to extract bribes from travelers. Zarqawi's network in Eastern Syria had expanded their efforts in this regard and, at the last meeting, 302 had promised Ginger that he would bring additional information on this network. Ginger reported this up the chain of command and the SOF Center in Balad decided this was one of the best leads they had heard of on Zarqawi. That meant that Ginger's case was the priority for now and he had a full complement of SOF resources. Dohuk safe house residents in the past had been a 171 collector, three members of the surveillance and reconnaissance squadron, mostly there to keep Ginger safe, and a dozen Peshmerga to run the safe house. The Peshmerga were responsible for feeding, guarding and generally keeping the curious of Dohuk out of the neighborhood. In the past week, the safe house added another dozen SOF personnel sleeping on cots. It included a full raid team, two intelligence analysts from SOF headquarters in Balad using multiple collection platforms, and a full S&R team to keep everyone safe and sound.

So, Ginger waited for the Syrian. He was dressed in classic local garb which included loose trousers, a shirt that he thought made him look like a character out of the Three Musketeers, and a long leather vest. His Kurdish turban covered his red hair, though it was not as critical as he had first imagined when he arrived in Kurdistan. During Ginger's previous trips to Iraq, he was based in Balad and really only saw the countryside through his night vision goggles as part of a raid team that would arrive after midnight at a target location and be back in Balad by daylight. Still, the Iraqis they captured were always precisely what he expected: copper skinned Arab men with black hair and black beards. Here in Kurdistan, there were many light skinned, blue eyed Kurds and more than a few had red hair. Everyone he met said that they were all the descendants of Alexander the Great's army, so he worried less about his own light skin. He learned a few Kurdish phrases and hoped for the best to disguise his identify.

The ear bud in his right ear clicked twice. "Stand by, stand by. Mike3. Bravo sighted moving from Red3 along the north side of the street, through the market toward your location, Echo2."

Ginger used the microphone switch and clicked twice to acknowledge. The café was halfway along the main city road and identified on the Zakho map back at the safe house as the "Red Line" running from Red1 to the East to Red 7 in the West. Each number identified an intersection along the Red line. The S&R operator named Deke was watching from the roof two buildings down from the café. He had driven the team to Zakho in a team minibus supporting the 171 mission.

"All call signs. This is Zero. Mike3 has our Bravo moving toward the meeting site. Anyone see any threats to our Klingon?"

Chief Warrant Officer 5 Jameson was the S&R team leader. This was his third rotation in Iraq, second in Kurdistan and tenth rotation since 9/11 to various warzones that made up the "Global War on Terrorism" or GWOT in SOF parlance. He wouldn't stop calling Ginger "his Klingon" (named for the cloaking device of the Klingons in Star Trek and the "cloak and dagger" attribution of US intelligence officers). Ginger had given up after about a month of bitching. Also, you didn't mouth off to a senior chief who looked like a refrigerator with a head. When Jameson wasn't running operations or sleeping, he was working out. He looked like he might be able to lift Ginger off his feet with one hand and then, well, Ginger didn't want to think about what might happen next. He became "their Klingon."

Jameson's team had been together since before 9/11. Ginger had worked with S&R back when he was on a raid team, but this team was the best he had ever seen. They seemed to know each other's movements before they happened, and they were the most patient and careful "watchers" that he had ever seen. Not an easy mission when you might be watching for hours at a time. Ginger had learned over time that if "the Mikes" were on his side, he was safe. Jameson had made it clear the primary mission for this meeting and any other support to Ginger was to keep "their Klingon" safe.

"Mike7 — nothing from my location." Nate was sitting in a Mercedes cab on the cross street facing the café. If things went sideways, Ginger knew that Nate would pull the Mercedes with its armor-plated doors in front of the café, Ginger would get in and they would leave the chaos to the S&R and raiders on site.

"Mike8 —nada." George was on the rooftop across the street sitting next to a SOF sniper who was covering the café with his Remington M24 bolt action rifle. Between the sniper's skill and the .308 rounds in the Remington, there would be little that they couldn't engage.

Ginger saw the Syrian coming forward and entering the cafe. He seemed relaxed as he greeted Ginger in broken English. "My friend.

Are you well? Do you have time to meet with me?" Ginger poured the Syrian a glass of sweetened tea from the large stainless-steel teapot at his table.

"Thanks be to God, Mr. John." Ginger had decided on arrival in Dohuk that he needed to have a throw away name for each of his sources. To keep it simple and easy to remember, he simply used the names of the apostles. His Catholic school upbringing meant they were permanently scorched into his head. 302 was Ginger's fourth source, so he was "Mr. John."

"Can we sit here, my friend? You are comfortable?"

"Yes, yes. Why not?"

"You have brought me something?"

"And you have brought me a gift as well, no?" The Syrian was a businessman first and foremost. With most Arabs, 302 would have spent an hour drinking tea before any business. With an American, he wanted to see his green first.

"Inside the napkin, my friend." The Syrian pulled the paper napkin from the table and placed in his lap. Inside were three one hundred dollar bills. The Syrian's monthly salary.

"You said you would pay for information."

"And you said you would bring information. The napkin was simply to say thank you for coming." The Syrian smiled. He had a full mouth of yellow teeth. He lit another cigarette from the burning stub that he just removed from his lips. It was not a smile that held any emotion.

"So, the Arabs you are interested in are set up on the border. They are just a few kilometers west of here. You should go visit them." An ironic smile. "They are bad men, but they are well armed, and the people are afraid of them."

"Where, exactly?"

"On the Zakho road. Between Faysh Kabir and Daryabun. They move the checkpoint each day, but always on that road, always between the two towns and, always in Syria. They are always there around sunset when everyone wants to get home before dark. They only allow you to go when you pay."

"They are Zarqawi people?"

"They say they are his people." The Syrian paused and searched for a word in his English vocabulary. "His...bodyguard?"

"You have seen Zarqawi there?"

"Thanks be to God, I have never seen that man. I want to keep my head attached to my shoulders, my friend. As a Christian, I am kaffir to them. I can pay the bribes to his men, but to Zarqawi, I would be dead."

"Anything else?"

"Nothing about them. Do you know the Syrian Army in Al-Malikiyah has an American with them?"

"What?"

"Yes, I have heard. I have a cousin who is in the Syrian Army. He says there is an American held prisoner there. He is like you, mukhabarat...intelligence?"

"Not a soldier? A prisoner."

"They say he is prisoner."

"You have a name for this American?"

"No, but maybe I get it for you. It will cost some money to bribe my cousin and maybe his friends."

"Please look at my book that I have here at the table. I think you will find it interesting." The Syrian reached for the book. Ginger grabbed his hand.

"It is for the Zarqawi information. The American information comes with another gift." The Syrian smiled again. He took a long drag from the cigarette and smoke slowly drifted from his nostrils.

"Of course, of course. It is not fair to expect you to pay until you have seen the goods. "302 opened the book and found two more one hundred dollar bills in the flyleaf. No magician or card trickster could have palmed the bills better than the Syrian.

The Syrian shook hands with Ginger and stood up. Ginger heard the round arrive that tore apart the Syrian's chest and the sound of the second round aimed at him. He never actually heard the shots fired that sent those bullets toward him. Later, Ginger admitted that he had no idea how he avoided the sniper round. Perhaps years of working in SOF had made him realize that sometimes "muscle memory" saved you well before you could think through a situation. Ginger never would have a memory of whatever caused him to hit the ground. He was on the ground with his pistol out, but he couldn't figure out where the rounds were coming from so he just started to low crawl across the patio among the chairs and tables upset by the other patrons as they ran away from the fight. Bullets were hitting pavement, tables and chairs. Ginger did notice one thing. This was not some punk with a Kalashnikov firing on full automatic. This was aimed fire and he was the target.

"Echo2, you hit?" Jameson was not about to lose another team member to a bad guy's rifle, not if he could help it. He still remembered the Jalalabad episode where Sue O'Connell was wounded. You could hear his concern in his digitized voice coming through the team comms. Another round cracked past Ginger's head. This time well above his current cover which was a concrete pillar at the front of the coffee shop.

"Not yet."

"Roger. Mike7, get our Klingon out of there." That was not an order that Jameson had to give. Deke was already driving down the street running from gutter to gutter on the road hoping that this was just a sniper and not a sniper plus an IED.

"On my way, boss. Ginger, the left rear door is going to open when I pull up." Two clicks from Ginger was all anyone heard as the Mercedes roared across the street.

"Mike3, you identified our shooter yet?"

"Zero, 3. We have identified the shooter on the rooftop at the intersection at Green3. Muzzle flashes only at this point. These are long shots…maybe 500 meters. I can't tell if he is still in action."

Another round skimmed off the Mercedes as Ginger jumped into the back. "Zero, 7. We can definitely say he is still in action." Another round hit the front windshield — spider web on the outside glass, but no penetration through the armored glass. Nate confirmed Ginger was in the car and accelerated diagonally across the street, did a forward 180 turn across the entire street and headed away from Red3 toward the intersection at Red4. Another round hit the trunk of the car as it left.

A new shot, a different sound and this time going toward the shooter.

"Zero, 8. Whiskey7 just engaged. Target down."

"8, Zero. Roger, Whiskey7 engaged, target down. Whiskey6, over to you."

A new voice in the mix. "All Mike call signs, Whiskey6. Exit now. Whiskey team will continue on target. Confirm."

"Zero"

"Mike3"

"Mike7"

"Mike8"

They regrouped at the designated rendezvous location at Red1 in Zakho center. Deke had picked up George as he left town. Billy was driving the command minibus with Jameson. He pulled in to the rear of the three-vehicle convoy as they headed back to Dohuk. It was a quiet ride along the broken pavement back to base.

Ginger sat in the van writing up his notes. He knew that short term memory was susceptible to failure caused by adrenaline. He figured there was precious little that he could get from the meeting other than two very different points. First, Zarqawi may (or may not) be working both sides of the Syrian-Iraqi border. Certainly, the temporary check points were claiming to be his men. Secondly, the Syrians had a Westerner as their prisoner. An American? Well, that was for another day and, now, another source to determine. Ginger could easily imagine any Syrian mistaking a Russian or a European mercenary for an American. Still, it was something that he would have to report and see if anyone knew what was going on.

By the time they had returned to the safe house, the initial report from the SOF raiders was on Jameson's desk. While Ginger and the Mikes had infiltrated and departed via cover vehicles, once the raid team took over they had called for helicopter exfiltration. They were probably already showered and changed into their sweats working out at the airbase in Mosul. Jameson showed Ginger the report.

The raid team worked quickly to identify the shooter's location. When they got there, there was only blood and a few spent cartridges of 7.62 x 39 consistent with a Kalashnikov or an SVD sniper rifle. No body and no rifle. Given the accuracy of the shooting, the raid team assumed it was a sniper and spotter team. Also, next to the cartridges was a small IED left behind to do more damage. One part of the team blew the IED in place, while a second tracked the blood trail to a small garage one block off "the Red line." Just before the team got there, the garage exploded. The explosion ended the search since what little evidence might have been left behind was now in pieces. The intelligence cell in Dohuk, Mosul, and Balad all agreed, it had the clear signs of an AQ operation. The only thing that they could determine for certain was this sniper team had been in Zakho for at least 48 hours before the meeting and probably up on the rooftop for 24 of those 48 hours waiting for the meeting.

"Why in the world would an AQI hunter team spend any effort attacking the Syrian? And, who knew that AQ in Iraq had hunter teams?" Ginger knew as soon as he said it that Jameson would give him the "stink eye."

"Ginger, what do you reckon the Al Qaida in Iraq has as a bounty for your head or any of SOF operator's head? 5k US? 10K US? Your Syrian was just the bait. You were the target."

"Which means someone in the network was either sloppy or talked."

"Or both, Ginger. It is entirely possible that it was both. Either way, your Syrian died because of a security breach and you need to sort this out soonest before we go out again to meet one of your sources. Good thing you had your guardian angels out there, huh?" Jameson took a sip from a stainless-steel mug of tea.

"Chief, no arguments there." Ginger walked out of Jameson's office just as Command Sergeant Major Mario Garcia walked in. He turned to Ginger.

"Listen, the next time you are working a case like this, how about using that cloaking device, huh?"

"Good idea, Sergeant Major. I'll put it on my packing list." Ginger now had to use the main comms system to set up a secure video tele-conference with Smith and Massoni in 171 back at Bragg. He wasn't looking forward to that conversation.

T his was day six of the sessions as near as Dave Daniels could tell. He had lost track of day and night after the first few sessions. They never let him see daylight, only the flat white light of the recessed neon bulbs in the ceiling. They played with him by turning the lights off for a few minutes...or was it a few hours...every day. Just enough for him to relax and then lights and white noise until he was fully awake. Daniels wasn't sure where he was. The last thing he remembered was the needle stick that hit him in the Strassebahn streetcar in Munich. After that, black until he arrived in the room.

He was not looking forward another set of interrogations. At least they weren't actually torturing him. No one had actually touched him other than the gentle, almost hospital like, grip that guided him from his room to the room where they started asking questions. He was holding up pretty well under the lack of sleep and the isolation, but it was getting harder and harder to sort out what he wanted to tell his interrogators and what he must never tell them. Sleep deprivation was a strange enemy. He had already started to hallucinate a bit as he lived through hours of isolation. Yesterday, just before they returned to interrogate him, he was certain there was a coke machine in his cell. So certain, he walked over to get a soda from the machine using coins that he didn't have in his pocket.

"Mr. Daniels, it's time for us to have another conversation." Daniels hadn't heard him come into the room. The voice was muffled by the balaclava that the guard in black always wore. Perfect, sterile English; neither North American nor UK. Daniels learned the first day that physical resistance to the guard was a bad idea. He was still sore from the "wall to wall" counseling that he received to reinforce who was in charge. Daniels meekly accepted the goggles and headset that would prevent him from seeing or hearing anything until he arrived in the interrogation room. As his world went dark, he focused his concentration on what he could tell his interrogators today. One step at a time was all he could think.

FAMILY BUSINESS

S usan O'Connell was in the dirt hide location with George and Nate overlooking the road that ran from Wana in South Waziristan to Khowst in Pakistan. It was a dirt road that was no more than a lane and a half wide, yet the locals through some sort of genius or madness were able to push five-ton and ten-ton trucks side by side along the road. They had been in place for 36 hours waiting to identify a convoy of SUVs that were carrying Uzbeks from the Islamic Movement of Uzbekistan into Afghanistan and into the war. The routine was fairly simple. One surveillant on the electronics including a digital photography wonder and a portable sensor tracking the Uzbek mobile phones and one surveillant pulling security for the hide and one resting or conducting "personal hygiene" outside the hide. Four hours a shift.

The Uzbeks were the most violent and militarily competent of the Al Qaida surrogates in Eastern Afghanistan. Exiles from Uzbekistan, they had moved to Kabul with Usama bin Ladin, set up camps in Jalalabad and then moved into Waziristan after 2001. For whatever reason, the Waziris and the Zadran tribesmen welcomed them and now they trained in North and South Waziristan and fought in Khowst. The targets S&R were hunting were senior IMU leaders coming to a meeting with their troops in Khowst.

Sue was laying on her stomach watching the computer screen. The top of the hide was just inches above her head. "No commando in the movies lives like this." Sue whispered to Nate who had just returned from his visit outside the hide.

"But no movie commando is as good looking as you are, either." Sue was covered in dirt and sweat. Her short hair was under a tan watch cap and her hands were also covered in tan Nomex gloves.

"Thank you, dahling," Sue said in her best Diva imitation.

The banter ended as the headset in Sue's ear crackled and then cleared to transmit two voices speaking Uzbek. Sue switched to her internal communications microphone. "Stand by, stand by. Bravos are on the air and within intercept range."

Jameson's voice came through all the earpieces in the hide. Jameson was in another hide location with the rest of the team in a series of local vehicles including the magic bus with its full intercept and Comms package. "Stand by, stand by. Mike4 sends Bravos inbound."

"Zero, this is Whiskey6. We are 2kms West of the hide. We will engage on Mike4 signal and when we have visual."

"Whiskey6, Zero. Copy. Mike4, 5, 7 acknowledge."

George first. "5."

Nate next. "7."

Sue last, "4."

The vehicle convoy entered the pass. "Stand by, stand by. Three Charlie's: black Toyota land cruisers, whip antennas. Approximate speed 30kmh. 2 minutes to target. Mobile signal coming from..." Sue checked the monitor as they got closer. "Mobile from third vehicle, I say again, third vehicle."

"4, Whiskey6. Roger. We have control."

Jameson's voice over the radio said, "4, 5, 7. Break down the hide and begin exfil on contact. Confirm."

"4"

"5"

"7"

They heard the claymore mine set by the raid squadron go off and started to move. George pulled off the cover of the hide. Sue disassembled the electronics and loaded them into the three rucks. Nate started to clean the site of any sign of their presence.

Crumph! Crumph! The two mortar rounds hit just below and just above their position.

"Shit! Let's get outta here!" Nate had been closest to the impact and was not his normal implacable self. In a gunfight, Nate was always the one quietly taking the target down. Clearly mortars were something he didn't like.

"I'm ready, let's go." George had already shouldered his ruck with the radio, batteries and hide screen and was on point heading on the reverse slope of the hill toward their vehicles, Nate closed in and looked over his shoulder at Sue.

"Sue, let's go!!"

Sue rolled onto her back and sat up, shouldering her ruck. She looked down and realized she was missing her left leg. "Ungh, ungh, I can't!" The mortar round exploded nearby.

Sue woke up from the nightmare. She reached down to scratch the leg that wasn't there. Phantom pain had transitioned to phantom itch. What hadn't transformed were the nightmares. Sometimes Afghanistan, sometimes Cyprus, sometimes the Farm. It always ended more or less the same. After months, she realized that "the dream" was always near dawn. Today it was 0420. Sue got up from the bed, hopped over to the shower to rinse off the sweat. After that, she would do a workout and shower again, make some coffee and get to work.

S ue looked at Jed Smith behind his desk. He was holding his head with both of his hands reading a series of reports on the Limassol operation. Sitting next to him was Massoni. In typical Massoni fashion, he was making faces at Sue behind Smith's back to see if she would crack up in front of their boss. They were all in the plywood and frame modified commander's office inside the warehouse that was the home of the SOF Human Intelligence Collection Unit (SOF/HICU) simply known by its street address at Ft. Bragg — Warehouse 171.

"O'Connell, when we sent you to Cyprus to conduct operations, I expected you to understand the concept of clandestine operations. I have read the reports. What precisely about clandestine DO YOU NOT UNDERSTAND?"

Sue had been relatively relaxed when she came into the office. She had already delivered an informal note to Smith and Massoni while she was still in Cyprus and on arrival back at Ft. Bragg, she had spent the weekend writing a full, formal report. She thought that she had done pretty well, considering the circumstances. Out of long standing habit, she now shifted into a position of parade rest. If this was going to be a formal discussion, she decided that she would handle it better if she was in a formal military stance.

"So, you are in country for a month and you are involved in a murder, you are kidnapped, you encourage your British colleagues to blow up one of our cars in a public junkyard, then, you actively get involved in the takedown of a smuggling ring, get shot at again, and are involved in the murder of what appears to have been a Russian mafia boss. Very low profile, DON'T YOU THINK?"

"Boss, on the up side, she disrupted the entire smuggling network that was delivering high tech parts for Iraqi and Hizballah IED production and she didn't piss off the station," Massoni intervened.

Smith gave Massoni what was commonly known in SOF as "the stink eye." However, Smith was also enough of a formal Army officer to never, ever criticize his Sergeant Major. He hadn't made it to

Colonel making enemies of senior non-commissioned officers. He turned back to Sue.

"OK, O'Connell. These are your reports, so I expect they are accurate and detailed and haven't left anything out. I don't need any more explanation. My next question to you is "what's next?" Are you going to start a war, disrupt the NATO alliance, or simply get back to working for 171?"

"Sir, given those choices, I would prefer to get back to work for 171." Massoni started to laugh though Sue had tried to avoid anything resembling a hostile response.

"Right. So, now that we are all in agreement that you worked for and will work for 171, let's get down to business. First, it turns out that the Commanding General has heard of your work and he has recommended you for another Bronze Star. I have agreed, and we will see what the chain of command decides. He also wants you to work for him, though I don't know how you would like staff work at Balad."

Most civilians assume that gaining notice from the Commanding General of any command, but most specifically from the CG of Special Operations Forces would be a good thing. Sue knew that was a completely false assumption. If the CG noticed you, it could only mean he would want you close and you would live among his staff and spend your days doing staff work from the time you woke up until the time you went to bed. In this case, in SOF forward headquarters in Balad Airbase in Iraq. For Sue, it would be a return to the work she did at 18th Airborne Corps. Long hours working behind a computer in a windowless joint operations center. The only difference this time, it would be in a large air-conditioned tent in the middle of Iraq. Dandy.

"Sir, if I have a choice, I would prefer to continue to work for 171."

"O'Connell, that was what I told the CG. I have reached a terminal grade in my career and I often tell him things he doesn't want to hear. Not career enhancing, but always good for the SOF mission. He hasn't fired me….yet." Smith paused and, it was his time to smirk. "I did promise him that I would continue to give you work that would support the SOF mission in Iraq and Afghanistan. I hope you will be willing to do that."

"Yes, sir."

"OK, now that that is settled, I need you to do something first. I need you to find Dave Daniels."

"Sir?"

"Your predecessor in Cyprus left on British military air from Akrotiri and was scheduled to fly from London to Washington Dulles after a few days of R&R in the UK. He was scheduled to report to the warehouse on 26 March. He is still missing. We have alerted the FBI, Army CID, OGA and the Brits. So far, they have come up with nothing. Since you got along so well with Dave before he left, I figure you might have better luck."

Sue realized that Smith was not joking and he was worried about a 171 officer who was missing. "Sir, I will start right away."

"So why are you still in my office?" Sue turned and walked out as quickly as she could. Massoni followed and spoke to her as soon as they were both out of Smith's office.

"I thought that went well, didn't you?"

Massoni returned to Smith's office later that afternoon. "Boss, I get the "need to know" bullshit, but are you really going to have O'Connell out there hunting Daniels and not know why she is doing so? I mean, the real reason why?"

Smith looked long and hard at Massoni. He was a great sergeant major and a terrific combat leader. He had been essential to any success that 171 had up to this point. However, sometimes, Massoni saw the world as a simple game of good guys and bad guys. Unfortunately, in the world of espionage, there were no good guys or bad guys. There were only targets and operators.

"Jim, the problem is I don't even know for sure what the real reasons are for using one of our operators to hunt down another operator. Don't get me wrong. I fully understand that idea of leaving no man behind, but right now, the CI gurus say the evidence is pointing to a defection not a kidnapping. I think he is an asshole, but I can't believe he is a traitor, " Smith paused to drink from his coffee cup.

"I honestly think we would be better served using O'Connell as a 171 asset going after AQ or Hizballah or some other set of enemies of the USA. Unfortunately, that is not how the folks inside the

Pentagon and at the FBI see it. They convinced the CG that they want O'Connell involved and the CG told me what was going to happen. Now, I don't think it is a good use of O'Connell's time, but I didn't get a vote. "

"Boss, do you think Daniels defected? And, if so, to whom?"

"Jim, I think he left of his own accord to someplace. If anyone is going to find him, O'Connell is the person. She is relentless. If Daniels is a traitor or if he was captured, it has bad written all over it no matter how you cut it."

Massoni left the office with no clearer understanding of what was going on than when he entered the office. He decided to go bother Marconi. At least when he talked to Marconi, it made sense.

Later that evening in her apartment, Sue called her mother. After the usual pleasantries, Sue decided that she needed her mom to know that at least one of the Beroslav family was dead.

"I heard that from Patty, dear." Barbara O'Connell's voice was steady through the digital signal. "I'm not sure that we know for sure what it means for us, but it can't be bad news. Especially since Patty was able to arrange for his own folks to take care of the problem."

Sue thought it interesting that over the phone Barbara simply referred to the deadly game of revenge between the O'Connell's and the Beroslav family as simply "a problem" the way one might talk about a leaky roof or a car accident. "Mom, any further news on Gramps or those creeps you handled in your neck of the woods?"

"Nothing worth talking about on the phone, dear. My biggest concern at this point is how many more family members are out there. I'm hoping the fact that their actions have been," Barbara paused, "….addressed by their own government and that might slow things down some, but I don't know for sure. When can you come visit? I do have some things to talk about and they are better accomplished face to face."

"Mom, I don't know when I will get any more leave time. I have some unfinished business here."

"Can I visit?"

"Anytime, mom. I will know in the next couple of days if I will be traveling anytime soon. How is Wild Bill, our family lawman?"

"He seems to be happy as can be chasing criminals in the DC area. I would like to think he will eventually see the light and slide over to FCI work, but we'll just have to let him make that decision."

FCI — foreign counterintelligence — was the FBI work focused on official and non-official targets of hostile countries. The Washington field office was considered one of the best in the country though New York and San Francisco would always argue that point. Before she attended the Farm, Sue would not have had idea one on FBI acronyms.

"Mom, I have an early start tomorrow, so I'm going to ring off now. I will call you as soon as I know how long I'm going to be here."

"Ciao, darling."

Sue put her cellphone down and went into her kitchen to make a pot of coffee. She had more than a couple of hours of work to accomplish before she called it a night. Once the water boiled, she put it in the French press and was ready to put the rest of her coffee together when someone knocked on the door.

Sue looked at her watch. 2130hrs. Lots of possibilities and none of them good. She put down the tray with the coffee pot, milk, sugar bowl and mug. She reached into a kitchen drawer — past the wooden frame holding her silverware — and pulled out a Glock26. It was in home storage condition, so she quietly worked the slide and put the gun into battery. Next, she turned on the small TV set on the counter. She used the remote to switch to the AV setting and the screen filled with a green glow as the wireless night vision camera over her door delivered an image. Man. Tall. Military style jacket. Knocking again.

Sue walked to the door with the Glock at "low ready" with the Glock pointing slightly downward with her right elbow locked at her hip and the gun easily put into action. She went to the door and released the bolt. Her main door was steel made to look like a composite. The outer door was an attractive metal frame that was actually manufactured by a company that made prison doors. No one was going to get through that door unless they used a grappling hook and a truck to pull the door out of the solid steel frame. Still, you could shoot through the glass. After Cyprus, Sue was taking no chances. She opened the interior door, keeping behind the steel door except for her face and her gun hand.

"Sue, you are never going to get men to come visit if every time you meet them at your door, you have a gun in your hand." Stan Cyzneski's voice was slightly muffled through the glass, but recognizable. Once again, he was in an old field jacket, watch cap, jeans and boots. He looked like a cross between an old veteran and a hobo.

"If you would call in advance, you might receive a better welcome. Also, if you are going to come visit, can you please dress a little better — you will make my neighbors nervous." Sue opened the door to let Stan in. He had been her classmate at the Farm and was her inside handler for the double agent operation ELEKTRA in Cyprus. Sue was not clear why he was here now. After he came in, she closed and locked the outside door and then did the same for the inside door. She put the Glock on the table beside the couch and invited Stan to sit in the chair opposite the couch.

"I just made some coffee. Do you want some?"

"Do you really need to ask?" Sue was already pouring a second mug — adding milk and two sugars — Stan's preference.

"Once again, you aren't here for fun, are you?"

"Sue, seeing you is always fun. How can you think otherwise?"

"Bullshit, Stan."

"Nope, true, Sue." He took off his field jacket and pulled off the paddle holster holding his Glock 19. Stan was big enough to carry even a full-sized Glock in a concealment holster and get away with it. Of course, as a CIA counterintelligence officer, he had no authority to carry a gun in the US except in extreme circumstances, so Sue was more than a little surprised to see the pistol.

Sue reached into a cabinet under the bar that separated the kitchen from the living room. She pulled out a bottle of Jameson's Irish whisky.

"Irish coffee?"

"Sue, you know better. You know the drinking age of an officer on assignment."

It was an old joke and Sue knew the punch line. "55" was the correct answer - standard retirement age for all federal officers. Sue nodded and added a small dash to her coffee — it was probably going to be a long night.

"Stan, I actually was working, so if this is not a social visit, I have to press you to get to the point."

"Working? You just got back."

"And I've got to start hunting for a missing 171 agent."

"Daniels? Well, that fits nicely into what I came here to talk about."

"Stan, when I left Cyprus, the COS said that ELEKTRA was finished, and I could return to being just plain O'Connell of 171."

"Did she now? I don't know how Dentmann could know for sure that ELEKTRA was finished. We certainly couldn't say that, and Army CI wouldn't say that, so why would the CIA station chief say that?"

"Probably because Beroslav killed my handler and I suspect the GRU wouldn't believe me if I told them that this is about a family feud that goes back two generations."

"Ah, well, there is that."

"So, why are you here, Stan."

"I suppose you remember that we still have Mary Sanderson in play." Mary had been Sue's instructor at the Farm as well as being a GRU agent and, while at the Farm, a talent spotter for the GRU. It was Mary who "pitched" Sue to be a GRU agent and that pitch was the start point for ELEKTRA as a double agent operation with Sue as the bait.

"How could I forget?"

"Right, you were the one with the pistol to her head when I came through the door."

"A minor disagreement."

"So, we have kept Mary in communication with her handlers. We couldn't let her go to her COS job in North Africa, but we did arrange for her to be the nominal DCOS in Vienna. She has plenty of opportunities to enjoy Austria, under our supervision of course and plenty of opportunities for her to meet with her GRU handlers.

So far, she had played it straight, at least we think so. We gave her the report on Beroslav's attack on their handler and, what a surprise, he ends up dead in the water off a pier in Limassol, most probably from an SVD Sniper rifle. Coincidence? We think not."

"They bought that I communicated with Mary?"

"And why not? You had access to the Agency communications in Cyprus, Mary is in Vienna, easy enough to send an email asking for advice. It all fits, no?"

"So, does all the goofy data saying the CIA captured an alien in Roswell in the 1950s, but I don't believe it."

"Why not? It could be real, Sue."

"Not while J. Edgar Hoover was alive."

"Touché."

"OK, so what does the GRU think they can do with Sue O'Connell? After all, I would think being locked in the trunk of a car bomb and then being shot by Beroslav on the docks would reduce a potential agent's willingness to collaborate, no?"

"Ah, but you are forgetting the point, Sue. Part of your motivation is to work for the GRU not for the SVR or the KGB thugs who became the Russian mafia. Now, your motivation is to figure out ways to screw those guys and, Mary has convinced her contacts that if they offer you that opportunity, you can be brought back into the fold."

"Is this sounding like a Russian novel to you?"

Q"It is a Russian novel, Sue. You are the author…along with yours truly, of course," Stan smirked as he completed the sentence.

Sue ignored the smirk. "So, how are they going to get in touch?"

"Well, that's why I'm here. I wanted you to know the state of play now because I have no idea when, where or how they will be in touch. They told Mary that they were going to reach out to you in their own time and in their own manner and that's all we know. Mary's last meeting with her handlers was Friday night, so it could happen any time now. "

"Perfect. Now, what does this all have to do with my job of finding Dave Daniels."

"Classic crime mystery question: did he fall or was he pushed?"

"Eh?"

"Is Daniels missing because he was kidnapped or because he is on the run or, to be more Cold War about it, because he defected."

"Daniels? Are you sure we are talking about the same guy? Good agent handler, excellent Arabist, egomaniac, jerk? That Daniels?"

"Indeed, Sue. We have had some sensitive reporting from an Agency source in Moscow for some time pointing to an Army intelligence penetration in the Eastern Mediterranean. SVR is supposed to be running the source and it pisses off the GRU mightily since they figure US military penetrations by right ought to be their business. Don't you think they might be irritated if Daniels has defected and the SVR is running the debriefings without GRU participation? Oh, I can imagine how irritated they might be."

Sue responded even more forcefully, "But, we don't know that Daniels is the guy. He might be simply AWOL, he might have quit, and the resignation letter hasn't reached us yet, he might be kidnapped by one of a dozen sets of bad guys who he worked against for years."

"Or, he might simply have decided it's time for his dacha in the birches outside Moscow."

Sue shook her head. "Now you are really getting Dostoyevsky on me. You aren't really suggesting that I use Daniel's status of missing in action as feed material for my first meeting with the GRU? I can't do that for lots of reasons. He is a 171 agent, he might be fighting for his life right now in some prison someplace, and my commander would cut my head off and shit down my neck."

"What if we got Smith to agree?"

"What if the earth was hit by an asteroid and all life on earth was destroyed?"

"Sue, you get to work on the Daniels hunt and be prepared for some GRU schmuck to reach out to you. I will engage Smith and Massoni and see what they say. You do realize they already know that the FBI and Army CI think Daniels was a mole, right?"

"Nope. They just told me his was MIA and my job is to find him."

"And find him you shall. Perhaps with a little help from the GRU."

"Stan, this sucks."

"Yup, Sue. It sucks to be Sue O'Connell, but, I can't help that, and

I do think ELEKTRA is worth it for many more reasons today than ever before. "

Sue and Stan finished their coffee looking at some blank space in the room to avoid looking at each other. Stan put down his mug, stood up and put on his holster and then his field jacket.

"Sue, I'm not here to talk you into or out of any of this. You have to decide how you want to play this hand you have been dealt. All I can do is try to help. You still have your phone that I gave you? One way or the other, give me a call tomorrow. We can meet for coffee someplace in Chapel Hill on Wednesday. It will give you a chance to get some fresh air. Meanwhile, you leave your commander to the ELEKTRA team. He will hear from us separately."

"OK, Stan. I'll give you a call tomorrow. "

She walked him to the door, locked up and returned to the large legal pad sitting on the coffee table. She still had to figure out Daniel's possible options when he got off the Royal Air Force cargo aircraft on arrival in the UK. One thing she had already decided. She wasn't going to wait for the FBI to reach out to Smith. She would be talking to him on arrival tomorrow.

S ue was surprised when Smith agreed to keep ELEKTRA going and even to use Daniels' disappearance as possible feed material. His explanation was typical Smith, deliberate, blunt, and aggressive.

"We've tried everything else. I've known for months that there was a possibility that Daniels or some other Army HUMINT officer in the region was a double. I don't believe it was Daniels, but no one gives a shit what I think. They expect me to be loyal to my team. If we can resolve this one way or the other, then I will be ready to accept the consequences. That said, you don't throw Daniels to the wolves unless you believe there is some sign from the opposition that they already know something about him. Meanwhile, I want to know how in the world your mafia creep found out you were coming to Cyprus in time to cap the real GRU handler and take his place. Too weird, no?"

Sue made it to Chapel Hill the following day and let Stan know that the operation was in place and to let him know that she had already told Smith the plan. She figured it was important to get some degree of control over the operation at this point and telling Stan that ELEKTRA was going to operate on her terms was the best way to make this happen. He took the news about as well as she could expect. Luckily, they were in a coffee shop near the University. He wasn't happy, and he tried the "I'm in charge" language for a while. Sue made it clear that she wasn't buying this and if he wanted to get too stupid, he could talk to Smith or, better still, the Commanding General of SOF. Sue didn't like this game much, but at least she was playing with a colleague she could trust, at least a bit.

She spent the rest of the week going through Daniels' records in the 171 spaces. She checked the admin records as well and found out one of Daniels' personal documentation packages was missing. Signed out for a previous TDY to Istanbul and never returned. The assumption had been that he simply kept the documents in his two-drawer safe at Akrotiri and would have used the military attaché's diplomatic pouch to get them back to Ft. Bragg. In fact, there was no record he had ever used the documentation during any TDY in the last six months.

"What do you think?" Sue was sitting across from Flash at one of the folding tables that served as workspace, lunchroom, and general source of clutter in 171. Flash had been the analyst handling Daniels' work and had worked with Sue before her departure for Cyprus. In exchange for Flash's help on this effort, Sue first had to tell her everything she could remember about the TDY to Cyprus. Flash tried not to show it, but she was impressed by Sue's adventure. Sue tried not to show it, but she was impressed by Flash's brilliance as well as her audacity when it came to her uncompromising, extremely black wardrobe.

"OK, so he didn't use the docs on the Turkey trip. And, he didn't ship the docs out of Akrotiri. So, what did he do with them? You think he used them to disappear in the UK?"

"Well, did anyone start looking for Daniels as a US military dependent in the UK?"

"Nope, we didn't because we hadn't captured the fact that Daniels still had this set of documents." They finished their coffees and Sue and Flash walked over to Flash's cubicle with multiple keyboards and screens.

"Let's look at where he used the dependent docs in the past." Flash typed a series of commands on the keyboard to her left. A series of case files opened up.

"He's had this document package for a long while. Well before he arrived at 171. I can't say when he got the package, but I know that it arrived with him when he came to us from the Army CI outfit in Germany. "

"Cold War docs?"

"Sister, I may be good, but I'm not that good. I can only say that he had them when 171 first started and we cherry picked intelligence officers from the services. I remember Daniels came from a Counterintelligence detachment in Germany. That's all I know and that's based on my memory not on any records here. Daniels' electronic life starts here with his first case files for 171."

"OK, so where did he use US military dependent documents once he was in 171?" More clicks — this time on Flash's middle keyboard.

"Doesn't look like he ever used them. That set of docs is for a civilian assigned to Germany. Not the most useful set of documents for 171. Daniels was our primary Hizballah hunter. He mostly used NATO docs to get where he needed to go and to work with liaison services. His record shows he worked with every NATO service, the Kuwaitis, Omanis, and the Israelis."

"So, he always uses an official passport when he is working. The fact that he worked with multiple services also is useful. He may have more than one explanation for his disappearance and more than one enemy out there."

"OK, sister. Thanks. I reckon I have to do some writing to London. Perhaps we can get a new lead at this point."

Flash looked up from her screen. "You know I thought he was a creep, but I never thought he was a traitor. Is it possible he has been kidnapped?"

"As they say in mysteries: Did he jump or was he pushed? Flash, I just don't know. I thought he was about as annoying a partner as I have ever had, and I did have to give him some wall to wall counseling in Cyprus. I think we just have to follow this trail and see what happens." Sue didn't point out that one part of the trail might be to throw Daniels' name in front of a GRU handler and see what happened next.

S ue had been confident that if Daniels used the civilian documents, the Brits would know it. After the years of IRA terror in Northern Ireland and in London proper, the UK had the most detailed electronic surveillance system in NATO. You couldn't go anywhere in the UK and not come across some type of camera or sensor or police surveillance program and you certainly couldn't leave the country unless you provided appropriate documentation. The new documentation was the first time when Sue began to believe that she might be able to unravel the history of Daniels' disappearance.

When Sue arrived at the 171 warehouse at 0600hrs after an abbreviated workout at home, she found the document in her in-box. The Brits did deliver on the lead, passed it to the Military Attaché who passed it to Sue via the 171 email channel. The Brits captured a Daniels with the appropriate passport number buying tickets for a Lufthansa flight from Gatwick to Munich the day after he arrived as Daniels at RAF Lakenheath in the UK. Sue was convinced that Daniels had used the day to run a cleansing route by buying new clothes, and getting a haircut. Eventually, the Brits would be able to trace his travels and, Sue was convinced, find his official documents someplace, most probably someplace clever.

In the electronic file Sue got from the MILATT, there was an MI5 photo of Daniels passing through Gatwick on 20 March. The photo was proof that he was using his tradecraft skills. If Sue had not matched the photo of Daniels with Daniels she knew, she probably would not have identified Daniels from this surveillance footage. He looked older and very European in style. He had a heavy wool coat, hat and what appeared to be wool slacks and heavy shoes. Sue knew the methodology: go to the closest used clothes store and buy clothes that are both used and consistent with the personae that you want to assume. Daniels was not an upper middle-class world traveler named Dave Daniels. Instead, he was a harried, Daniels as a spouse serving in Europe. The clothes made the man. He looked like he was just returning from some shopping trip — he had two shopping bags from Marks and Spencer. Perfect. But the question remained. Why?

It was 1900hrs and Bill O'Connell was finishing his shift at the Washington Field Office Gang Task Force. He had spent the day looking at files from the Washington Police Department and the Virginia State Police. The files focused on the latest data from their confidential informants on the transformation of the Central American gangs, especially M13, from narco-trafficking and murders for hire to more organized criminal activities including extortion, human trafficking, and, in two cases, bank robbery. In the past, each of these crimes would have been investigated by different law enforcement agencies with different jurisdictions. Now, the Washington Field Office Gang Task Force included a room full of lawmen from every possible federal, state, and local organization that could work against a single target. It meant complete transparency as well as opportunities for joint operations where the Drug Enforcement Administration and the FBI and Secret Service might work the same case from different angles along with DC Metro, Virginia and Maryland State Police and several smaller local police departments. Better still, it meant that they shared intelligence reports from their very different sets of confidential informants or "CIs" as Bill learned in the first few days of his assignment.

Bill was still the newest guy on the Task Force, actually the "fucking new guy" or FNG according to all the local lawmen on the floor, and that usually meant doing the grunt work that no one else wanted to do. He had spent the last year preparing the paperwork and then serving warrants, conducting witness interviews, and then completing the endless paperwork that guarantees when a lawman puts cuffs on a villain, the paperwork is complete for the prosecutor. Bill came from the Marines. He learned early on that the youngest officer in the battalion always did the dumbest work. He also learned in the Corps that there was no room or tolerance for whiners, so you just did the work as best you could until you could hand it over to the next FNG.

Bill sorted the files into three trays labeled "new case," "ongoing case," and "dead case." He finished cleaning up his desk, shut off the light and left. He was the last agent out of the task force bay. As he walked out, he heard a voice from the far end of the bay.

"O'Connell, who said you can leave without my permission." Mr. Jeremy Ferguson, Supervisory Special Agent for the Task Force. Twenty-five years in the FBI. Twelve different field offices. A career street agent and a terminal GS-14 because he would not leave street work. Also, a Marine for ten years from 1981 to 1991 who still kept his high and tight haircut. He was six-foot in his socks, 200lbs and still built like the light heavyweight boxer he was in First Marine Division. White shirt, dark tie, dark suit, black shoes. Word was that he still carried a Smith and Wesson Model 13 revolver as his backup, a 3" .357 that he was his service revolver when he entered on duty. He went to Quantico when all the instructors had pictures of J. Edgar Hoover on their green metal desks. To most of the Task Force, he was a dinosaur still roaming the jungles and terrifying to all the new agents. Bill liked him the same way he liked and feared all of his senior NCOs in the Iraq.

Bill shouted across the squad bay toward the single office that still had lights on. "Sir, its 1900hrs, I finished the file reviews and figured I would call it a night. I still have to get to the gym before hitting the rack."

"You need to get up earlier and work out before you get to work. That will keep you healthier and allow you to work longer."

"Check, sir. I will start the new routine in the morning."

"O'Connell, do you really think you are going to leave this office without coming into my office?"

"Thought so, sir, but I guess not."

"Correct, Marine."

Bill worked his way through the maze of cubicles toward the one office in the corner. One thing that SSA Ferguson had going for him was seniority. If there was an office with a view in the Task Force spaces on the third floor, he was going to have it. Bill walked through the open door.

Ferguson looked up from his desk. He had about foot of brown files on the right side of his desk and another foot of files in his metal box labeled "outbox." The outbox would be filed in the morning by some lesser being on the Task Force. Most of the members of the Task Force worked off their computer files, but there still wasn't a good way to transfer files electronically from the DEA to the FBI, the Secret Service to DEA, or any state or city law enforcement files to any other member of the Task Force. That meant every case that was active had a paper file and every paper file had to go across Ferguson's desk every month for a review, sometimes cursory, sometimes thorough. It depended on his mood and how much he thought of the case agent.

"O'Connell, I wanted you to know two things. First, I have found your work to be satisfactory over the last year and I have recommended you are moved off of probationary agent status. I heard today from the Hoover building — you are a full special agent as of now and on 01 May you will be paid as a GS-13. I also thought you would like to know that there are two new agents coming into the Task Force from Quantico this week. Your days as the FNG are over."

"Thanks, sir."

"Oh, by the way, you have to train the two new FNGs, that's what you get based on your new promotion to GS-13." Bill knew that was part of the deal as soon as Ferguson told him of the arrival of the new pair. Still, it was part of Ferguson's leadership style to always offer the worst case up front.

"Roger, sir. They will receive my best Marine training routine for FNGs."

"I figured as much, O'Connell. Now, go work out and get in early tomorrow. The FNGs arrive at 08."

"Check…." Bill had intended to say "Sir" as he did a quick about face to leave when he realized he was lying on his back on the floor of Ferguson's office. Ferguson was kneeling over him using a white handkerchief to apply pressure to Bill's chest. Bill thought about what the old timers had told him at Quantico — a good agent always has two handkerchiefs — one in his right pocket to keep his hand dry before a handshake and one in his back pocket to use or to give to a lady. Bill wondered which one was on his chest and why was it so red.

"Marine, you need to keep focused on me. You got it. You are going to be all right. Medics are on the way."

Bill was having trouble focusing on Ferguson. He didn't understand what Ferguson was talking about or why he was in civilian clothes when he should be in utilities. He remembered giving that same line to one of his Marine's in Ramadi. He was using a compression bandage on a sucking chest wound at the time. "I've been shot?"

"Bill, just keep focusing on me. You have been shot, but the medics are on the way. We will have you in the trauma unit in no time. Just stay with me."

"Where else would I go, gunny?"

Ferguson had been a Marine in Desert Storm and part of the first unit in Kuwait City. He had seen enough gunshot wounds in the Corps and since to know that O'Connell could survive if he didn't go into shock. The fact that O'Connell was already losing his grip on where he was and who he was definitely was not a good sign. He needed to keep his man alive and calm until the medics arrived. He assumed the personae that he hadn't had for over 20 years.

"Exactly my point, Marine. We are staying right here until the corpsmen arrive. Now, I'm going to switch to another bandage, so I need you to hold on to this one while I switch." He took Bill's right hand and put it on his wound, then pulled his other arm over the top of his chest. "Pressure, Marine."

"Yes, Gunny."

The medics arrived before Ferguson could change out the bandage. They were from the DHS clinic in the basement Federal building and all former servicemen working now for DHS emergency services on the night shift in case of a terrorist incident. They handled O'Connell professionally and had him out of the office, down the elevator and into their ambulance in the time it took for Ferguson to call the Field Office Special Agent in Charge and tell him there had been a sniper shooting at his office. After that, Ferguson called the team leader of the field office evidence response team and told him to get back into the office. He called his deputy, Molly Norton.

"Molly, I don't know what you are doing right now, but you need to get to the trauma unit at Washington General right now. O'Connell's been shot. A sniper hit him in my office. I don't know if there is any chance of a second attempt, but I want full coverage 24/7 on O'Connell until we find out. Check?"

Norton had been a sergeant in the Texas Department of Public Safety before joining the FBI. She had considered the Texas Rangers, but figured there was a better chance for a woman in the FBI than the Rangers. She had worked as a street agent, an undercover agent, and as a FBI SWAT team leader in Louisville office before coming to DC. She was all FBI, all the time.

"Boss, you got it. I'm out the door right now. Do you want the coverage from the Task Force or do you want a separate squad involved?" Ferguson knew what Norton was thinking: that the shot was related to some leak from the task force. At that moment, he realized he had called the right person. He hadn't even considered an insider threat.

"Give Jack Stevens a call. His FCI squad isn't all that busy. He can pony up the agents. If he gives you any guff, he can call me."

Norton put on her best Dallas belle accent. "He won't give me any guff, boss." Ferguson could hear that she was already in her car with lights and siren on headed to the hospital.

"Thanks, Molly. More to follow."

"Check, boss."

Ferguson shut off the lights in his office. There was no need to give the sniper another target and then he sat down in his chair behind his desk and poured himself a cup of coffee from the pot he made six hours ago. It was going to be a long night. He used his desk lamp to pull out his address book. He had one person he had to call right now: Barbara O'Connell.

Sue and Barbara were sitting outside Bill's hospital room. They were just down the hallway from the pair of armed lawmen sitting outside Bill's room. He had been moved from the ICU to a regular room yesterday and was now expected to make a good, if not complete recovery. The sniper's round had hit him on the left side of his chest, broken his clavicle and lodged against his shoulder blade. A few inches to the right and it would have been entirely different.

Sue had been working in 171 when the Massoni came up to her. His serious face told her that it was not the normal Massoni coming to see her. He told her about her brother, told her Bill's wound was not life threatening, but she needed to get to DC right away. He also told her that 171 didn't need her to do anything but get there, take care of her brother and not to worry about when she got back. She left immediately, went home, packed her bag and headed north in the Thunderbird.

Barbara and Sue had just had a brief conversation with Bill and had been chased out of the room by a young nurse who said he needed to rest. Molly Norton had introduced herself to Barbara and Sue as she checked in to be sure that the armed guards were both legitimate and alert. Molly put on her best Texas lawman "I'm in charge personae" as she worked the DC metro policemen. Sue was certain that they didn't know what was hitting them as she probed and prodded them into a greater degree of diligence than they had previously considered necessary. Sue liked Molly from the beginning and she wondered if some of her interest in Bill's security might just be a function of her interest in Bill for other reasons. That's the nature of our business she decided. You just don't get to meet strangers in this world, so you better find a mate from inside the system. At one point, Molly had been close to hurting the insistent nurse when Barbara intervened, and she and Sue moved Molly out into the hallway.

While Molly Norton was working on the DC metro uniforms, Barbara pulled Sue aside for a family discussion. "Sue, they said the shot was from the building next to the FBI offices. It was a high velocity

.22 hollow point. Not typical of local gangs who live by their machine pistols and AKs."

"But typical of hired killers, right?"

"Yes, Sue. Typical of hired guns."

"Like our nightmare."

"Yes, dear. Like our nightmare."

"What does the Bureau have to say?"

"The same thing they said about your grandfather's murder. They will catch the perpetrator because villains always make mistakes."

"And what you do think?"

"I think this is getting out of hand and its time I did something about it."

"Mother, what exactly do you intend to do?"

"First, I'm going to move back to the area to take care of your brother. While the round didn't hit any vital organs, it did a fair bit of damage to muscle and bone. It was not your typical .22 — it seems it was a special load. Bill is going to be in rehab for some weeks if not months. I'm thinking that we need to move him down to the house on the river. Just remote enough, but not too remote."

"Sounds like a plan. I can take some leave to be with you."

"You need to get back to work tracking these men using the official systems. I intend to start tracking them using an…unofficial system. We have a number of different resources that we need to bring to bear on this effort. If you work the inside, I will bring some my old contacts into the mix."

Sue and Barbara spent the next few days building a plan while they worked with Bill to help him understand the reason for the attack. It took him some time to understand that the attack had nothing to do with his work on the Gang Task Force. Eventually with the help of Jeremy Ferguson and Molly Norton, Bill accepted that his world had just gotten substantially more complicated and more dangerous. Once Ferguson and Norton left, Bill discussed his new world with Barbara and Sue.

"So, let me get this straight. This is a family feud? O'Connell's versus Beraslovs? Like something out of a Western movie?"

Barbara sat in the chair next to Bill's hospital bed. Sue was standing behind her mother. Barbara was about to speak when Sue stepped forward.

"Something like that, though more like a Japanese samurai movie. It is also about espionage and Russian organized crime."

"Well, that makes it so much easier to understand."

"Hey, don't be such a baby." Sue stuck her tongue out at Bill.

"You are such a creep, sis."

"OK, you two. Cut it out."

"Sorry, mom." They said in unison.

"Bill, the doctors say you can leave the hospital in two days if there is no sign of infection. They want you to start as soon as possible on some physical therapy, but that can be accomplished anywhere. I want you to move down to your grandfather's place on the Potomac River and live with me while we sort out what we do next."

"What we do next? Isn't this a job for the Bureau?"

"Some of it is Bureau business and some of it is our business. In the meantime, we need to get to someplace safe and your grandfather's place is as safe as it comes."

"Really?"

"Yes, really." Barbara and Sue said at the same time.

Ferguson sat in his office thinking about how he was going to frame his presentation. He looked at his coffee cup. He had been pondering this same question for the last three cups and still didn't quite have the answer. Might as well just get started and figure it out on the run. Not exactly how he liked to work cases, but it would not be the first time he had decided to go with his gut rather than with evidence. He stood up, put on his suit coat and walked out into the squad bay.

"Meeting right now. In the conference room." His voice echoed across the entire squad bay, against the windows and the cipher locked door that controlled access to the task force. Ferguson saw the team had heard him and were heading into the conference room. As soon as he knew he had their attention, he went back into the office and sent the power point presentation from his desktop computer to the computer in the conference room. He then walked out of his office and into the conference room. He looked around. All of the team who were on duty today were in place: seniors at the table , more junior officers at the chairs on the periphery.

"First off, I need to know who here has a case about to go to prosecution?"

Two of the thirty officers raised their hand. Mike Sanders was a senior FBI case agent and Norm Bukinski was attached to the task force from the Virginia Highway Patrol. Molly Hanson spoke up. "Boss, Mikey and Norm have two different informants from M13 who have provided a breakdown of their transportation network. We intend to take down the transportation jefe tomorrow morning at about 0200hrs. The US Attorney says it could be the break he has been looking for in attacking their drug, gun and people smuggling outfit. We have the indictments, the warrant and already have eyes on the M13 safe house where this guy lives. I already have SWAT and the special surveillance group (our SSGs) ready to go. Mikey and Norm will be the arresting officers."

Ferguson already knew the case and what Molly had been working on as his "duty relief," basically as his number two. He just wanted to have the rest of the squad up to speed on this case and it was as good a way to do so as any. "Thanks, Molly. OK, you three focus on what you have to do now. You get back to your desks, get the job done and I will circle back with you on Monday. Good luck tonight. Take 'em down and bring back the goods."

Molly already knew what he was going to say when they left. She didn't want to be out of the room, but as Ferguson put it, sometimes deputies do what the boss doesn't want to do, and this was one of those times. The three left the room and Molly closed the door. Ferguson eyed the rest of the team. It was as good a working outfit as he had ever run and better than any he had ever worked on.

"You all know that Bill O'Connell took a round in the shoulder." Ferguson hit the controls and crime scene photos came up on the screen behind him. Pictures of Bill on the gurney, pictures of Ferguson's office covered in blood and pictures of the office window with the bullet hole. "We all live with that risk every day. I get that. Bill is doing fine. I saw him at the hospital yesterday and he will be released this weekend for outpatient care. He will be back on duty in about a month, light duty first and then back to full duty by early summer. "

Ferguson looked out over the team. He made two fists and pounded as hard as he could on the conference table. Coffee cups, note books, and pens jumped around the table. Ferguson raised his voice to half way between his work voice (always loud) and his Marine voice (very loud). "Some asshole had the balls to go after one of us in our own house. I want that asshole and anyone who works for him caught and I want him caught by this squad. I know the management has transferred the work to the FCI Russia squad because they think the shooter was a member of the Russian mafia…." Ferguson paused to raise both hands, palms up. "and he may have links to Russian Intel."

He hit the screen control again and a network diagram came up on the Russian mafia in the greater Washington area. On the diagram were three different lines that ended with question marks. These were the supposed links between the mafia and the Russian intelligence officers at the Embassy. Ferguson had been trying for two years to get the Russia squad to give him some names. Everyone in the room knew the Russian squad had stiffed their boss for the last two years.

Ferguson looked at the team again, making eye contact with each one of them. "We are the gang task force. We deal with violent criminals every day. We have files on the Russian mobsters in our town. You have informants out on the street. I want you to drop whatever else you are doing until I say otherwise. I want you to search every place you can think of to find out who attacked our house. I want it known on the street that we are pissed, and we intend to make it more and more difficult for the Russians to work until they give up the assholes who attacked our house. " Ferguson paused just long enough for the team to register the point.

He said, "This is not a normal case. We are not going to be patient. We are not going to be deliberate. We need to get out on the street and let everyone know that we are insulted, pissed off and looking for answers and willing to do harm. If your contacts are wondering who we intend to arrest, you let them know, we will arrest them. We already have some cases ready that we were holding for more evidence. I'm ok with those targets knowing the men who shot Bill made us angry and less willing to make a deal. Now, you need to be careful. We already know they intend to shoot at us. I want this to be buddy teams from start to finish. No one goes out alone to do this," Ferguson paused again for effect. He knew he had their attention. "And I want a case. I want to bring these mopes to justice. I want them on trial, I want the newspapers and the television to be at the courthouse when we bring these guys forward in orange jumpsuits, shackles and leg irons. And…I want the Russian mob to know they don't own this town and they definitely do not own us. Now, team up and I want you in front of my desk this afternoon outlining how we are going to make this happen. Get outta here!"

The team left the room. Ferguson was pleased with his performance and their response. Molly stuck her head into the conference room. "Well?"

"I think they got the message that we are the ones who are going to take these guys down, whoever they are. You know, I really do want them arrested for the simple reason that bringing villains to justice is what I do for a living."

"But?"

"Well, if there is going to be shooting, I'm going to be the one who does the shooting, you can count on that."

"That's what I figured, Boss. I just want to be there in the stack when we go through the door. "

"Molly, you don't have to worry about that. You will be the only one I will have at my six."

"Deal. Now, on the M13 case..." Molly dropped a two inch file on the conference room desk. "There are some complications."

Ferguson sat down and opened the file. "There always are complications. How about you get us both some coffee and we'll work through them. We need a good result here so that we can move on to the real case."

Molly was already out the door when she looked over her shoulder. "Two coffees on their way."

Sue called Massoni from Washington and told him that she would be returning to 171 no later than 26 April.

"Sue, take as long as you need to with your brother."

"Jim, the reality is that my work may help us figure out what happened."

"Really? Oh, the boss is going to love this right?"

"Precisely."

"Brilliant. I will let him know you are coming in on Wednesday, 26 April and you will have a surprise for him. He loves surprises."

"Oh, thanks Jim."

"I'm always there for you, kid."

Sue drove the Thunderbird down to the house, opened it, set up the guest rooms and filled the fridge and the pantry. She wasn't sure how much her mom would want to cook from scratch, so she filled the freezer with various frozen options as well as about a dozen frozen pizzas for Bill. She expected his appetite would be back to normal by the time he arrived. Sue also set up one of the downstairs rooms that previously had served as a small study as a small gym. Sue remembered her lengthy physical therapy effort and figured Bill would need someplace to work out as he rebuilt his shoulder and chest muscles damaged by the gunshot wound trauma. Barbara and Bill arrived at the house on Monday as scheduled and they settled in quickly. She had already identified a retired Agency medic living in the area who was now on the Agency EMT reserves. He would play the role of "nurse" for Bill.

The first of the strategy sessions took place in the house on Monday night after Sue made the only dish she was certain would always come out right: Chicken Marbella. Sue had learned this dish from her mother over the years. It was a foreign service staple that was easy to create, simple to double or triple in case of visitors, and what Massoni once called a "fire and forget" meal. After she cleared the table of the dishes and brought out the coffee and the port, Sue joined her mother and Bill. Barbara took charge from there.

"Here is what we know for sure. The Beroslavs have been successful twice in killing O'Connell's. Your father and your grandfather were both targets." She looked at Bill. "Sue was nearly killed in Cyprus and you were just targeted as well."

"Sue, can't you stay out of trouble even in Club Med?"

"It's just my nature."

Barbara looked at them both with her hands on her hips. "Enough. These guys are serious, they are former intelligence officers that makes them good at infiltration, and they are ruthless. So, you have to be serious. These are not guys who are going to quit. "

Sue reached out and grabbed Bill's left hand. She looked at her mother. Barbara was taking on a role of team leader the way anyone else might put on a favorite winter coat for the first time in a November morning. It fit well, easily conforming to the body.

"Here's is how I see us moving forward."

"First, Sue, you need to get back to your unit and start working out how the Beroslav's got your name and location when you were supposed to be on a compartmented 171 mission and an even more compartmented CIA-FBI counterintelligence mission."

"What FBI mission?" Bill hadn't been read into the double agent operation called ELEKTRA and neither Sue nor Barbara had remembered to tell him until now.

"Bill, for now, just accept the fact that your sister was working on an operation targeting the GRU. The rest is a story for another time. You didn't have a need to know and unless you decide in the long run to work CI targets, you are going to have to accept there are going to be operations that Sue runs that are just not for us to know about, at least not immediately."

"Cloak and dagger stuff. I hate it."

"Dear, I'm sure you do, but you aren't going to get a choice for at least a little while. Even your boss has accepted that for now."

"Ferguson knows what is going down?"

"Ferguson was briefed into what he needed to know by the Washington FCI squad. Honestly, I think he was glad to hear that the attack had nothing to do with the Gang Task Force and everything to do with FCI. "

"I can see that."

"Molly certainly worried about you, no?" Sue couldn't help but insert this little bit of elicitation effort to see how Bill would react. She noticed he blushed.

"Enough already." Barbara saw through Sue's gambit with little effort. "Now, while Sue is working on the inside trying to sort out what this all means, Bill will be getting healthy and, eventually back to work, though at a desk working for an old friend of mine, Janice Macintosh."

"FCI Russian squad."

"Bill, I'm glad you see where this is going. Janice is a good friend of the family. She was the Legal Attaché in Prague on our last overseas assignment. "

"She is also a man eater." Bill did not look pleased.

"No doubt. But I doubt that Ferguson is all that easy to work with if you are not 100 percent at work, right? So, for now, I can only say get over it and get with the program." Barbara paused. "And, since you will not be on the Gang Task Force any more, you can date Molly." Sue hadn't seen that last comment coming, and she broke out in a snort that caused her to cough and turn red. Bill just blushed again.

"While you two are working the US government side of the equation, I will be working with some of our family friends who can help. The first will be an old friend of the family and Sue's as well. Max Creeter. Max has already offered to help after your grandfather was murdered and now he has insisted. He will be coming down tomorrow to join us along with another old friend who you might remember from our time in Kenya, Beth Parsons."

"Beth Parsons? Wasn't she a senior at the mission in Nairobi?"

"Yes, Bill. She was the deputy chief of mission — basically the senior foreign service officer in Nairobi. She continued to advance in State Department and was the Ambassador in Kiev and again in Warsaw. She ended her career as an undersecretary of state for European affairs. She is now a highly paid consultant for a legal firm with clients interested in partnering with Russian firms in the Former Soviet Union states. Beth's connections within the FSU and in Moscow proper are better than anyone else I know. She also just happens to be your godmother, Bill."

Bill looked at Sue. "Who knew?"

"So, tomorrow, we gather in the library for lunch, we sort out the different parts of the mission and then proceed along multiple tracks." Barbara looked at Bill. "For now, I think the next best action is for Sue to show you some of the special aspects of the house while I check the security before we call it a night."

"This is getting more and more like a spy novel every minute." Bill was still not entirely certain that any of this was real or, at least, not as serious as his mother said.

Sue looked at her brother with his arm in a sling and the pressure bandages pushing up from his shirt. "Bill, trust me, this is far more serious than any spy novel you have ever read. These guys are cut throats and they are after us. Nothing more than our deaths will satisfy them and, having lived through a direct meeting with these guys, they have no more emotion about killing than you have when you kill an ant in your bathroom. No emotion at all. Now, you need to see the wine cellar."

"Wine cellar?"

"OK, it is a wine cellar, but it also happens to be the armory."

The two of them walked away while Barbara started to pick up the remaining dishes. She wondered when her world got so crazy. It only took her a minute to realize that her world had always been this crazy from the time she married Peter O'Connell and entered "the trade." She hoped her children would survive the next few months. She wasn't sure any of them would, but she intended to do everything she could do to keep her children alive.

Max Creeter arrived on Monday night after dark and before Sue had finished cleaning up the dishes. Sue realized that her mother had made some electronic modifications to the Potomac River house when a small alarm started to go off and the television screen in the kitchen came on to display an ancient Land Rover Defender coming up the driveway. The sensor must be at the end of the driveway that lead from the road to the house on the river. Sue pondered how many other sensors were yet to be discovered.

She watched as Max Creeter got out of the Defender, it was an old right-hand drive version. He walked to the back of the truck and pulled out a square long gun case and a black duffel bag. House guests at the O'Connells appeared to come with their own arsenal. Sue met Max at the door.

"Greetings, stranger. Please provide the password to enter Castle Despair."

"Templar" was all Max said as he pushed through the door with his two bags — neither seemed to be under 50 pounds.

"Any chance there is a garage that I can store the battlewagon?"

"Around the back and under the house. I will open the garage door to Bay 3. I'm in Bay one and Mom's rental is in Bay two."

"Check. Meet you down stairs after you lock up."

No hug, no greetings, not even the normal banter that Sue was used to from Jalalabad. It must be a serious if Max was this serious. Sue always knew that there was trouble in Jalalabad when Massoni stopped joking.

Max returned from the garage, carried his kit up the stairs to his room when directed by Sue and then returned to kitchen. By this time, Max had changed into sweats and trainers and a nylon shoulder holster holding an ancient 1911A1 .45. Sue had a cup of tea and a couple of home-made oatmeal cookies waiting. Before Max had a chance to sit down at the kitchen bar, Barbara and Bill came into the kitchen. Max stood and gave Barbara an enormous bear hug and then grabbed Bill's left shoulder and slapped him gently on the cheek.

"I think by now you both realize being a bullet magnet is not ideal."

Sue and Bill nodded and Barbara said, "Too true."

"Barb, I don't remember you actually catching any of the bullets shot at you."

"Mom??" Bill was still learning that his mother was more than someone who made great food and did a little spying on the side.

"Max, you were not supposed to reveal all of my secrets in the first hour of this family reunion."

"Sorry." Max did appear to be sorry, though Sue was not entirely certainly because she had never seen Max Creeter show any remorse. "I just meant…"

"Let it go, Max. She will let us know when she is ready." Sue decided to give both Max and her mom a break.

"Now, tea and biscuits! Perfect." Max did a pretty good imitation of a British accent though to Sue's ears it sounded more like a South African accent. Another bit of curious history?

They spent most of the night listening to Max tell stories about his transition from warrior to academic. They laughed out loud as he portrayed everything from his first day at Georgetown University to the arrival of his first set of graduate student interns. When they had their fill of tea and tales of academe, Barbara brought them back to their currently reality.

"Max, for now, I need you to be our security as we build a plan and then, I suspect, I will need your help building a small team that can do certain…investigative activities in Europe which will allow us to find the source of the Beroslav resources. I realize you are an academic right now. Can you make the time without drawing any attention?"

"Barb, the life of the academic is always fraught with challenges," Max paused for effect. "…but disappearing for a few weeks or months is not one of them. I'm currently on an unpaid sabbatical from Georgetown. I'm supposed to be researching a new book and preparing for classes next Fall when Georgetown honestly intends let me loose on their undergraduates. They intend to use me as a full up professor if you can imagine that."

"Max, that is terrifying." Sue had been careful not to speak too much or too often — this was her mother's show. Still, she couldn't help it when her "inside voice" leaked out. Sue thought back to her time in William and Mary. No professor she had doubled as a Special Forces operator at least as far as she knew. Max was currently sitting across the table, relaxed with his hands wrapped around a ceramic mug filled with Earl Grey tea.

Barbara received a call on her mobile at the breakfast table at 0630hrs. Everyone was up, more or less, drinking coffee, watching the sunrise hit the river and generally lost in thought. "Beth will be here at 0800hrs. I'll start breakfast. Sue, please get the study ready for our meetings. Bill, you can set the table even if you only have one arm to do it right?"

Bill had been trying to lose the sling for his arm for the past two days. Every time he took it off, his mother put it back on. Last night, Max took over that duty. Max promised that he would give Bill a workout that would make him cry as soon as they could break free, but only if Bill kept the sling on for another 12 hours. "Right, mom."

Beth Parsons arrived with the fanfare you might expect from a visiting dignitary. At precisely 0800hrs, a black, long wheelbase Jaguar XJ pulled up in front of the Potomac river house. The driver stayed in the car while a young, fit man got out of the passenger door. He paused for a second, looking around the driveway and the house and then opened the right rear passenger door. Beth Parsons had arrived.

Barbara was waiting at the door to the house. She watched Beth walk up the stairs to the house in her black power suit. Barbara knew it was "Washington armor" but Beth moved as comfortably as if she was wearing jeans, sweatshirt and Nikes. Beth Parsons was a slim, fit woman of indeterminate age, though Sue was certain that she had to be 60 plus. She had her hair cut in a blunt pageboy that, unless she was very lucky, had been dyed jet black.

Looking from one of the windows in the study, Sue noticed Beth was carrying a well-worn, black Coach shoulder bag that looked large enough to handle a laptop, a submachine gun or, perhaps, both. After greetings and introductions, they had a late breakfast created out of nowhere by her mother and moved into the study. Sue delivered a fresh pot of coffee and a pot of Earl Grey tea, made to order for Max. Sue started another kettle of water to boil; this was not going to be the last set of pots of the day.

The meeting brought several factors into some degree of clarity for Sue, in a "through the looking glass" sort of way. Her mother demonstrated over the meeting that she was not just a former operations officer, she was calling in unspecified debts from powerful enough obligations that both Max Creeter and Beth Parsons simply couldn't refuse to help. Sue had spent enough time with this old/new version of her mother that she was not as unnerved as her brother. Bill had accepted that he was the target of the assassin, but he hadn't accepted yet that his mother was someone who could and, in fact, may have pulled a trigger in the past.

Barbara shifted almost immediately into "work mode" and explained the situation to the visitors. Sue found it interesting that she avoided any discussion of her father's death or, for that matter, Sue's recent confrontation in Cyprus. Instead, she made it relatively simple — Peter Senior had run afoul of seniors in the KGB who became the Russian mafia. Now, they had murdered Barbara's father in law and appeared to be coming after her son. The US government didn't seem to be able to capture the connections, so Barbara was asking help from her friends to do things that the intelligence and law enforcement communities couldn't accomplish. Once this very abbreviated and only slightly true story was outlined to Max and Beth, Barbara addressed what needed to be accomplished.

"Max, as we talked about last night, the first order of business is security here until Bill is back on the job and then, challenges as we try to sort out the Beroslav network."

Max nodded. He had started to shave his head again and had well groomed, very short gray beard. He was dressed in jeans, a white button down collared shirt and a set of New Balance trainers that looked like they had definitely seen some trails in the last few weeks. He looked more like a Silicon Valley venture capitalist than a commando, except for the small revolver grip that was peeking out from a deep concealment holster in the small of his back. She wondered what his students would think the first time they saw this man at the front of the class, sans gun of course. Sue decided she needed to add something if for no other reason to demonstrate she was part of the equation.

"Max, we have a few items down in the basement you need to see."

"Sue, I helped your grandfather build that part of the basement, so I'm thinkin' that it won't be a big surprise for me." Sue blushed as, once again, she realized that the O'Connell family history was full of surprises.

"Beth, now that you know the deal, do you think you could help?"

Beth had taken off her black suit coat and was sitting in a brilliant turquoise silk shirt. Sue was convinced that the shirt along with the suit jacket, black wool pants and black pumps was worth more than virtually everything in Sue's closet at home and, perhaps her Thunderbird as well. Sue had always thought her mother was very stylish, but next to Beth Parsons, she definitely looked the part of the retired government officer. Of course, the murder of her husband, her father in law and the attempts on her children's lives might have had something to do with it.

"Barbara, you know I can and you know I will. Sterns and Mandeville have resources that will be essential to our better understanding of the Beroslavs and their business. I can imagine we will even be able to get billable hours out of this as the firm has a number of clients who would very much like to know what firms in Europe are linked to the Russian mafia — just for their peace of mind, of course." Beth smiled. Sue could imagine it was the sort of smile that might have been captured in a portrait of one of the Borgias.

"Doing good work and getting paid for it? Nice." Sue was convinced that this was Max's inside voice suddenly leaking out. Sue wasn't entirely sure that Max's comment was sincere or sarcastic. Beth looked at him. Again, that same non-smile smile.

"Well, Max. We can probably figure out a way to get you that sort of deal for the length of this job. Interested?"

This time it was Max who was at a loss for words. Beth cocked her head to the right and started writing down some notes on a small Yves Saint Laurent notebook that she had pulled from her enormous bag. She passed a note to Max. He looked at it, nodded and put it in his shirt pocket.

This meeting of her parent's generation of colleagues had thrown Sue into the deep end. She couldn't tell what was going on at any level and this latest serve and volley between Max and Beth Parsons was definitely evidence that there was nothing that she knew today that they didn't know and had practiced for years. On her way out for another pot of coffee and a separate pot of Earl Grey for Beth, Bill followed her out to the kitchen.

"What in the world was that all about?"

"Pretty strange seeing Mom in her real element, eh?" Sue remembered the first time she actually saw her mom in action as they traveled to New York to attend her grandfather's funeral. It was as if someone decided to tell her that the sun rotated around the earth. It made everything seem unbalanced. Now Bill was facing this same challenge.

"Mom's transformation is one thing. But, what about Max and Beth? Are they for real and, should I be worried?"

"Not as worried as the Beroslavs, I reckon." Sue had filled the pots, rinsed the glasses and took the tray back to the study.

By the end of the day, Beth had returned to her car and left for DC and Max was already checking the alarm systems and the perimeter with the ancient .45 now holstered on his hip. Sue hadn't seen what was in the long gun case, but she expected it was already in place somewhere in the house. Perhaps to the "widow's walk" structure at the top the old Victorian? No telling.

Barbara, Bill and Sue gathered in the kitchen as Barbara assembled dinner with Sue played the role of sous chef and Bill played with the corkscrew that had opened a bottle of well-aged red wine. The meal was a simple one of lamb stew with early spring vegetables from the market that they picked up on the way to the Potomac house. The smell of onions, garlic and turmeric filled the kitchen. Barbara had the rice cooker on and working and she had made four small rounds of flatbread for dinner. Sue remained amazed, six hours of war planning hadn't slowed her mother's cooking down one bit.

Bill said, "Mom, how long do you think this is going to last? Being on watch for the Beroslav's and living in this house as if it was a safe house and we were some family in witness protection?"

"Bill, we are only staying here until you are cleared for light duty by the FBI. Probably another ten days. That .22 didn't do much damage, so you can return as soon as the doctors at Walter Reed say you are cleared. After that, I will return to the bungalow in Chicago for a bit and regroup with you and Sue when we start to make progress. Our efforts against the Beroslavs will take some time so I'm not expecting a quick resolution. According to your grandfather, they have been after us since World War II. We have to realize we need to take our time, use all available resources and, perhaps expect that we are never going to resolve this completely. That's the problem with tribal feuds. Unless there is some enforced resolution, revenge is always the most likely scenario."

"Hatfields and McCoys?"

"More like Waziris and Mahsuds, I reckon." Sue was beginning to realize that this was well and truly a tribal feud like she saw in the mountains of Afghanistan. Brutal, violent and unpredictable.

"For now, we are safe here with Max on watch, the electronics we have in the house and recognizing that we have to be on our guard 24/7. Once we return to work, we get some real traction. Sue, that's why you have to return to work tomorrow. We need you in the game, the official game, with the resources of the Agency and SOF on your side. "

"Check, mom."

Sue had returned to Bragg as promised on time and refocused on challenges of her two jobs: one for SOF and one the single most important player in ELEKTRA, the double agent operation targeting the GRU. Her farewells to her mother and Bill as she left her grandfather's house had been harder than she thought but she acknowledged that her ability to work inside the system was essential to the overall safety of the family. Now that she was back "inside the system" she wasn't all that sure.

"Hey, kid. What's the news on Bill?" Massoni was the first to greet her on arrival inside the warehouse. No matter what time Sue arrived at 171, Massoni appeared. It was 0600hrs, Massoni was in his sweats and looked as if he had been working out in the warehouse gym for at least an hour. He was holding a mug of coffee in each hand.

"Want some?"

"Your coffee, Jim? Really?"

"More for me then." He downed the first mug and started on the second.

"Bill is fine. It was a .22, designed for a head shot. Just luck that he was turning away when the shot was fired. That and the glass deflection resulted in a shoulder wound. He will be fine. Desk duty for a few months during rehab and he'll be back on the street as the O'Connell family crime fighter."

"And you?"

"Jim, it wasn't easy going to the hop or hanging with him and mom. Still, it was even harder leaving."

"I understand Mad Max is now on retainer protecting your family."

"Jim, the SOF jungle telegraph is better than ever. Yes, Max is helping mom and Bill. The perpetrator is still out there, and we don't know why they targeted Bill. Max offered to help." Sue decided to change the subject before she had to answer any more questions. One thing she always wondered about Sergeant Majors was how they always were ahead of the game. At the beginning of her Army career, Sue thought it was simply a network of NCOs that Sergeants Major kept as their internal intelligence network. After years in the Army, Sue accepted it was just magic.

Sue said, "When do you get here in the morning? Or do you just sleep here hanging upside down like a bat from the steel girders?"

"Sue, you know better than that. It's part of the mystique of a Command Sergeant Major always to be there. They teach it at the Sergeant Major's academy. Secret of the guild."

"Fair enough. Now, I'm going to make some real coffee in the squad bay, so if you want something other than your diesel oil, you can come by later. "

"Thanks, kid. Time for me to return to the rafters."

Sue smiled as she went back to her desk. There were certainly compensations for working "inside the system" and working with Jim Massoni was one of them. When Sue got to her desk, there was a note from Flash. It said, When you log on today, check the files I sent you last night. We need to talk.

Sue went to the safe, opened the drawer with the hard drives and pulled out her drive. She put the hard drive in the shell and fired up her computer. She checked her mail. Flash sent her two different emails with attachments with a time log of 0220hrs 26 May. Sue said out loud "Am I the only one in this place that actually goes home at night."

A voice from farther down the warehouse said "Yes, as a matter of fact."

"Flash, what the heck are you doing?"

"Give me coffee and I will tell. No coffee, no tell."

Sue walked over to the team coffee pot which was almost finished brewing a blend she bought while in DC. Sitting next to the pot was Flash's mug — red with a yellow lightning bolt on both sides — the logo from the DC Comics hero. Sue grabbed her mug with the 18th ABN Corps Dragon. She filled the two mugs and walked to Flash's cubicle.

"Coffee!" Flash looked like she had been in place all night. She was in jet black sweats, jet black crocs and was wearing red framed reading glasses.

Sue delivered as instructed and added, "Coffee, good. Sleeping in cubicle not good."

"Sleeping period is not all it is cracked up to be. Especially when you have work to do."

"Now you are going to make me feel bad that I get 6+ a night."

"I doubt you have any bad karma left, Sue. It's not like you haven't already had enough already. I'm just a simple computer genius trying to do my part."

"And, if you ever tell me what that part is, I will be amazed, I'm sure."

"Coffee first, then facts." Sue watched Flash work on the mug — black with three sugars. As far as Sue was concerned, about the worst possible mix of acids she could think of, but that's what Flash wanted, so that's what Flash got.

After a few minutes of silence, Flash started in at her normal speed — basically, New York City conversational speech pattern on steroids.

"While you were up North…," Flash paused. "Sorry, how is your brother?"

"Good. Cranky. Safe. Under care by my mother and a former SOF operator named Creeter."

"Mad Max Creeter? The hero, Max Creeter? The published author, Max Creeter? You know him?"

"Flash, it turns out that he is an old friend of the family, though I didn't know that. He was in J-bad when I was there with Massoni."

"Girl, you need to check out his history. He is one amazing dude. National Pentathlete, Gold medal winner in college. Green Beret, Ranger, SOF operator. Distinguished Service Cross, Silver Star, a couple of combat jumps, retired Squadron Command Sergeant Major, PhD, advisor to SECDEF, well, it goes on and on. "

"And where did you find this out and why?"

"We have some very interesting access here at 171 brain trust and we need to know everything," Flash turned to Sue and stuck her tongue out.

"Nice. Very professional." The voice from the opposite side of the cubicle wall was Jedidiah Smith, 171 commander.

"Boss, I was just giving Sue the updates we identified last night."

"Flash, it was early this morning, but that's good. She has to get up to speed quickly because she needs to travel." Smith turned to Sue. "Sue, how's your brother."

"Fine, boss. He will be back at work on light duty shortly. He was lucky."

"So, I heard from our FBI liaison at SOF." Sue was always surprised at how small a world the special operations, intelligence and federal law enforcement communities were and how incestuous they could become. It was so much easier when she was just another S&R operator on TDY someplace tracking some villain.

"Boss, I will get the dump from Flash and then come by your office, K?"

"Sounds like a plan, O'Connell. Flash, make her smart."

"Tough duty, boss." This time it was Sue that stuck out her tongue. Once Smith left the area, Flash held out her coffee mug. "More coffee."

"Yes, ma'am."

Sue returned from the squad bay after filling Flash's mug. Flash nearly finished the second mug before she started. "While you were gone, I started by accessing Daniel's email logs. You do remember Daniels, right?"

"Flash, I may appear to have been distracted by the fact THAT MY BROTHER WAS NEARLY MURDERED, but I do remember our missing 171 operator."

"Ok, just checking."

"So, I checked his emails and it turns out that he received an encrypted email from the Pentagon on his last day in Cyprus. "

"Eh? Who sent it?"

"Well, it was encrypted, so it took pure genius to sort that out. I only got it open last night. But, first things first, while I was doing that heavy lifting, we got a report from Ginger working out of Dohuk. "

"He's doing Kurdistan and AQI, right?"

"Check. He has four sources that he is running — well, he had four sources. One was killed last week. Before he was killed…"

"Wait a sec, kid. How did it happen? Is Ginger all right?"

"Now, girl, if he wasn't all right would I have jumped over that part of the story? After all, Ginger is the heart throb of nearly every chick in SOF, so you are not the first one to ask that question. Yes, he is all right. His source was shot during a meeting. The S&R crew and a raid team took care of the rest of the story. The whole report is on your computer as one of the attachments I sent…" Flash looked at her very large, very black, watch. "I guess the Boss is right, it was this morning."

"OK, so what did Ginger have to report?"

"The Syrian source said that an American is being held prisoner in Syria in the city of Raqqa — Northeastern Syria. NFI." No further information. Sue was still puzzled by why this was more important than Daniels' emails.

"So, I check with the Fort, OGA and even the FBI and they are all hearing the same thing — an American prisoner, possibly intelligence officer, held by one of the dozen or so Syrian intelligence services. No one is missing an IO except…"

"171"

"Correct. Now that doesn't mean anything much at this point, until I start going through Daniels' encrypted correspondence."

"And…" Sue realized that Flash was enjoying pulling the threads of the case out one at a time, but it was starting to get a bit annoying.

"Hey, girl. Remember, I'm the one who hasn't been home for the last two nights."

"And your clothes tell the tale."

"Thanks for that, Ms. Fashionista." Flash looked Sue up and down — black fleece, long sleeved polo shirt, jeans, Merrill light hikers.

"Fair enough. So?"

"So, it turns out that Daniels has ties to a special team inside the Pentagon. The ties are based on his old work in Army CI back in the day working against the Evil Empire. Well, the team is focused on the weapons of mass destruction threat from AQ. They appear to be cherry picking assets from all over the IC except OGA and the FBI (who appear to be out of the compartment). DoD only resources. They are trying to hunt down possible leads. "

"And Daniels?"

"Well, they reached out to him because one of his old Army CI cases had to do with KGB operations focusing on our tactical nuclear units in Germany in the 1980s. This Pentagon team thinks that the old KGB guys, now Russian mafia guys, are willing to sell just about anything to anyone for a price. Perhaps including radiological material. Including radiological material from Saddam's old program. "

"But we didn't find a program in '03 or '04 when we were looking for it. "

"Not bombs, silly. Just rad material, especially hazardous rad material. Plenty of that in Iraq, Syria, just about anywhere in the former Soviet Union. "

"So, Daniels was working on a case for them?"

"The emails suggest that he was given a lead of a former Soviet, now Belorussian scientist who was out shopping his skills on the criminal marketplace in Bavaria. That's why Daniels was in Germany. "

"And he didn't tell anyone in 171?"

"Nope and the boss is pissed."

"I would guess so."

"We don't know that Daniels is the guy in Syria, but we do know that he was last seen in Bavaria and no one in the US or German security system can find him. We also know that we are the only part of the US intel community missing an agent. Now you know the rest of the story."

"More in the files?"

"Plenty in the files, but I think you ought to see the boss before you spend the morning reading the files. He was pretty agitated last night, or…early this morning…when we sorted this out."

"Flash, you are a super genius."

"That's me. Wile E. Coyote. Super Genius."

Sue went back to her desk with her coffee cup. She didn't like Daniels before and she didn't like him now. One thing that SOF and the Farm taught you was you always told your boss what was going on, no matter what and no matter who told you to keep your trap shut. Otherwise, there was no way the system would work, and this was a perfect example. If it wasn't for Ginger, 171 would never have known that there was someone, possibly Daniels, in a prison somewhere in Northern Syria. Dandy.

Security was one thing. Secrecy for the sake of secrecy was another and often was designed more than anything else to hide stupidity. When Sue was in college, she had read case studies in her national security studies program outlining how political figures often made bad decisions, tasked law enforcement, the intelligence community or Special Operations to execute the decisions and then hid behind compartmentation to avoid scrutiny. She had heard of the same thing while in SOF and at the Farm. At the end of the day, you need to be sure that everyone that needs to know knows what is going on. Still, how different was this from the secrets she was learning about her family? How do you make a distinction? Where do you draw the line? It made Sue's head hurt, so she decided to get back to the basics. She would engage Smith and Massoni, they would tell her what they wanted done and she would do it.

It wasn't even 0800hrs yet and she was already deep in a project and in Smith's office. Not exactly the easy transition that she had hoped for and certainly not a quiet opportunity to work "on the inside" for the family business.

"OK, O'Connell, I take it Flash brought you up to speed."

"Boss, I still haven't read the files yet, but I know the specifics. "

"I'm not going to tell you how much of a moron I think Daniels was in this case. I will save that for when we find out where he is, get him out, and I can choke him with my own hands."

Sue realized that Smith was using a metaphor, but it was still scary.

"Based on the data we have, we have the following plan." At that point, Massoni walked over to the white board which normally was filled with scribbles outlining where everyone in 171 was that day — erased each night and replaced each day with more scribbles. Today, the board was empty. Massoni had the pen as Smith started to dictate. "We have set aside a series of operations assuming that Daniels is in Syria. I have the Fort, DIA, CIA and the FBI trying to confirm this. For now, we are going to work on finding and rescuing whoever is in that prison. If it is Daniels, great. If not, then you get back to searching for him."

"I know Flash already told you, but this started as a Pentagon operation with White House interest. If AQ has material for a radiological weapon, we are really in the shit. So, along with everything else, your job is to sort out if this Intel is crap or real. If real, how real."

"Lucky you, " Massoni said quietly in an effort to avoid a projectile headed his way. It didn't work. Smith launched an eraser at Massoni's head. It missed or, perhaps, Smith never intended to hit his sergeant major. Smith continued, "Ok, here is the way it stacks up right now:" Massoni started to write.

"Adam Burkhart is in Jalalabad — he stays there and continues to work the Afghan targets. Same with Paul Mulroney and Patricia Gomez working in Kabul. Our team in the Bahrain, Bill Makropolos, Terri Majors, and John Markwell all stay there — their work on the Gulf targets are just too important to pull."

Sue knew the names as simply pins in the map. They had all been deployed when she arrived at 171 and hadn't been back when she was working in the warehouse. Now they were on the white board on one side of a line that Massoni had drawn.

"Andy Jacobs, Joe Peterson, and Marty Vincente are working cases from Baghdad and we are sending your pals, Peter Knoblach and Joe Shepard, to take up the slack. Andy and his team will move forward to Mosul to work with Ginger who is working in Dohuk. Jerry Tiermann and Will Sanderson will deploy to Incirlik and Pigpen Taylor goes to Beirut. " By this time, the white board was filled with names and locations that all circled Syria. The only name not on the board was Sue's.

"Boss, where do I go?"

"Well, O'Connell, I thought long and hard about this because I have to consider where we can stand to have trouble." Sue winced. "Here's the plan. You are going to follow Daniels' footsteps. First, you go to the UK and work with the Brits for a day or two. I want to know as much as they will tell you about Daniels. It It shouldn't be much since he basically used London as a transit hub. After that, you go to Germany and work with the Army CI team that is sorting this out with the Germans — mostly through their Bavarian state police and state security — the LKA and LFV. I'm hoping you can get something out of that team that hasn't arrived by electronic reporting. After that, you follow wherever the lead takes you. After all, Daniels disappeared in Munich. So, we don't actually know that he is in Syria. Remember, when I last talked to you, we thought he might have defected. We still don't know whether he was kidnapped, defected or is eating a dirt sandwich in some forest outside Munich. Sort that part out and follow the trail. Try not to destroy the NATO alliance while you are there, O'Connell."

"Check, boss."

"Oh, and by the way, you need to drop this ELEKTRA shit with OGA and the FBI until we sort out Daniels situation. I never liked this double agent mumbo jumbo anyhow and right now, we have to find our guy pronto. The rest of the cases can wait. Is that clear?"

"Yes, sir." For once, Sue used the formal military reply because it was clear she was getting a formal military order. In all honesty, she was happy to have that order.

"I am sending a note to the MILATT in London today. When do you think you can get there?"

"Commercial or military hop, boss?"

"Whatever is fastest."

"I can let you know by noon. I can pack and get out of here today if I can get a flight."

"Then get to work. Oh, and make sure you tell your mom and your brother you may be on the road. I don't need a call from OGA asking about you. You do know your mother has some juice, right?"

"No, boss. But I'm learning." Sue left Smith's office wondering what more could happen. Plague? Pestilence? Earthquakes? Hail? Suddenly she heard a muffled sound of thunder and realized the T-bird was outside with the top down. She got outside just in time to put the top up before the rain started. She moved the car under one of the covered spaces behind the warehouse before the hail arrived. She ran for the back door as hail pelted her and rain soaked her to the skin. "Perfect" was all she could say.

Barb was in the hallway in the house watching Bill and Max Creeter working out in the ad hoc gym set up in the front room of the old house. Bill was improving every day and she suspected Max Creeter's "physical therapy" sessions as well as his mental therapy sessions with her son were the cause for this improvement. Bill's shoulder wound had not been serious, but he had arrived at the house with more than a bit of paranoia and much less confidence than she had previously seen in her son when he was a combat Marine.

Max was standing in front of Bill. He was wearing a black Under Armour t-shirt, black sweatpants and tai chi shoes. Bill was in the same workout gear except his t-shirt was navy blue and his sweats were navy blue as well. They were a mirror image, both holding kettle bells and working a routine of lifting the bells from waist level through a full range of motion to head height. Max's bells were black 25 pound bells and Bill's were red 5 pound bells.

"You need to start working toward a full range of motion, Bill. I know it seems silly with just 5 pound weights, but the motion is more important than the weight. We are rebuilding your full range of motion first. We can always rebuild strength later."

"Max, it isn't that it seems silly, it is because any arm motion above my head hurts."

"Remember, pain is simply weakness leaving the body."

Bill shook his head. "Max, don't forget I'm a Marine. I know plenty about pain and weakness."

"Bill, you sure the pain is what is preventing you from a better effort? It isn't every day that you get shot." Barb backed down the hallway. She wanted to hear this conversation, but she didn't want to be seen.

"Max, I saw plenty of Marines wounded in Iraq."

"But this is your first, isn't it?"

"First? Like I should expect more?"

"Bill, I can't tell you. I never expected more than wound and ended up with two."

"Where?"

"You aren't going to use this conversation to stop the workout. Keep up with my routine. If I can work and talk at the same time, you can certainly listen and workout at the same time."

"Yes, Sergeant Major."

"So, the first time I was shot was in Central America in the early 80s. My SF team was supporting a training mission in El Salvador. We were training young Salvadorian soldiers to fight the insurgents trying to expand leftist control beyond the borders of Nicaragua. Remember to keep that full range of motion."

"So, one night at the training compound, we get a mortar attack. I was a young weapons sergeant and had heard the stories from my team sergeant who had served with SF in Viet Nam. Mortars first, then a raid through the wire. My job was to get the Salvadorans up and into their positions. Specifically, to get a machine gun team into their firing positions and ready to engage. There was no raid, Bill. Just mortars and young sergeant Creeter took a piece of shrapnel in the calf. Hurt a lot, but hardly life threatening. Once we were able to stand down from the alert, the team medic did the initial triage work and the next day I was flown to San Salvador to a military hospital. Hey, what the heck are you doing. Control the return of the weights back to your start position."

"And...?"

"Well, it taught me that anyone can die in a war zone and there is a fair bit of randomness in the story of who lives and who dies. Once you accept that, you can either become paranoid or come to terms with it is the nature of the trade. We had a great operational psychologist at Bragg who made that clear to me during my recovery. It took me about six weeks of physical therapy to get back to rucksack run strength. I spent that time at Smoke Bomb Hill at Bragg doing PT, talking to the shrink and starting my history degree. "

"What about the second?"

"I am only allowed to provide one war story per day. It's in my contract. But I will tell you that this first wound taught me that I wasn't invulnerable and that it didn't do any harm to talk to someone about my fears. When you return to DC, I'm sure the Bureau is going to insist you talk to a Bureau shrink. Do so. It will do you good."

"I wondered about that…"

"Meantime, we need to move from resistance training to some stretching. OK, put the kettle bells down. Assume the warrior pose. Follow me through this set of moves…"

Later, Barb talked to Max just before he started what he called his mid-day check of the perimeter. He had on camouflage fatigues, jungle boots and was finishing a cup of tea before heading out. She was sitting at the kitchen table holding a cup of coffee. "You are doing Bill good service, Max."

"The least I can do for the kid, Barb. You guys are like family and I suspect there are very few in the Bureau who have been shot at and even fewer who have been hit. Based on what Bill says, I think his former boss Ferguson is one of those guys, but he isn't going to have the time to have this sort of conversation or to help in the rehab."

"Bill should be ready to return to DC…when?"

"I reckon he will be ready by next week, but mentally ready to leave by the end of this week. Up to you whether you can convince him that if he goes north, he has to keep up with the routine."

"I suspect you have more influence than I will."

"Maybe, but it's not my place."

"Max, will you continue to help us when Bill returns to DC?"

Max finished his tea and walked over to the refrigerator. Leaning against the appliance was a civilian version of an M4 carbine. Max picked up the weapon, reached into the side pocket of his camouflage pants and recovered a 10 round magazine. Max fed the magazine into the magazine well of the rifle, worked the charging handle to load a round in the chamber and put the weapon on safe. With the loaded weapon barrel now faced toward the floor, Max pulled the sling over his head and pulled out a black watch cap from the opposite pocket on his pants. He looked directly at Barbara.

"I'm in for the long haul, Barb. You always knew that, but now I've said it."

"For whatever it takes?"

"For whatever it takes." Max turned and walked out the kitchen door toward the woods. In a few seconds, he had disappeared into the woods. Barb relaxed. As Max had been loading the rifle facing away from her, she had pulled her Smith and Wesson revolver from a holster that was in the middle of her back and had it in her lap. She now returned it to the holster. She still didn't trust anyone yet.

MACE

The cockpit of the C17 was a mix of green and red dials, multiple controls and two very large seats for the pilot and the copilot. They were both very awake. The sponson on the KC10 refueling bird had just separated from the C17 and both aircraft were pulling away — the KC10 to the left, C17 to the right. The aircraft had not actually needed refueling, but the crew of both aircraft needed the training for quarterly certification, so the two aircraft met over the Atlantic in the middle of the night and completed the refueling mission.

"Nice job, Sarah." The pilot in command, LTC Mitch Matthews, had been "hands off" as his copilot, 1LT Sarah Jasper, and navigator, CPT George Ames, completed the refueling. He had been flying for over 20 years, mostly multiengine jet aircraft. First B52s, then C141 Starlifters, and now C17s. He needed to see his crew in action and they were famous for letting the "old man" do the work. This time, he turned the controls and the operation over to Jasper and Ames and enjoyed the view as the KC10 pulled in above them and sent the refueling sponson into place.

"Boss, you want some coffee and one of Pope Air Force Base's best box lunches?" Master Sergeant Derek Chavez's voice came over the internal comms. He was down on the flight deck in what was called a galley and what was arguably better described as a closet. Chavez had worked as Matthew's loadmaster for 10 years. They had been based out of Ramstein for five and Pope Air Force base, the USAF component of Ft. Bragg, for another five. Matthews had asked for Chavez to come with him back to CONUS. Chavez agreed, reenlisted, and stayed with Matthews following his "tail number" for years.

"Sure, Derek. Hey, what is our passenger doing back there in the cargo hold?"

"Boss, as near as I can tell, she is reading some files. SOF operator, right?"

Ames chipped in. "Hey, what gave it away? Perhaps, when she got on board in the flight suit with no insignia, carrying a black suitcase and a laptop?"

"Smart ass." Matthews tolerated Ames because he was the best navigator in the Wing.

"I asked her." Jasper chimed in.

"And?" This time Matthews was paying attention.

"She said she works for a logistics outfit assigned to the US Army Special Operations Command. Nothing interesting, just moving cargo from one USASOC headquarters to another."

"Well, if that's what she said, then that must be the truth." Matthews said it with what his crew called "the voice" which meant "Enough!" Before his assignment to Ramstein, Matthews had flown two years for the "air commandos" at Eglin Air Force base. Part of the USAF component of the Special Operations Command. It was fun, flying various two engine turbo props, painted slate grey with no markings. He delivered more than his share of "logistics specialists" to parts of Central America in the late 1980s. "Derek, please check with our passenger to see if she wants something from our luxurious galley, OK?"

"Check, sir."

Matthews looked out the windscreen and could just make out a sliver of dawn on the Eastern horizon. Somewhere over Europe, it was time to wake up.

The inside of a C17 cargo aircraft is flight is never comfortable. Sue had jumped out of a few when she was assigned to the 18th Airborne Corps, but then the jump seats were set up for four rows of jumpers from front to back. Shoulder to shoulder, knee to knee with the smell of adrenaline and fear as the paratroopers prepared to jump. One of the reasons that Sue had volunteered for jumpmaster school was to get away from the crowd and have something to do in the aircraft before the jump. Otherwise, she would have had to wait and fret and watch paratroopers turn green, or worse.

On this flight, the aircraft was filled with cargo pallets for the 82nd Airborne on their way to Afghanistan. First stop, Lakenheath AFB, UK. Sue was jammed in a sling seat between the fuselage wall and a series of cargo pallets packed with boxes, covered in plastic and strapped down with cargo nets. Bullets? Meals? Uniforms? No way to tell under the wrapping. No matter what they were, they weren't giving Sue a lot of legroom and that was always a bit problematic with her prosthetic. She was facing forward with her left leg propped up on her suitcase and day pack. The night flight would get her to the UK in the morning and Sue was using the time to catch up on reading some of the files the brain trust had loaded on her 171 laptop.

The loadmaster walked up to her working his way along the skin of the aircraft. In a green flight suit like her own, but in a nylon flight jacket covered with his squadron patches. He was wearing a headset and trailing the headset cord behind him. He stopped at Sue and dropped off a box lunch. Over the noise of the jet engines, he shouted. "Chief, anything else I can get you?"

Sue had been wearing a Bose headset playing some Mozart from her iPod. She pulled them off and shouted back. "Thanks, but I'm good. I filled my thermos before we left Pope from your squadron coffee pot."

"That is hard core, Chief. I know an Air Force box lunch isn't appealing, but the pilots get ours from the Pope Officer's club, so they are pretty good. We are about four hours out from Lakenheath. Just come forward if you need anything."

"Thanks." The Loadmaster turned away and Sue looked inside the cardboard box. Two sandwiches, one roast beef and one chicken, an apple, an orange, and a half dozen cookies. He was right, it was far better than anything she ever ate from an Air Force box lunch. Sue opened the cookies, poured herself a cup of coffee from her thermos and turned back to the laptop. The blue light from her Mac was the only light in her part of the aircraft.

Before she left 171, the Brain Trust loaded an encrypted flash drive for her to get her started on the project. The notes were from Hawkeye since Flash was still off shift when Sue asked for help from the Brain Trust. She started with the first file.

Sue, here are the basics. Once you check with either the London MILATT or the Army CI offices in Munich, I can send you some other material. Do your best to keep your skin attached to your bones. Hawkeye.

RAD CT THREAT

Summary: Material captured from computers in AQ camps in Jalalabad included discussions on several WMD programs. Most of the material focused on chemical and very simple biological weapons — especially disabling biologicals. There were notes regarding use of hazmat material to create a radiological vice nuclear weapon. It would be an effective terror weapon because it would cause radiation poisoning, set off RAD detectors and create havoc in the cleanup phase. It required some basic understanding of special handling, but little else.

Access to hazardous materials: AQ continues to explore the availability of radiological waste from the Former Soviet Union (FSU). The Islamic Movement of Uzbekistan (IMU) and the Chechen AQ links are exploring the options. OGA and DIA have focused their efforts on partnerships with FSU services to cut that potential pipeline. More data in the files - I can't load that on this computer.

DANIELS' ACTIVITY AND LEADS:

During his last few weeks in Cyprus, a Pentagon based team working out of what seems to have been a subsection assigned to the Office of the Undersecretary of Defense for Intelligence started to engage Daniels on a special project. He received a number of emails sent through the 171 server, but sent only to him with none of the 171 management on the addressee line. One of the members of the section apparently knew Daniels from his time in Army CI. They read him in on the project to determine the level of WMD threat from AQ and other terrorist enterprises. Daniels appears to be the only 171 officer involved. Since you were already in country, he started to work on this effort during his last days in Cyprus and planned his own operation in Europe before he returned to CONUS. We only have his official correspondence with the USD(I) section and, as you know, Daniels was not a big one for writing down his plans, so we don't know a lot about his efforts, other than he intended to reestablish contact with an arms smuggler he handled during the US European Command Kosovo effort.

Sue looked up from the laptop. She remembered her work in Bosnia when she was with the 525th MI detachment and working in the Joint Operations Center. The collapse of Yugoslavia created chaos that the world saw as ethnic cleansing and ground warfare throughout the 1990s. The US intervened after the UN efforts failed to stop the genocide. The US expanded its efforts into Kosovo and eventually brokered a ceasefire. In the middle of all of the chaos, multiple criminal enterprises, some Serbo-Croatian, some Bosnian, some Albanian all began to trade in arms, drugs, and humans. Since Daniels was a CI case handler at the time, she had no doubt that he had sources inside those networks if for no other reason than "force protection" — the watch word at the time as US forces moved into the region with the full understanding that there were no friends, many enemies and, mostly, spoilers who were working all sides for profit.

Daniels reported back to his Pentagon contacts that he had reestablished that contact and intended to meet him near the St. Michael's cathedral in Munich on 24 March at 1930hrs. That was his last electronic transmission.

I checked what records we could get from the US Army Europe headquarters. Daniels had two major cases when he was in Kosovo. Only one is still alive. His name is Miroslav Dubyatch. Open source has him as head of a trucking firm that carries cargo along routes between Munich, Vienna and Zagreb. The firm's name is Dingach Trucking. I have already sent the material to the Army CI focal point for you. The focal point's name is Major Earl Bantler and he is based in Garmisch.

Sue, good luck on this. I will send you more through the MILATT in London and through Bantler. Hawkeye.

Sue looked up from the screen. Not only did she have to work to save Daniels, but her focal point in Garmisch was her former boy-friend from Ft. Bragg. What could be better? Sue remembered their last meeting.

She and Earl had decided to go to selection at the same time. The 525th commander was unwilling to send both of them at the same time, so he sent Bantler. Earl hadn't made the first cut at week two and returned to the 525th. He was angry and convinced that the S&R selection staff had been shits and prejudiced because he was an MI warrant officer not a "gunslinger." He told Sue as much and argued she was wasting her time. He thought she needed to stick with the conventional MI assignments and, eventually, go to OCS and become an officer. Sue disagreed and went to the next selection. When she returned from selection, Bantler was gone, back to Ft. Benning for Officer Candidate School. He never wrote to her or called her again. Earl is now a Major, running a CI unit and would be her focal point in Bavaria. Shit. She could expect him to demand a salute from a SOF warrant officer and would probably make it clear that he was "in charge." Shit. Shit. Shit.

Sue shut down the computer and opened one of the sandwiches from the box lunch. Might as well try the Air Force chow. It might be the best part of the trip.

S ue had dozed off shortly after she finished the box lunch. She woke when the C17 made its final approach to RAF Lakenheath and touched down with small jolt that rattled the cargo pallets. She did her best to put herself together. She would be facing someone from the US Military Attaché's office at the airbase and she didn't want to look like the way she felt which was as if she had been dragged through a knot hole, backwards. Not a lot she could do, but at least she could appear to be a bit put together. As the aircraft moved from the active runway to the taxi way, Sue stood up and tightened the Velcro waist straps on her flight suit. She pulled a nylon flight jacket from her main bag — complete with nametag and the USASOC shoulder flash. Tucked into the pocket of the jacket was her red beret with a corresponding USASOC flash and her warrant officer rank. Not exactly ready for a sergeant major inspection, but at least presentable once they opened the rear of the aircraft. The loadmaster came down the aircraft carrying her black nylon duffel bag.

"Chief, we always try to deliver door to door, but I'm not sure where you are going so I can't promise anything except a refueling spot on the tarmac."

"Master Sergeant Chavez, you are the heat. No worries about what happens next. I honestly don't know myself. I suspect I will be met planeside, but if not, I'll just walk over to the Base Ops and figure it out from there. "

"Probably not the worst place you have ever landed, eh Chief."

"Now that would be telling, wouldn't it?"

"Right on, chief."

Chavez walked past Sue and headed to the rear of the aircraft. He turned back to her and pointed to his ears — time for hearing protection. Sue put her Bose headphones on and turned on the sound suppression feature. Not exactly government issue, but they would work fine. Chavez reached up to a panel near the clam shell opening of the aircraft, pushed a button and suddenly the world appeared in the rear of the aircraft like a movie screen. Sue was reminded of the first time she "tailgate" parachute jumped out of a C130. The aircraft stabilized at 1000 feet and the loadmaster opened the tailgate of the aircraft to reveal a view of Sicily drop zone, the Pine Barrens of North Carolina and blue sky. When you exited from a jump door, you didn't see anything until the parachute opened. This time, she and 40 other jumpers from the 18th Airborne Corps walked off the ramp of the aircraft and it was brilliant.

Today, the view was far less dramatic. It was a grey morning with a light drizzle so the C17's tires left a substantial track along the taxiway. The air was cold and damp, but Sue was pleased to be breathing fresh air after seven hours on the aircraft. "Fresh" was tinged with the smell of jet fuel, so it was not all that pleasant. Finally, the aircraft came to a halt and the loadmaster lowered the tail gate to the ground. He pulled a set of yellow landing chalks from their stowage compartment near the end of the roller conveyor system that secured the cargo pallets. He waved to Sue and she started down the space between the cargo pallets and the skin of the aircraft. Never easy, even when she had two legs. Now, it was even more problematic. Worse still would be the drop from the tail gate to the ground — not much more than 20 inches, but just enough to jar her prosthetic. Sue gingerly walked to the end of the tailgate and jumped down. Definitely a pain.

"Welcome to sunny England!" Sue recognized the voice if not the uniform.

"George, what are you and Dozer doing here in Lakenheath?"

"Sue, we are here to greet you, isn't that obvious?" George and Dozer had switched from their desert camouflage uniforms to the European green and black camouflage known in the British Army as DPM, disruptive pattern material. Both were wearing the same tan watch caps that Sue had seen them wear in Cyprus when they helped her work against the IED smuggling project.

"Actually, I'm here to greet you, Chief O'Connell." A USAF Lieutenant Colonel in a flight suit, leather flight jacket and an overseas cap greeted Sue. "LTC Bill Maklovich, Air Attaché from London." Sue put on her beret and rendered a salute.

"Thank you, sir. I was just a bit surprised by my British colleagues from the Special Boat Service."

"As was I, Chief. Still, they are part of the team here and I will introduce you to the rest of the team shortly. Let's get away from the aircraft and let the loadmaster do his job."

"Yes, sir." Sue quickly walked back over to the loadmaster.

"Master Sergeant, thanks for the hospitality. No telling when we will meet again." Sue offered her hand and the loadmaster offered his nomex gloved hand.

"Always a pleasure to have some company on a flight, Chief. See you on the other side."

"Roger that." Sue caught up to Maklovitch as he walked toward a British Army Land Rover Defender parked just outside the yellow safety lines. George had already started the vehicle and Dozer was standing next to the rear passenger door to let Maklovitch and Sue in. As soon as they were in the vehicle and Dozer had thrown Sue's gear in the back, George drove off at what Sue was convinced was not the regulation safety speed for vehicles on an RAF taxiway.

"We are headed to the Joint Operations Center for OP MACE." Maklovitch shouted over the whine of the Defender's turbo-diesel. "It is our headquarters for this operation."

"Mace? Like the pepper spray?"

"No chief, like the medieval weapon."

Dozer turned around from the front passenger seat. "That was the first question I asked as well. George here knew it was the weapon. He has had a proper British education, at least as proper as it can be in Newcastle."

"Welsh bastard," was all George said.

"Chief, this project has come into place pretty quickly — mostly over the past 10 days as we started to work out some of the details of the disappearance of Mr. Daniels. Washington and London decided if we were going to address the potential for a WMD threat, we needed to work together. MACE is the joint code word for the operation. It is a collaboration between the American and British civilian intelligence services and both US and UK Special Operations Forces. The SOF piece at this point is just your unit and parts of S&R. If we get closer to a real target, other SOF units will be engaged."

Sue realized that the "other SOF units" wouldn't be pulled from their ongoing missions in Iraq or Afghanistan until and unless there was confirmation of a WMD threat and a specific location. After that, there would be some degree of political wrangling to determine first if the raid mission would be a US or UK team and then which service would get the nod. The Defender pulled up next to a hanger with a door big enough to accommodate a C17. There were no vehicles nearby nor any sign of life other than a massive antenna bank on one side. George pressed a garage door opener clipped to the visor on driver's windscreen. A portion of the hanger door opened, and they drove inside.

Sue had lived in a hanger in Cyprus with her 171 shipping container and the SBS container at opposite ends of the building with a small gym and four cars parked inside. Nothing from Cyprus prepared her for the operations center for OP MACE. In the center of the hanger had three, black roll on/roll off containers that would fit into the hold of the giant C5A aircraft. They were linked together by a three, separate passageways that looked more like vacuum hoses than anything else. On the left side of the hanger were three standard shipping containers placed end to end. There were no windows and only one door at the far end. A series of very large conduits came out of the container roofs and passed through the wall of the hanger. Sue figured that if she was oriented properly, that outside that wall was the series of antennas she saw on the way in. On the right side of the container were eight vehicles of various makes — both left and right hand drive. Four sedans, two vans, one Toyota Land Cruiser and one four door Range Rover. They were all combat parked and looked ready to roll at a moments' notice.

"Follow me, " Maklovitch lead the way to one of the doors to the black containers. They walked through the door into a room filled with computer monitors back to back running down the center of the room with analysts working at each monitor. Along the outside walls of the room were 1:500,000 scale maps covering the world. Clearly, the left side of the room was responsible for North America and South America, SE Asia and Western Europe. The right side of the room was responsible for Africa, the Middle East and Central and South Asia. The maps were filled with colored pins tied to other pins by colored string. "I know SOF would prefer big screens and digital monitoring, but we don't have the space or the time to set that sort of classified system here. So, we are making do with the old ways of keeping track of possible targets, shipments and materials. I would introduce you, but these folks are busy and in another forty minutes, there will be a shift change and we will have an entirely different crew."

"MACE is more advanced that anything I thought was going on."

"More advanced than I knew about a week ago as well. They flew half the US and Canadian crew in last week from one of those "unknown locations" that you read about in the newspapers. The other half of the crew is British. I still haven't been able to get any of them to tell me where they were set up before they arrived. Hardly matters. The entire facility is air transportable to any location that can handle C17s. If we narrow down the threat to a single location, we will all be there in 36 hours."

"Sir, I thought you were the air attaché for London?"

"That's what I thought as well until last week. This was supposed to be a quiet assignment after flying AC130s and MC130s in Afghanistan. Gunships and Intelligence birds. They are all Hercules aircraft, so if you are in Air Force Special Operations Command and you are multi-engine certified, you are flying them. I was on a crew out of Karshi-Khanabad in Uzbekistan in '01, '03, '04, and then in Balad in '05." Sue knew that Karshi-Khanabad — K2 in SOF parlance had been the jump off point for most of the early SOF missions and all of the air support to SOF until Bagram and Jalalabad airbases were secured and opened.

"This was supposed to be my extended crew rest. Then MACE came up and they needed a AFSOC officer in the UK with the right clearances. You are looking at him."

"Sir, just FYI. I was in Afghanistan in '02 and '03 and I suspect you guys saved my life more than once. So, thanks."

"Don't mention it. I never knew who was on the ground, I just flew the birds in the orbits needed and the gunners did all the work. "

Sue felt a finger tap her rather dramatically on the right shoulder. It was more like a tap from some bad stage play than the normal, friendly soft punch she was used to inside SOF. She had learned over the past few months how to pivot on her good leg and swing her prosthetic more or less naturally.

All Sue heard was "Wolf tribe rules!" before she was grabbed in a bear hug around her waist. Melissa was much shorter than Sue, so she couldn't accomplish a typical "abrazo" shoulder to shoulder. It was much closer to shoulders (Melissa's) to waist (Sue).

"What is the world are you doing in England, Melissa? The last time I saw you, you were headed back to a basement cubicle in Langley." After graduating from the Farm together on a team that Melissa had decided to christen "wolf tribe," Sue and Melissa had been part of the counter IED operation in Cyprus. Now, this expert in computer operations was in OP MACE.

"For some unknown reason, the bureaucracy has identified my genius and MACE is the operation they decided I should support. I'm actually running the midnight to morning shift on the tech side. I was heading back to the barracks when I saw your boney body in the hanger. Plenty of time to talk later. I'm done."

"G'night, M," Melissa responded to Dozer's greeting with a smile and a fond wave. Sue decided there was a back story that she was going to have to get out of Melissa or George. Dozer would never tell her what sort of barracks romance was brewing with him and Melissa.

"Chief, are there any other members of your personal entourage that I should know about before we proceed?" Maklovitch offered the question in good humor, but he was clearly ready to move on.

Sue returned to more formal stance and replied. "Sir, I certainly hope not."

"Then we need to get you processed into the team, add your 171 computer into the network, and get you a room."

"Especially a shower, sir."

"Remember, chief, you said it, I didn't."

In processing in a special operations base generally took less than an hour. Register you weapons with the armorer, draw communications equipment and get an ID card and you were done with the administration side of the in processing. For OP MACE, it took two hours of in-briefings, IT briefings and power point presentations. It was painful, but when it was completed, Sue had a much better idea of the project, the various operational sectors tracking the WMD threat and the intelligence power being thrown at the project. Still, when George drove her to the team barracks, Sue could barely stay awake. George made no effort to converse as he drove at breakneck speed across the airfield in what she now knew was an RAF security police Rover that MACE had "acquired." The blue strobe that George had on as he drove was a clue along with his reckless abandon.

"Get cleaned up, put your head down for a kip and I will pick you back up for dinner at half six, OK?"

Sue's mind was a befuddled jet lagged fog. "Half six? Is that 1730 or 1830?"

"1830, Sue". George shook his head wondering when Americans would learn proper English. Sue grabbed her duffle bag and OD helmet bag that served as her field briefcase and stumbled into the barracks, accessed through her new ID. It was noon. If she moved quickly, she could get a solid four hours before George came by for dinner with the mates.

Ferguson was working through the paperwork, as usual, and on his second pot of coffee. He was trying to remember why he decided five years ago to become a supervisory special agent running a squad as opposed to staying a street agent pursuing villains. He decided it was probably an effort to keep his second marriage together, an effort that didn't work out in the long run. Still, when the squad was working as a team, he liked being the team leader managing the resources and teaching the younger agents street smarts taught to him by FBI special agents from back in the day when you had photos of J. Edgar Hoover on the walls.

"Boss, we got a lead on the shooter." Molly was the only person in the Gang Task force who was allowed to just barge into Ferguson's office. Everyone else was told on day one, knock on the door if it is closed or knock on the wall if the door is open.

"Nice to see you, too, Norton. "

"Boss, seriously, one of our confidential informants inside the local Russian mob talked to Blake last night and offered up a name." Blake Johnson was from the Virginia Highway Patrol on detail to the Gang Task Force. He was good, and Ferguson had been trying for the last two years to get him quit his job and go to Quantico. The Bureau needed guys like Blake.

"And, did the name mean anything?"

"Serbian named Ivan Miroslav Dingach. We've never been able to build a case, but he is muscle for a Slavic extortion and smuggling gang working out of Baltimore harbor."

"And, he is where right this moment?"

"The CI offered up his cell number. The locator says he is in a warehouse in the Dulles corridor near the airport. "

Ferguson stood up. He opened his desk drawer and pulled out his paddle holster with his Glock and slid it on his belt. He reached deeper into the drawer and pulled out a 2" barrel Smith and Wesson revolver in an ankle holster. He pulled up his left pants leg and strapped the ankle holster on. He had his coat on and out the door at a trot.

"What sort of backup do you want, Boss?"

"I want Blake and you. We'll go in my Explorer." He was already in the elevator punching the button to the garage as Molly called Blake.

April in Northern Virginia should be a season of apple and cherry blossoms and leaves on trees. Winter had held through March and the leaves were just starting to come out. Ferguson was speeding down the Dulles Toll Road with the blue/red lights but no siren on. The lights were in the dash and in the back window, called a wig wag as the lights switched from red to blue and back again.

"Blake is already in the general area. He wants to know how we are going to play it." As Molly spoke, Ferguson pulled into the far left lane of the toll road and accelerated. The noise from the high revs of the Explorer's engine made talking really shouting.

"Tell him to keep at least a half mile away. We will meet up at a Denny's on Route 15 just outside Dulles. We have anyone else nearby?"

"I called up Mikey and Norm. They are close by. They were interviewing a M13 lead in Herndon. They just want to know where."

"Well, tell them what I just said." Ferguson pulled the Explorer out of the left lane, crossed three lanes of traffic, blasted through the EXPRESS PASS booth and entered US 15 going north.

The three cars were parked behind the Denny's. Ferguson had never been one for displaying lawman activity to the public, but this time he didn't have a choice. The five task force members were behind their vehicles, putting on their body armor and checking their weapons. Ferguson had a pump shotgun in his hand, all the others were loading their M4 carbines.

"OK, Molly just checked, we have confirmed that this mope's phone is still active at the warehouse. The office has cleared the raid with the US Attorney and we have a warrant on the way. Once we have all the paperwork, we work the case like any other. Blake and I will knock on the door, Molly, you, Mikey and Norm cover the back. Ideally, everyone inside raises their hands and we are done. Just remember, we think one of these guys shot Bill. We want him in custody, but I also want all of us going home tonight, so don't take any risks. Got it?" The team nodded. They continued to do their basic gear checks for another few minutes when a Black Crown Victoria pulled up. Everyone but Ferguson was surprised at the occupant.

"I hope you are happy, Ferguson." Joe Manucyck, the FBI assistant special agent in charge of the violent crime, major offenders squads of the field office stepped out of his car. He was a short, square bodied, square headed cop. Ferguson was not entirely certain he had ever seen Manucyck's tie tight around his throat — it was always loose, and the sleeves were always rolled up past his elbows. He looked more like a union boss from the 1950s than an FBI supervisor in the 21st century.

"Boss, I hate to think we upset your lunch."

"Shut up, Ferguson. You know I work out at lunch. I had to put my suit back on and go see the judge myself. Here's your warrant. Now what's the plan?"

"Blake and I go in the front. Molly, Mike and Norm go in the back. Where do you want to be?"

"Covering your back, Ferguson, like I have been doing for almost a decade." The ASAC had already opened the trunk of the Crown Vic and was putting on his armor. He pulled out a shotgun.

"OK, let's go." Ferguson and Blake loaded into the Explorer with the ASAC in the right rear passenger seat. Molly jumped into the back seat of Norm's car and they were off.

The warehouse was a metal sided pole building. It was 20 by 60 feet with access front and back through large metal rolling doors and a "man door" next each of the rolling doors. The parking lot in front of the warehouse was made up of chipped macadam and had two late model pickup trucks parked in front. The back yard of the warehouse was surrounded by six foot fence with rolled barbed wire. Three wrecked cars were parked in the back.

Molly's voice came on their internal radio net, "Boss, cutting the lock on the back gate now."

"Check." Ferguson, Blake and Manucyck were already in a modified stack formation against the wall of the warehouse. Blake said, "No sign of cameras."

"OK. " Ferguson knocked on the front man door. "Hey, anyone home? I need some parts and the local junkyard sent me here. "

Ferguson continued to hammer on the door which rattled against the frame.

"Dude, we are not a parts store. Get lost."

"Oh, man. Sorry, the junkyard guy must have been wrong." Blake had the hand-held ram ready. Ferguson nodded to him as soon as he said "wrong."

The door collapsed from the shock of the ram. Ferguson and Manucyck came in with shotguns at the ready. "FBI. Put your hands where we can see them." Two men in t-shirts and cargo pants working on a table full of small arms looked like their eyes would pop out of their heads. They immediately raised their hands.

Blam! The noise of the pistol in the metal building was loud. Somewhere in the back of the building, a third man with a pistol had decided to fight back.

Blam!

Ferguson, Manucyck and Blake moved from their stack position to different positions in the building behind whatever cover they could find. Blake was the first to get to the table. He shouted at the two men still with their hands up. "Hey, morons. Get down on the floor, face down. Your pal is just as likely to shoot you as me." Blake was on one knee behind the table as another pistol round hit the weapons on the table shattering one gunstock and burying itself in the sheet metal that served as the table top.

The noise from the ram hitting the back door rattled the building. Blam! Blam. This time the shooter had turned to face the new threat and Ferguson finally had a good look at him. He was hiding behind a series of rolling tool boxes.

Ferguson thought about what his Marine platoon sergeant told him years ago. "Marine, do not ever confuse concealment with cover. If you have cover, I can't kill you. If you have concealment, I can't see you, but I might be able to kill you." The torso of the shooter was behind metal tool boxes that provided some cover but mostly concealment. However, his legs were concealed by some fabric and cardboard.

"Not good enough, asshole." Ferguson said as he went to one knee and aimed the shotgun at the shooter's legs and fired, worked the pump and fired again. The noise of the shotgun filled the building, followed by the cry from the shooter as the number 10 buckshot ricocheted off the floor and filled his legs.

"Drop the gun, now!" Molly had led her stack from the other end of the building and was now about ten feet from the shooter with her M4 aimed at this chest. He followed instructions.

"Ferguson, that was a nice party. When can I come to the next one?" Manucyck was shouting at Ferguson. Everyone was still suffering from the concussions of the firing in the building, but Manucyck and Ferguson were closest to the shotgun blasts. Ferguson shouted back.

"You're welcome, boss." He looked to his right as Blake used flex cuffs to secure the two individuals at the table and Norm was using handcuffs on the shooter. Both agents were reciting the Miranda rights as they worked. Mike had returned to the car to get their trauma kit to stabilize the shooter who had a dozen different wounds from the shotgun in both of his legs.

Molly looked across the warehouse at Ferguson and Blake and held up a driver's license. "Dingach. "

"Let's get them back to the office."

The sun was just sinking below the tree line when Barb was on the phone to Beth. "I just heard from the Bureau, they arrested the shooter today. Links to the Russians, of course, but he isn't talking much." The mobile phone connection was iffy. Barb assumed Beth was in her car using Bluetooth. It was clear enough, but her voice sounded like it was being sent through a tin can, eliminating all of the nuances that you need to judge a response.

"My sources are still sorting out the financial links, Barb. I will have something for you in a day or so, but I'm not sure it will do much to clarify where we go next."

Barb was pleased to hear Beth use the pronoun "we." Up until this call, she wasn't sure how invested Beth was. It wasn't that she didn't trust Beth, but she wasn't entirely certain why Beth took the job. "We can start with whatever you find and then I will work with Max."

"He is a dish, dear. Hot pursuit on your part?"

"Business, Beth. Just family business."

"Perfect. I have to go, Barb. I am at a Georgetown party that I chose to be fashionably late, but I need to get in there or I will be rudely late. Ciao."

"Ciao, bella."

Max looked across the room at Barbara. He was sitting in a straight backed chair with his back to the library bookcases. He was wearing his standard "night shift" uniform — jeans, long sleeved black t-shirt, black trainers. He looked at Barb. "Family business?"

"Are you going to tell Beth or the kids that we are couple?"

"Couple of what?"

"Exactly."

S ue was finally fully over jet lag and was, more or less, up to speed on MACE. Melissa was the designated briefer and she worked hard to give Sue what she needed to know and avoid the more esoteric side of this hunt for terrorist WMD.

At the end of the briefing yesterday, Melissa summed up the points. "Here are the key points. I know your little case officer brain can't keep more than a few ideas in your head at one time, unlike a super genius like yours truly." Melissa ducked at the empty Styrofoam coffee cup blasted by her head. "First, we are looking at nuclear waste, not bomb making material. AQ might have been able to move forward on some sort of real atomic bomb if they had time and money to buy one. 2001 operations in Afghanistan ended that possible threat."

"Instead, they are looking to strap highly toxic and radioactive waste to a conventional weapon, mostly likely car or truck bomb, and create large scale terror at a time and place of their choosing. The waste is coming from the Former Soviet Union. The FSU states are filled with this sort of waste from reactors, weapons plants, research facilities, etc. Most of it is for sale or at a minimum, unsecured and easily stolen. So, the first mission for MACE is to find the available sources."

Melissa paused to take a drink from her Diet Pepsi. She started again, "Next, we need to sort out who is in the market. At this point, the likely subject is Zarqawi's bunch, Al Qaida in Iraq. He has the money, a relatively stable safe haven on the Iraq-Syrian border and he is just the sort of creep who would like to create this sort of terror. We have seen some of his funds transferred to bank accounts in Lebanon and then heading to offshore accounts held by front companies for FSU mafia groups. Might be for better guns but might be for this sort of purchase."

"Finally, we tracked Daniels' electronic trail to the German-Austrian border. He appeared to be working to revive old contacts from his days in Army CI in Munich. The contact was a smuggler and general ne'er do well with links to the old KGB and their front companies in Vienna that became the first platforms used by the Russian mafia in the early 1990s. If Daniels got in touch with these contacts, he might have ended up on the wrong end of the operation, not the hunter but the hunted. We just don't know."

"Melissa, what's your best guess on Daniels? Alive? Dead? Gone to ground or captured?"

"I think he was kidnapped somewhere in Southern Germany or Austria. I know that Ginger's report suggests he or some other military operator might be held in Syria. That's good news because it suggests he's still alive. I just can't figure out who might have taken him there or why or even how. "

"So, the trail goes cold in Central Europe."

"Well, if I did all the work, you wouldn't have a job, would you?"

"MACE is a dangerous game, sister. We have terrorists and villains hanging out together. Not exactly what we were trained for and certainly not what Daniels was used to in the 1990s. "

"Sue, I do believe the Daniels case is directly linked to sorting out a key part of the MACE requirement which is disrupt the delivery of radioactive material to AQ. After that, we destroy the pieces as part of the larger mission. Find Daniels and you will find the key part of the puzzle."

"Great. One guy disappears in Southern Germany and may be in Syria…or not. "

"If it was easy, anyone could do it."

Sue had slept on that thought and woke up at 0500hrs to work out before the day began. She was working out on the Stairmaster in what was called "the gym" inside the MACE hanger. It was just a corner of the building that didn't have equipment or offices or cables running through it. It was dark, it was damp, and it was small. There were sets of weights, a bench, two Stairmasters, and a rowing machine. One of the young RAF analysts was on the other Stairmaster. She was in sweats and was wearing ear buds listening to something that was so loud, Sue could hear it over the noise of both machines. Maklovitch walked to the front of the Stairmaster. He was in his flight suit and leather jacket.

"Good morning, chief. Late workout?"

"Sir, I'm just a laggard."

"Well, how soon can you get yourself cleaned up, in your flight suit and ready to travel? I have a day trip planned."

"A drive around the country?"

"Not exactly. I have arranged flight time on an RU21 at 0900hrs. We can fly to Ramstein, meet the Army CI guys from Garmisch who are supposed to be helping us find Daniels and get back by 2100hrs. That's assuming you can get ready to go in the next hour."

Sue was off the machine and already jogging toward the hanger door when she looked over her shoulder. "Sir, I'll be ready by 0800hrs. Where do you want to see me?"

"At base ops. I will be working up the flight plan and getting clearances. It's just you and I and the clear blue sky…well, actually the rainy sky. If we get out of here by 0900hrs, I reckon we can be in Ramstein at 1200Z — which is 13hrs local for you Army types. I have already sent the message. Major Bantler will meet us there. We will have about four hours on the ground and then need to get back in the air. Think that will do?"

"It will do nicely, sir. See you at Base Ops."

Sue was about as pleased as she could be. The meeting with Bantler would be short, it would be official, and it would be shared with Maklovitch. No old times remembered, no recriminations. Just business.

Sue had been a fair number of USAF aircraft, but always as the "trash in the back." She had to admit she was enjoying flying in the right seat of the Beechcraft twin engine turboprop with nothing to do but watch the scenery and keep Maklovitch company. The only ones she had ever seen ferried general officers and civilians around Afghanistan. No wonder the AFSOC pilots always seemed happy.

After they cleared UK airspace and were almost to the French coastline, Sue keyed the mike on her headset. "Sir, how in the world did you get this aircraft for today?"

"Chief, how about you call me Bill and I call you Sue. It may be formal in OP MACE spaces, but I have been in AFSOC too long to enjoy being called sir."

"Bill, it's a deal." There were very few places in the special operations community where officers stood on protocol, but it was never a mistake to wait until they tell you so. "Again, how did you get the plane?"

"Well, this RU21 needed a NATO check flight. You probably noticed the various antennas on the airframe and the wings. This is an old timey intelligence collector from the Cold War. It was designed to intercept Soviet and Warsaw Pact signals. This U21 is nearly 20 years old. It's been recently fitted with the newest cockpit design and updated radars and IFF. It needed to be flown into European NATO airspace to insure it all worked right. I used the juice from MACE to get the approvals and our flight plan. Everyone at Lakenheath thinks we are doing the check ride. That's why we can't overnight in Germany. The flight plan was limited to twelve hours."

"No dramas from my side, Bill. I think this is a great way to get what we need from the CI folks in Germany and get back to work. Did you say this is new identify friend or foe equipment? We aren't going to cause the French to scramble fighters, are we?"

From behind the boom mike, Maklovitch smiled. "I certainly hope so. I always wanted to see if the special engine capability on the RU21 was real or just propaganda." The sky cleared as they entered French airspace and Sue settled in to watching the scenery from a comfortable 10,000.'

Malkovitch interrupted her thoughts by saying "If you look down right now, you can see the remnants of the trench lines from World War I. Look over at about 2 o'clock. We are nearing Metz. At 11 o'clock there is Romagne sous Montfaucon. There is a US cemetery there for the dead from the Meuse —Argonne battle. "

"Bill, it sounds like you know this place."

"My grandfather left Minnesota, joined the Army and fought in the Great War. When I was a young pilot, I flew C130s out of Ramstein. I toured the battlefields. My dad was a pilot in World War Two. He flew modified B24s for what was called the Carpetbaggers. Basically, it was Army Air Corps special operations. I tried to sort out his flight routes over France from England — not as easy as finding by granddad's trenches. "

"Your Dad might have flown my granddad. He was in the OSS."

"Sue, now you are making me feel old. That would make me the same age as your dad."

"Not exactly." Sue realized this conversation was going in a direction that she might not enjoy. Time to change topics. "How is the plane flying?"

"Rock steady. On our way home, we'll have to see what she can do. Sue, we are about a half hour out from Ramstein. In a bit, I will be spending my time with air traffic control. Tell me your plan with the Army guys at Ramstein."

"Bill, here is what we have. It looks like Daniels was using a set of old contacts from his Army CI time when he was based in Munich in the 90s. The records are not accessible — at least not yet. So, we need to get as much from the Army CI detachment commander as possible on what sorts of cases they have from that era and whether Daniels made any contact with them as he was passing through. If we have a lead, a name, ideally a phone number or an address, then the wizards back at MACE can start pulling the threads. Hopefully, we will have a lead that we can follow to wherever Daniels is located and, just as important, to whatever Daniels was tracking."

Again the smile behind the boom mike, "Hope is not a plan, Sue."

"Right, Bill. But right now, it is all we have."

The rest of the flight was uneventful, and the rolling hills of France transitioned into deeper hills and valleys of Western Germany. Ramstein had been a center piece of Cold War defense with Air Force fighter bomber squadrons and cargo wings. In a post 9/11 world, it was more an intermediate stop for cargo headed to either Afghanistan or Iraq. Just as important, but not on the front lines.

As they pulled into the designated parking spot, Sue looked out to see Earl Bantler in his army combat uniform, boots and Gore-Tex jacket. Major's oak leaf on his patrol cap and USAF blue ear protection. He looked older than she remembered and much less fit. Life in Germany had treated him well, perhaps a few too many beers or too much schnitzel. That was his problem with the Army, not her problem anymore.

Once the engines were shut down, Maklovitch hung his headset on the yoke of the aircraft and led the way to the back of the aircraft and opened the crew door that folded out and became steps. He walked down the steps, put on his USAF blue overseas cap and walked toward the flight line NCO that was putting chalks on the wheels. It took Sue a bit longer to get out of the copilot's seat. Her prosthetic made movement in/out of the cramped quarters a challenge. Eventually, she found the pull handle behind her headrest and used her arms to leverage herself into the crew compartment. The rest was easy enough so long as she remembered not to trip on the stairs. She hit the tarmac slightly harder than she had hoped, but had her maroon beret on by the time she joined Maklovitch and Bantler.

"Sergeant, we are here for a couple of hours. Our flight plan has us departing at 1700. Will that work? "

"Yes, sir. Base ops already sent the plan to us. You will be able to turn and burn at 1700hrs on the dot."

"Great."

Earl Bantler walked up to Maklovitch and rendered a very formal salute. "Sir, welcome to Ramstein."

"Thanks, Major. It's not my first trip to the depths of the Black Forest."

"I understand from base ops you have about four hours on the ground. I reckon we can cover what we need to cover in about two hours and that will leave us some time for a meal — assuming you still like stuben grub. "

"It will be a pleasure. Sadly, no beer for me since I have flight time back to the UK. Still, I'm sure you will be able to share a beer with Chief O'Connell." Maklovitch turned to his left where Sue had "assumed the position" of the subordinate — one step to the left and one to the rear of the principal.

"Excellent. Greetings, Sue."

"Sir, it is good to see you."

"It's been a long time since Bragg, Sue. You are looking fit."

"Too kind, sir."

"I heard you were wounded in Afghanistan. Not too serious?"

"Serious enough, sir. But it didn't keep me out of the fight."

"Excellent." He turned to Maklovitch. "Let's go over to the office in base ops that I have arranged for us." Earl turned quickly and started walking toward the building to their front.

Maklovitch slowed his pace just slightly until Sue was even with him. "Baggage?"

"A little. I'll explain on the way home."

"Perfect. It will keep me awake. Just don't make me cry."

"Not likely."

The briefing was even less helpful than either Maklovitch or Sue had expected. Bantler had included his senior field agent, Mike Sherman, and his detachment sergeant major in the mix. Neither Maklovitch nor Sue were certain what the Army team knew or needed to know, so they just listened to the briefing hoping that by the end, they would have a clue if anyone in the room knew of OP MACE. It became clear after the first twenty slides on the PowerPoint presentation that this was not going to be anything more than an explanation for why they knew nothing about Daniels or his contacts. "Death by PowerPoint" was a technique used across the US military to say plenty while saying nothing.

Maklovitch knew the game and finally interjected, "Do your old files show us anything that might help in tracking Daniels down."

Sherman responded, "Sir, Daniels was here in mid 90s. The focus for the team at the time was Balkans. I arrived about six months before Daniels left the Det. He was a freak when it came to OPSEC. He kept his own files, controlled access to his safe and only the Det commander at the time knew what the heck Daniels was doing. Honestly, I didn't like the guy, he treated me like shit and I was happy to see him leave. After 9/11, we all focused on Force Protection here and began regular rotations to Bagram. None of us knew that Daniels was here and, if we had, I would probably have reported him to the MPs to have him detained and questioned."

"Major, what's your best guess on Daniels?"

"Sir, I don't know why he was here and I can't honestly say if it was on personal business or official business. If it was the latter, he didn't inform anyone in the chain of command in Germany. I checked with the US Army Europe G2 shops here and even the NATO headquarters J2 at Mons. They had no record of his travel. No orders, no contact, nada."

"OK, I guess that's about it. Let's wrap up and have some lunch. I'm starving."

"Now you are talking." Sherman said under his breath, but loud enough for everyone to hear.

Maklovitch might be an AFSOC officer, but he was still an Air Force Lieutenant Colonel and not about to let that sort of thing happen in front of him. "Agent Sherman?"

"Nothing, sir."

They drove off base in an Army Suburban to a local German pub known in German as a Stuben that had been serving as the off-base venue for US soldiers and airmen since 1950. It was a simple two story building — brown clapboard with a heavy oak door. Inside, the room was decorated in a Black Forest hunting lodge kitsch with stuffed boar and red deer heads, carved wooden shelves and dozens of beer steins from the various US military units that had favored the location for fifty years. It was designed not as a "typical German pub;" it was designed more to be what an American serviceman thought a German pub should look like. Bantler had already arranged a side room for the five of them and it appeared he was a regular. The pub owner brought in a tray with five pilsner glasses of a local beer and set them around the table. Maklovitch passed his glass over to Bantler and said, "I'm sure one of you can find some use for this." He then turned to the pub owner.

"Ein caffe mit milch, bitte."

"Jawohl."

The meal was served family style and included classic Swabian fare: Maultaschen, beef and onions with spaetzle, wurst, black bread and, for the Army members of the table, more beer. Maklovitch had no problem finishing off his plate and had two more coffees before they were finished.

Sue had never been a fan of German food. Perhaps she was

spoiled by living in Frankfurt as a child where the German restaurants were off limits to children, so her meals were always at home made by her mother using the terrific European fruits and vegetables that she found in the markets. The closest thing she came to German food on that tour was when the family went on "volksmarch" walks in the German countryside. The ten and twenty kilometer walks through German forests always ended at a local sports hall where the local sports club used their food stalls to raise money for the local soccer team. After a day outside and a 10 kilometer walk, her mother allowed Sue to eat any wurst and hard roll she wanted fresh from the grill and one piece of pastry that the local women made to sell to the participants of the walk.

Here, Sue worked on her plate of beef, onions and spaetzle, but mostly pushed it around with the black bread so that it looked like she was eating as much as everyone else without filling her gut with a meal that would only argue with her on the way home. The toilet in the RU12 was not someplace she intended to visit while flying over France. She did find the local pilsner to her taste but kept it to one glass. She ordered coffee as well and called it good. Bantler and his two compadres worked hard to finish off all the food at the table and each ordered coffee and kuchen. Sue realized at this point that Bantler and his crew must barely pass their annual Army fitness test. Perhaps they never took one.

Once they were done, Maklovitch made the first move. "Gentlemen, as much as I enjoy your company and this stuben, I have to get the aircraft back to Lakenheath or the Air Force will start docking my pay for joy riding." Maklovitch walked over to the waiter, asked for the bill in German, pulled out a set of Euros and said "Stimm so."

They drove back in comfortable silence generated more by the number of carbohydrates that they had ingested than any other reason. Sue was convinced that Sherman was actually asleep by the time they reached the Ramstein main gate. Bantler dropped them off at Base Ops and Maklovitch walked in to reconfirm the flight plan and check weather. Bantler walked over to Sue. He clearly had something that he wanted to say to her that he didn't want Maklovitch or his men to hear. Sue was not looking forward to this moment.

Bantler started with the basics by saying, "Sue, I just wanted to say it is good to see you. We left our life together a long time ago and I wondered if you are interested in starting it again."

"Sir?"

"I understand you are currently assigned to RAF Akrotiri. It wouldn't take much to catch air hops back and forth using US or RAF aircraft. It could be just like it was."

Sue could see this was going in a direction that she wouldn't and couldn't travel. The challenge was to explain her lack of interest without creating a scene or getting sideways with a field grade officer who might turn vindictive on her. Once again, the Farm training came in handy. She opted for misdirection and flattery to control the conversation. "Sir, you know and I know that we can't go back to where we were. You are now a Major," Sue decided to heap the flattery, "and on your way to O5 and an MI command. I am just a CWO and an operator in the field. The Army won't allow it and you can't take that risk. I think it is best for the two of us to just remember the past and move in our different worlds: yours toward senior officer duties and mine, most probably, to staying in my own little world at this rank. I hope you understand." Sue put on her most sincere face and hoped for the best.

"Sue, you were always one tough career bitch and I should have guessed that you haven't changed." The acid in his tone was dangerous; Sue could tell this wasn't going to end well. Bantler looked over his shoulder to see Maklovitch within listening distance. Bantler decided it wouldn't do for him to look like a creep in front of the Air Force, so he decided to cool down and drop Sue O'Connell like a hot rock.

"Your Lieutenant Colonel is on his way. Good luck with this Daniels thing and think about what I just said."

Maklovitch approached and said, "OK, Sue, it's time to mount up and get back to the UK. Earl, thanks for taking the time to see us. I'm sorry it wasn't all that helpful, but you did your best."

Bantler saluted. "Safe trip, sir. I will continue to work the Daniels case from this end and let you know if we find anything else." Maklovitch and Sue climbed into the aircraft and Sue closed and latched the door. Maklovitch was already in his seat and running through his preflight checks. The last remnants of German daylight were turning into gloom. Sue climbed into her seat, put on her headset and buckled in for the flight back to Lakenheath.

On top of the steering yoke on her side of the aircraft was a small, heavily wrapped plastic bundle about the size of a half a pack of playing cards. Written on the package was the line "Personal for Sue O'Connell." Maklovitch looked over and said, "Fan mail?"

Sue slipped into her most formal military tone, "Sir, I have no idea, but given the last few months, I'm thinking it can't be good news." Sue picked up the package and guessed it was some sort of message and not some sort of bomb. She said, "Sir, I don't think this is a threat to us and I honestly think it should be opened only by professionals at MACE, assuming you have them."

Maklovitch focused on getting the aircraft out of Ramstein and on his flight route back to RAF Lakenheith. No one spoke for a long time. Finally, an hour into the flight, Maklovitch decided he either had to start the conversation or accept the fact that the trip would be one of stony silence. Stony silence was ok, but he was sufficiently intrigued that he decided to risk the direct approach. He keyed his mike and said, "Sue, why did you get a package delivered into my aircraft?"

"Bill, I didn't have anything to do with this and don't know how it got into the plane."

The green glow of the cockpit instruments illuminated Maklovitch's face as they headed West. The sunset turned the horizon bright orange as they flew over the darkened French countryside. Maklovitch said, "So if you don't know what it is or who put it on the airplane, what can you tell me?" He was expecting an interesting tale of romance gone South — at least it would pass the time while the auto-pilot got them to the Channel. What he didn't expect was Sue's return question.

"What do you know about ELEKTRA?" She spoke to him while staring out the cockpit at the sunset.

"I have the benefit of a classical education, courtesy of Jesuits. Elektra was the daughter of Agamemnon and a character in a

Sophocles play and I think a play by Euripides. Extra points if I know what it means as a code word?"

Sue smiled for the first time since they arrived in Germany. "USAF for extra points — what does the code word ELEKTRA mean?"

Once again the smile behind the boom mike. Maklovitch said, "ELEKTRA is a double agent operation using the 150th most secret agent in the world, Chief Warrant Officer Sue O'Connell."

"150th?"

"Well, maybe worse than that, but then again, I'm just guessing that the Cyprus explosion and gunfight and all the computer hacking that you did with Melissa might have raised our profile just a bit, no?"

"When and why did they read you in on ELEKTRA?"

"As the US team lead for MACE, I pushed for full files on all the US and UK players. Our cousins weren't as helpful as the US system. As to ELEKTRA, I had to sign a box of papers from both Army CI and the FBI. They figured someone in theatre needed to know what the heck you were doing. I drew the short straw. It doesn't hurt that I am also a graduate of the asylum on the Potomac."

"And you were going to tell me you are a Farm graduate…when?"

"I thought I timed it well. So, what does any of this have to do with your Army colleague back at Ramstein?"

"Bill, I don't think it has anything to do with him. Major Bantler was trying to revive a love affair that went south years ago."

"A little problematic with DoD fraternization rules, don't you think?"

"That's what I said to get out of telling him I always thought he was a creep."

"So we regroup back at Lakenheath. Who do you want involved in the opening of your package?"

"Does the FBI LEGATT in London know?"

"Nope. I was read in through a secure video teleconference from Washington. I do know that the station chief here knows about ELEKTRA because we had to confirm with Washington and with 171 that we were not going to get sideways with him."

"Does MACE have any forensics folks on staff?"

"Flaps and seals folks?"

Sue was surprised for a moment that Maklovitch used an old timey, insider term, but then again, he said he was a Farm graduate. Flaps and seals was a term used by the MI5, FBI, and OSS in World War II. It meant individuals who could clandestinely opened envelopes, photographed the documents and resealed the envelopes with no evidence of tampering. Hardly central to 21st century operations, but the name stuck to any forensics folks who handled packages.

"Exactly."

"We have a number of techs as part of the Agency team in MACE. I don't know if any of them are flaps and seals guys. We'll just have to wait until tomorrow and see. Anything else you want to talk about to pass the time? World domination? Natural disasters? Former murder convictions?"

"Nope. Other than to thank you for arriving in the nick of time so I didn't have to put a choke hold on an overweight field grade officer trying to put the moves on me."

"And your baggage with Bantler from Ft. Bragg? Is any of this why they did so little to help us on the Daniels case?"

"We were a number nearly a decade ago. We both went to selection. He didn't make it, I did. He went to OCS, I didn't. He left Ft. Bragg, I didn't. I don't know which of us made the first break for the door, but I was happy when he left. Honestly, I think he was considering making stuff up in the Daniels case so that he had an excuse to visit me at Akrotiri. Now, I am really happy we didn't stay in touch."

"Ya think?"

S ue was definitely getting tired of traveling in the back of C17s. This time, it was a little better because the aircraft was transporting half of OP MACE to Iraq. The other half was in a separate C5A that was carrying most of the bulkier equipment including a specially outfitted shipping container with all of the intercept and computer operations gear and two Level III armored Land Rover Defenders and a lightly armored Toyota sedan that was "pre-damaged" and designed to look like a taxi so that it would be low profile on the streets of Northern Iraq. The full team would arrive at Balad Airfield, set up OP MACE (Headquarters) and a portion of the team would eventually move to the SOF base operating out of Mosul.

Sue was surrounded by members of OP MACE — most of them asleep in modified airplane seats bolted to 463L cargo pallets. Some of the more seasoned members of the team brought their own inflatable sleeping mattresses and were stretched out in between the pallets, on the cargo pallets and on black plastic Pelican cases. George and Dozer refused to let anyone handle their vehicles, so they were in the second aircraft with the Defenders and the rest of George's SBS section.

Even after years in the special operations community, Sue was always surprised how quickly they could mobilize resources compared to the conventional Army. It had all started on 04 May when she finally opened the parcel left in the RU21 while it was parked in Germany. It was three pages of single spaced, type written notes. Sue recognized Mary's signature at the bottom, but an autopen or a good forgery would certainly fool her. Sue had learned at the Farm that handlers often sent messages to their agents from the original recruiting officer. These were messages of congratulations, messages of encouragement, even messages of disappointment. These messages were generated by the handler or headquarters but, rarely, by the original officer. Sue honestly didn't care.

This was the first time that the GRU had sent anything to her. She read it very carefully, wearing nitrite gloves so that she would not destroy any biometrics that the 171 team or, eventually, some Quantico wizards might get from the letter.

S,

I apologize for not reaching out to you sooner. Your work in Cyprus came to our attention and the office is quite pleased with the results. Let's not forget that the same triggers that were headed to Iraq were also headed North. The office wanted you to know that disrupting this network was a good thing. They showed their appreciation by assisting in the elimination of your primary adversary.

Sue thought back to the dock and the final gunfight with Nicolai Beroslav. She remembered being hit in the chest by Beroslav's suppressed Makarov. Too far for the tiny 9mm Kurz round to penetrate her body army. Close enough that it did knock her down. Then suddenly, rounds coming from out in the harbor. Large caliber rounds. Beroslav was hit and fell in the water. Rounds impacting near her forced her to take cover. Then suddenly, quiet and darkness. No one was every able to sort out who did the shooting other than the fact that Russian sniper rifle rounds were found at the scene. GRU? SPETSNAZ?

Now we are here to help you again. The mission that Daniels and you have is just as important to the office as it is to the US. We do not want Jihadis to have radiological material any more than the people in Washington do. There is no way to determine what city they might attack and what civilians they might harm. This is an operation that we all want to succeed.

By this time in the paper, Sue was certain this was not Mary writing this note. This was not her writing style. It was too directive, too impersonal and the writing style too stilted to be from an American.

Here is what we know. You have to determine how you will insert this information into your system. Perhaps you will use your own sources, or you will "find" material from Daniels that someone else has missed. This is your challenge. However, we recommend that you do it quickly, because the information is time sensitive.

Daniels has been taken by a team of Georgian criminals who are linked to a larger criminal enterprise based in Lebanon and Syria. They are the group that has the radiological material. We think they are the same group that is linked to Beroslav. They have Daniels. They are trying to determine how much he knows and how much he reported. After all, they are criminals and they don't want to be caught. They just want their money. Our resources have told us that the exchange is set to take place at the end of May in Al-Malikiyah. We believe it may be a sale to Chechens or possibly Uzbeks. They have already offered to give the Jihadis Daniels as well, a bonus if the Jihadis arrive in Al-Malikiyah with Euros 1,000,000 for the radiological material. The negotiations are still ongoing.

There is a former KGB safe house in Al-Malikiyah being used by the Mafia. The Center used the safe house to meet Turkish agents and as an intercept platform against NATO operations in Northern Iraq in the 1990s. The last pages of these notes provide a detailed map and interior design of the safe house. We want you to use this information to prevent this trade and, if you can, to save Daniels. We want you to succeed because you have a future and we want to help insure your success.

The only other information we have is the code for the satellite phones that the Chechens are using. The numbers are also listed on the map pages. We believe that if you start with this information, you should be able to explain how you get the rest of the story.

Good luck

M

Sue revealed the full contents of the note during a secure video teleconference with 171. Maklovitch and Sue at one end, Smith and Massoni on the other. She explained how she got the material and read the full letter. The screen distorted their faces and the speaker distorted their voices, but it was clear that Smith was pleased. Well, sort of pleased.

"So, we have a lead courtesy of the GRU, maybe. We know who

is keeping Daniels and why, maybe. And we may have a target that solves both our lost agent and one of the key parts of OP MACE, maybe. Did I get this right?"

"Boss, you need to look on the bright side…." Massoni started to interject.

"Not now, Jim. Please. OK, O'Connell. What is your recommended course of action?"

"Boss, we can give the satellite numbers to the geniuses here and the brains in 171 and hope they come up with something that looks like what we have been given. In the meantime, we start planning to move in on the safe house. The team in Dohuk is close enough that they may have intelligence on the site that just never made it to a level of quality to be reported. I think it is worth it."

Smith looked over at the screen image of the senior US MACE partner and said, "Maklovitch?"

"Jed, I think Sue has a thread that needs to be pulled. OP MACE was never risk free and this might work. Especially if we throw resources at it."

"Of course, it also gives the GRU a chance to monitor our resource capabilities, no?" This time Massoni was serious and his point was clear — we use the GRU information and the GRU watches how we use it.

"Jim's right. We have to work this carefully. Still, I've got a man being held somewhere and no one else has a lead. We follow this one to the end."

Sue looked into the screen and said, "Into Syria?"

"If that is what it takes to get Daniels out and to support OP MACE, we follow the lead into Syria."

"Check, chief."

Smith ended the teleconference by saying, "O'Connell, you will meet me in Balad NLT 06 May. If OP MACE can come, bring them. If not, just be there."

"Check."

That same day, Melissa in Lakenheath and Flash at Bragg began the hunt for the satellite phones and their owners. It would initially appear to be searching for a needle in a haystack of needles, but actually, once you have a code for a satellite phone, the rest is relatively easy, at least easy for the large intelligence community that supported OP MACE. Many of the resources that might not have been available in a normal operation were opened by a simple call by staffers at the White House and the British Prime Minister's office. Sue was surprised the juice that OP MACE had. Sue watched Melissa work and watched her set up a secure link to Flash and the two ladies worked their magic. Ten hours later, several pots of coffee and five pounds of M&Ms at Lakenheath and an equal number of red twisters in the 171 warehouse, and the analysts had a very good set of arguments that supported everything that the GRU note said.

"You realize that this could be a GRU setup?" Maklovitch commented to Sue as they watched Melissa's team and the 171 team work feverishly to determine a location and details that Smith, Massoni, Maklovitch and Sue already knew from the notes.

"Yes, but as my boss said: Do we have any other leads? Not right now."

Within 24 hours, Maklovitch had whistled up two cargo aircraft and was already starting to load plan how to move OP MACE to Balad. Sue was in direct contact with the entire 171 collection team involved in this effort and they were coordinating resources and a plan to meet Smith and Massoni in Balad on 11 May. Melissa and Flash were able to dig through a dozen years of history and found out more about Al-Malikiyah and its links to both the KGB and the Syrian internal security apparatus than they had originally received from the GRU notes. They also were able to track the satellite phones to a location on the German-Austrian border at the time that Daniels disappeared. There was something there, even if it was not precisely what the GRU wanted them to believe, it was definitely worth the effort. Daniels could easily be in Syria. They needed to find out.

B arb and Max were sitting in the sunroom, drinking tea and plotting. Bill had returned to Washington the previous day so that he could be back working at Washington Field office on the following Monday. Barb and Max had used the day to clean up the house, begin packing and enjoy the last bit of Spring weather together. Now they were focused on things far more serious and far more dangerous.

"So, what did you get from Ferguson?" Max may have been sitting comfortably at the table, but he was staring out the window of the sunroom. Barb couldn't sort out if he was just thinking or searching the terrain outside the window for targets, or both.

"They arrested the team that actually conducted the shoot. The team lawyered up pretty quickly and they haven't gotten anything out of them. Their computer forensics folks have attacked the cell phones and the computers found on site. Not a lot to go with other than vague tasking from a firm in New Jersey linked to an old KGB front company based in Vienna. Bank records show a payment from the New Jersey firm to the three villains. Not a lot of money. Twenty-seven grand a piece paid in increments of nine grand so that it fell under the Treasury anti-terrorism tracking programs."

"Ferguson offer that up himself?"

"You kidding? Ferguson lives and breathes lawman. He wouldn't give up this sort of data to a civilian under any sort of duress. I got this from Beth."

"She has that sort of juice at Justice?"

"Apparently." Barb's relationship with Max was long standing and growing deeper, but she was not ready at this point to tell him of her established connections at the Agency Counterterrorism Center. Beth had nothing to do with the data. Since Barb worked as a contractor for CTC, it was easy enough to get the data off the shared computer systems between the Agency, Treasury and the FBI. Perfectly legal... well, mostly legal.

"OK, so what's the next step?"

"Beth is using her connections in Europe to identify the location and the official managers of the Vienna firm. Once we have something that fixes these guys in place, we need to get to Austria and figure out a way to encourage them to tell us where the Beroslavs are and which family member authorized the financial transfer. Then…"

"Then we follow that lead until we find a way to have a discussion with that member of the family and…."

"We resolve this problem once and for all."

"Barbara, do you really think we can resolve this…diplomatically or kinetically?"

"Max, I think we have to sort out some leverage that allows us to avoid more rounds going downrange. At the end of the day, we both know that we have to do more than kill them because we can't kill them all."

"We could try, but I agree with you, it would probably not work over the long run."

"And, Max, I want this to end before my kids are worrying about this."

"Too late for that, dear." Max stood up slowly and backed away from the sunroom window. He nodded to Barb and she moved her chair back away from the window as well.

"How many?"

"Three so far. I don't know how many more. Call 911 or whatever lawman you have on speed dial. Tell them to come here as soon as they can. Tell them to bring an ambulance. There will be casualties." Max was already out of the room before Barb had the phone in her hand.

Barb found Max in the master bedroom. He had a table set up with a chair about five feet from an open window. A Remington bolt action rifle with bipod, telescopic sight, and a six-inch sound suppressor on the barrel was already in place. The stock was tight against Max's shoulder and he was scanning the wood line.

"No cell coverage. They must be using a short-range disrupter."

"OK, so we know for sure they aren't local house breaking punks."

"Downstairs is secure."

"Check."

Barb walked over to an oak armoire. She placed a small magnet against one of the sides of the armoire and a false wall opened up on a hinge revealing a shotgun, a M1 carbine that Pete Senior kept after the War, a Browning hi power and a four-inch Smith and Wesson Model 66 stainless steel revolver. Barb clipped a revolver holster to her pants and holstered the Model 66. She loaded the Browning and the carbine.

"You want the shotgun nearby?"

"Does it have a sling?"

"Yes and ammo as well." Barb used a sarcastic tone — of course it was set up properly. Peter senior was a lot of things, but he knew combat weapons.

"OK, wise guy. Yes, please put it on the desk behind me. You need the Browning and the Smith?"

"Not really."

"So, leave the Browning right here at the table. You cover my back and I'll take care of our visitors in the woods — at least for a bit."

They sat in silence for what was only five minutes, but it seemed like forever.

"Max."

He kept his eye on the sight reticle.

"Mm?"

"Thanks."

"No problem." The rifle coughed and the recoil moved Max's shoulder.

"One down."

The suppressor had reduced both the sound and the signature from the flash. Max could see the other two in the woods were confused why their colleague had just dropped like a stone.

There was a crash as the front door was hit with a man portable ram. The door held.

"They will be coming through one of the windows sooner or later." Another crash as the ram hit one of the windows that looked like 19th century glass, but was hardened armor glass. It would eventually give way, but not easily. Another cough.

"Two down."

"If you could deal with number three sooner rather than later, that might be a good thing."

"It takes some degree of skill for a head shot at 200m you know. How many on the riverside?" Barb worked her way down the hallway toward the stairs and one of the windows facing the river. She returned to the room to hear the third cough. "Three down. Now we have to see if there is anyone else in the woods."

"We have four out front. Three working to get in, one at the boat dock next to a zodiac."

Max moved from his shooting position. "Watch the wood line for a bit."

He walked quietly over to the bedroom that faced the river. He carefully opened the window three inches and then backed away from the window and assumed a kneeling position in the middle of the room. It was closer, but a harder shot because he didn't have a stable platform.

Cough.

"Shit." Max saw the boat driver spin. He had hit him in the hip and was now leaning against the outboard motor. Max worked the action on the Remington.

Cough. The boat driver slid into the water. Face down.

Max returned to the master bedroom and said, "Any other creeps out front?"

"No telling. But definitely no creeps willing to leave the wood line."

"OK. That leaves three out back."

The glass in the living room finally gave way to the ram. The three individuals in jeans, field jackets, and balaclavas climbed through the window as Max and Barb crept down the stairs. Barb had the carbine at her shoulder ready to fire. Max behind her with the Browning, shotgun slung over his shoulder ready to be put into action. Everyone met in the main entrance hallway of the old house.

Barb fired three rounds into the chest of the first assailant. Center mass. Dropped him quickly. Max fired the Browning over her shoulder — one round in the head.

Max shouted into her ear, "They are wearing body armor!"

The second assailant opened up with a short barreled AK . The first round whipped past Barb's head and the rest peeled the plaster in the ceiling. Another round from the Browning behind Barb. Another head shot.

Barb was ready for the third assailant as he came through the hallway door. One aimed round from the carbine. Two more just in case.

Max and Barbara looked at each other and then assumed a back to back position while they cleared the living room where the assailants made their entrance. Carefully, they worked their way out the main door.

As they cleared the main door Max said, "Check your phone."

"A little late, no?"

"Check it."

"Still no coverage."

"That's probably good. It means there is no one left to turn off the jamming device."

The round that hit Max came from the river. He fell on his side.

"Shit," was all Max said. Barb reached down to check Max. He waved her on.

"Get him or we are both toast." Another round cracked over their heads. Barb knew he was right, but...

A third round hit the dirt about ten yards in front of them. Barb tried to get the shotgun off Max's shoulder. It was mangled from the round that hit Max. Barb holstered the revolver and recovered the carbine from behind her back. She fired three rounds in the general direction of the shooter, kicking up dirt along the river bank and started to run toward the river.

The last assailant had started the boat and was working to get the zodiac away from the dock. A Russian sniper rifle was slung on his back. Barb dropped to the prone position. The M1 carbine was never designed to be a long distance rifle, but the Zodiac was less than 100m away. She fired seven .30 caliber rounds into the Zodiac itself. The rounds penetrated the boat and it began to sink as the man in the field jacket tried to turn the boat and accelerate into the river. She set up for an aimed shot at the driver. Click. Empty magazine.

Barb drew the Model 66. It would be a long shot, but the .357 round coupled with the four-inch barrel could do the job if Barb could. She drew the hammer back so it would be a single action shot. One shot was all that she needed. The man sank with the boat in the 12 feet of water near the dock.

Barb returned to Max. She was too late.

Barb realized for the first time in her career, she had to call the Cleaners for help. The jammer must have been in the Zodiac. Her phone had service. She dialed a number on speed dial that she had never used. Issued when she returned to the US. The Cleaners would make this disappear. Barb turned back to Max.

The airfield at Balad had been one of the premier military air-bases for Saddam's air force. By the time the US and its allies invaded Iraq, there was no air force and the US Air Force decided not to follow doctrine which instructed "day one, crater all airfields, destroy all airbases to insure air superiority." Air superiority was not something they had to worry about so other than a cursory attack on the airbase, Balad remained intact. In 2006, it was a major center for the US Air Force in Iraq and it was the headquarters of SOF and its constituent units. Smith sat inside a newly established, air conditioned, inflatable structure that was the headquarters for 171 (forward). Massoni and the analytic team remained in the 171 ware-house after the contact with O'Connell. Smith and Flash had grabbed the "first thing smoking'" out of Pope airfield at Ft. Bragg and arrived in time to move into an empty structure. They arrived midnight Iraq time and moved immediately into their space. The SOF administra-tive team wired the place, set up the folding tables and chairs and hooked 171 into the larger SOF local area network. Smith made a courtesy call to the SOF command cell, met briefly with the Com-manding General, and then went back to his new home: 171 Forward Operating Base or FOB/Balad. This wasn't the first time Smith had been to Balad and by no means his first time in Iraq.

Jedidiah Smith started his military career as a young private with a college degree. Throughout basic training in 1980, he was mocked by his fellow recruits as "the professor," but his drill sergeant and the rest of the basic training staff realized his value. The Army in 1980 was not a place where a college educated enlisted man would be common. It was an Army that was badly paid, badly supplied and struggling to decide what it would look like after Vietnam. Smith had enlisted in the Army mostly because he couldn't find any jobs for a 22 year old with a degree in German Studies from Cornell University. He passed all the basic tests, was determined to be fit, given his col-lege sports career in lacrosse and his intramural activities in the judo club that was no surprise, and he headed to Ft. Huachuca as a private first class going to Military intelligence school.

Smith worked hard at the MI school and was an E4 by the time he arrived in Germany working for V Corps headquarters staff preparing intelligence summaries for the command using his German language skills and his understanding of both West and East Germany. His work caught the eye of the Army Counterintelligence Detachment in Frankfurt and they arranged for him to move to their side of the house. Suddenly, Smith was no longer reading and translating material for operational and tactical planning for World War III in Europe. He was operating in Germany as a counterintelligence support asset, still in the office and still reading German documents. This was his first insight into "war in the shadows" that had been taking place in Germany since the creation of NATO and the Warsaw Pact. The Soviets and their allies were aggressively working to set up espionage networks in both the US and the UK sectors of the West Germany. It was well and truly spy versus spy. Smith was amazed, intrigued, and hooked. For the rest of his life, he would be involved in espionage.

Smith attended the Army Counterintelligence Schools and, when he made Staff Sergeant, he was sent to Officer Candidate School in 1987. It was the first time he had been resident in the US in over seven years and his time in Ft. Benning was totally different from anything he had seen or done in what was referred to as US Army Europe. Among the various schools at Ft. Benning was OCS, the Infantry School, Airborne School and Ranger School. Smith decided that he wanted to go to them all. The Military Intelligence Corps agreed begrudgingly. Someone inside the Department of the Army realized that Smith was worth the effort. They were right. Smith ended up running an Army CI team for the 18th Airborne Corps during Desert Storm and Desert Shield ferreting out Iraqi intelligence and special operations networks in Saudi Arabia and Kuwait. He helped to build the intelligence network that resulted in the US identifying Saddam's nuclear weapons program.

After that, the Army decided to send Smith to the CIA case officer course at the Farm. It was another good investment. Smith moved back to Germany and became the best recruiter of reporting sources on the collapse of the USSR and the strategic concern of "loose nukes" as weapons stockpiles were suddenly in the hands of local governments in the newly established states in the former Soviet Union. Smith's work came up on the screen of the commander of SOF. He wanted a man like Smith, now Major Jedidiah Smith, in his command. He went to the Army G2 — a classmate of his from the Army War College — and asked politely for Smith. Orders came down from the G2, Smith reassigned to Ft. Bragg and told to report to SOF headquarters. It was 1993 and Smith became part of a team working directly for Commander, SOF on how to build and sustain a sophisticated SOF intelligence network. SOF already had more than enough technical collection programs; the one thing that was needed was a stand-alone collection team that could go anywhere CG/SOF wanted and do whatever was needed. Smith helped design and build that team as he was promoted inside SOF to Lieutenant Colonel. That team became 171 after 9/11.

Now, Smith was setting up an intelligence operation that might prevent the ultimate terrorist nightmare, a radiological weapon attack on the US or a NATO ally. He had been working for 26 years to get to this point and he realized that he would have to use every bit of experience he had from Germany, Italy, Central America, Ft. Bragg and Afghanistan. He had most of his operators now on task to support this mission. He still had operators support SOF missions in other parts of the globe, but he needed to structure what resources he had to get a quick and successful resolution of this threat. 171 would find the targets, they would assist other SOF resources in fixing the targets and CG/SOF would determine how to finish the target. Smith had no doubt in his mind that resolution would be "kinetic." He just hoped there would be something left for his outfit to use after that resolution.

"Boss, coffee?"

"Flash, you know you have a real job."

"Not without coffee. I'm just asking if you want a cup."

"Sure, Flash. We need to be on our toes. O'Connell and her crew from OP MACE will be on the ground in about an hour."

"Its gonna' get crowded in here."

"For a bit. I expect to start moving some of MACE out as soon as we can. We don't have a lot of time to sit still."

Flash handed Smith a styrofoam cup of black coffee and said, "Boss, here's the go juice."

"Thanks, Flash."

S ue was riding in the back of what appeared to anyone on the street as a 50 year old Mercedes taxi. She was dressed in full hijab — black headscarf, black caftan and black abaya over the black dress. Unlike the Afghan burka, the outfit didn't smell like a wet dog. The disguise team at MACE in Balad had purchased the clothing at the highest quality store they could find in Baghdad and modified the outfit to fit Sue and her "onboard" items — body armor, communication package and weapons. She couldn't fit her weapon of choice, a suppressed MP5, under the abaya, so they agreed to an Uzi and her Glock.

So much of this trip was completely different from her time in Afghanistan. First, they were leaving the Green Zone in a highly pol-ished, up armored four door Mercedes GLK, something Sue had seen only when NATO VIPs arrived in Jalalabad. Then there was her clothes and the clothes of Melissa Nez who was sitting behind her in the third row of seats. High quality, new, and, probably most important to Sue, clothes that didn't smell like goats and donkeys. Finally, the fact that she was traveling with four men, two in the front and two in the second row. They were all dressed in a mix of Arab dress and "Baghdad chic." All of the men looked like they belonged in the region and their driver, Jamal was born in Baghdad and spoke in what she was told was the "Baghdadi" dialect. They were all from the CIA station.

Sue was headed to a CIA safe house in a particularly dangerous part of "bandit country" in Baghdad, South of the Tigris. The driver and man riding shotgun in their GLK ran this corridor at least once a week posing as rich Iraqi businessmen working the lucrative con-tracts supporting the US coalition in the Green Zone, the " secure" part of the city where the military commands, the coalition diplomats and the new Iraqi government lived and worked. Pass through the checkpoints and the security walls, cross the river and you were in Baghdad where the average citizen worked and the various hostile militias ruled.

"How far to the safe house."

Jamal turned his head and replied to Sue. "Too secret, can't say." He said with a smirk.

"OK, wise guy."

"It's about five klicks away as the crow flies, but we aren't crows." Jamie was riding shotgun. He was an CIA paramilitary case officer, trained to run agents, build secret surrogate armies, and, at night, go to diplomatic functions to spot and recruit new spies. The Agency paramilitary cadre were as close to real life versions of characters in spy movies, which was still not very close. Jamie had a full career in Special Forces and another ten working secret wars throughout the region. He looked to be a fit over 50 man who had seen more than his share of combat. He was also a team leader for operations outside the Green Zone and he was Jamal's boss.

Jamie had told Sue that Jamal came to the US as a child refugee after the first Gulf war, was raised by his uncle and aunt in Los Angeles, went to USC on a soccer scholarship, joined the Army, did a tour of duty with SF in Afghanistan and was on his first Agency tour. He might speak in a Baghdadi accent, but he was a California surfer dude at heart. He was young, good looking and, so far, seemed smart enough and arrogant enough to survive a tour in Baghdad.

The next row in the GLK were two Agency analysts assigned to MACE in Balad who were going to work with Sue and Melissa in the safe house. Both were assigned to CIA headquarters and both were near native Arabic speakers though both were born in the US. Sue still hadn't sorted out which was which, but one was Bill and one was Will. True names or aliases? It hardly mattered to Sue, but Melissa kept at them before they loaded into the GLK.

"Now who is Bill?" One of the two raised his hand. Melissa turned to the other Agency officer dressed in full thobe and head scarf in brilliant white silk. "So that makes you William?"

"Well, I'm William as well." Bill said. He was dressed in a suit coat over a thobe with a red and white checked headscarf.

"You can't both be William."

Sue had given Melissa a shove. "Let it go, will ya?"

Behind them was a second black GLK filled with three armed Iraqis who were a special security and investigative element raised by the Agency in 2004 and loyal only to Jamie. He trained them, he paid them, he deployed them. They were his men.

Before they loaded up, Sue asked Jamie. "You trust those guys?"

"Nope."

"Terrific."

Jamie smiled and said, "But if we get in a firefight once we get out of the green zone, they will fight with us. They don't have any relatives here, so they won't have a lot of choices but stick with us or die. Plus, the good news is these guys can shoot. That part, I guarantee. Welcome to Baghdad!"

They pulled up to the safe house gate which opened in time for both GLKs to pull in without stopping. The eight foot high metal gate closed and two more Iraqi armed guards in black fatigues with M4 rifles slung across their backs locked the gate and pulled a third GLK across the gate so it could not be forced open.

"Welcome to my home away from home." Jamie was out of the car and hugging the guards as Sue and Melissa got out.

"Nothing like Afghanistan, I promise. The villa's previous owner was a colonel in Saddam's Mukhabarat and no one liked Saddam's secret police, even the regular police. Needless to say, we purchased this at a bargain price and have used it as our little fortress ever since. The locals are well paid to keep us informed of unnecessary curious visitors and we keep them safe from the various gangs who were previously Saddam's henchmen. Of course, it could end up like the battle of Camerone someday, but so far, so good." Sue was not encouraged by his reference to one of the Foreign Legion's most celebrated defeats. Basically, a French version of the Alamo.

Once they were inside, Sue realized that Jamie was right, the villa definitely was not like their safe house in Afghanistan. It had four different meeting rooms, a dining room, a gym, and a kitchen on the first floor and six bedrooms on the second floor. On the third floor were another six bedrooms occupied by the "permanent party" mix of Agency officers from the station and Agency contractors working security. Each bedroom looked like a US motel room with its own bathroom and twin beds. Sue and Melissa put down their overnight bags and laptop cases and changed out of local garb and into jeans and camp shirts. Sue secured the Uzi in the gun safe on their floor, but both She and Melissa kept their handguns in their shoulder holsters.

Everyone in their GLK met back in one of the meeting rooms after 30 minutes. The other GLK had already left, taking previous residents of the safe house back to the Green Zone. Jamie opened the discussion. "Some house rules first. We only have emergency Comms with station and we don't use any mobile devices here. I know I said this before we left the Green Zone, but, as a reminder, when you return to your rooms, please double check your phones are shut off and the Wi-Fi on your laptops is disabled. We know that the Russians and the Iranians have been trying for some time to find this place. Eventually they will, but for now, I don't intend to make it easy for them. Check?"

Everyone nodded.

"Next, you are here to debrief one of Jamal's agents. This guy is critical to the station's work against the various militias and the IED threat on the road out to BIAP. So I need you to understand that while we are fully supportive of the MACE effort and we get the high interest in this effort, the first joker who tries to tell me that they are under the direction of the White House to get this done gets to spend the night with the guards in their quarters sharing their meal. We are all on the same team here, have all signed the necessary sheets to be cleared into MACE and all want to succeed. The only difference is that next week you guys will be gone and Jamal and I will be still here. It is not that we don't like you, we just don't like any tourists in our neighborhood wherever they come from because you don't know the rules on how to stay safe. Do not shit in my back yard. Check?"

Sue liked Jamie already. She knew the road to Baghdad International Airport or BIAP was called by the Army patrols a road of death and defeating the IED threat was job one for multiple case officers in Baghdad including the 171 case officers assigned to station. Saying this up front and making it clear was simply Jamie's way of insuring this team from Balad do not lose their focus. That was definitely fair enough.

"Sue, your turn."

Sue already knew everyone had some understanding of the

MACE mission, so she focused on the specific reason why they were there. "At the last meeting Jamal had with DUSTDEVIL, he offered to provide information on what he called a Russian mafia approach to the local militia leader affiliated with Zarqawi. He said he would provide additional information at this meeting. One possibility is that this approach has to do with our hunt for radiological material that Zarqawi wants to make a dirty bomb. We want to be available if he comes to this next meeting with material that supports this theory. If he brings his computer as he said he would, Melissa will squeeze anything and everything out of the computer before we leave."

"Another piece of the puzzle that you may not know is we think one of our targets in the MACE equation has kidnapped one of our case officers and is holding him someplace in Northern Syria. Any information on that would be critical because we have a SOF raid team in Mosul ready to get our man back if we can pinpoint where he might be."

Jamie was shaking his head and Jamal simply said "Shit."

Jamie looked at Will and Bill. "How about you two. Why are you here?"

Will spoke for both of them. "Jamie, we have been tracking the issue of radiological weapons for over two years at Headquarters. Our job is to listen to the debriefing and give Sue and Jamal queues through their ear piece in case DUSTDEVIL offers something that is especially interesting or consistent with what we already know about the Russian angle on this. We will be set up in the same room that Melissa will use when she works on his computer, so we will provide as much information as we can as soon as we can."

Jamie seemed satisfied. He turned to Jamal. "OK, kid. Give them a basic outline of DUSTDEVIL and where we stand on the case right now. I know they have all read the file, but we all know…"

Jamal, Melissa and Sue chimed in at once "Everything we tell headquarters is completely true, it's just not truly complete."

The two Williams seemed perplexed. They were headquarters analysts, they had access to all the traffic and they had assumed that all the traffic captured all the details of DUSTDEVIL. Suddenly, they realized that they were in case officer country where there was plenty that headquarters never heard.

Jamal started with the basics. "OK, let's start with DUSTDEVIL himself. He is an Iraqi Shia. During the Iran-Iraq war, he was a fighter in the Shia "Badr Corps" when he was in his 20s. Badr was hardly a corps, but it was trained by the special forces side of the Iranian Islamic Revolutionary Guards Corps, the IRGC. They were supposed to infiltrate behind the lines and conduct classic resistance operations — sabotage and subversion. Based on our debriefings of Badr Corps fighters and IRGC trainers, the training was pretty darn good. Operational security sucked. Most of the Badr Corps members were wrapped up by Saddam's Mukhabarat by the mid 1980s. DUSTDEVIL was an exception and that was mostly because he was smart enough to stay clear of his peers and keep quiet. "

Jamal paused and took a swig of bottled water. "He reestablished contact with the IRGC when Saddam invaded Kuwait. He crossed into Iran and met with a number of IRGC intelligence officers who were satisfied that he was the real deal and they tasked him to start providing detailed information on the Iraqi Shia community in Basra and the Marsh Arabs, mostly Shia, but not all, but certainly all hostile to Saddam. After the US defeat of Saddam in Desert Storm, DUSTDEVIL decided that it would be a good insurance policy if he also had a relationship with the Agency. He was clear about his motivations and his detailed understanding of the IRGC made him worth the hard work to run him. He knew plenty about both what was now called the al-Qods force, the IRGC special forces, and IRGC intelligence and counterintelligence. This meant that he could give us insight into the IRGC-Hizballah collaboration, the IRGC-Iraqi Shia operations and, perhaps, the IRGC operations in Europe. So far, so clear?" This had all been in the file summary that they had read in Balad, so everyone at the table nodded.

"DUSTDEVIL has been a solid source since 1991 — fifteen years providing detailed reporting. After Saddam's repression of the Shia in Basra, DUSTDEVIL emerged as one of the main managers of a transport company that runs cargo, legal and illegal from Basra to

Baghdad. The company was run by Saddam's henchmen, but they needed a "loyal" Shia to keep their operations running in Southern Iraq. DUSTDEVIL did the needful. Of course, he was reporting to his IRGC handlers and us along the way, so he was playing all sides at once."

Bill said "Is he still an IRGC source?"

"We believe so. His reporting for us has been consistent over the years and, honestly, right now the only reason we are running DUST-DEVIL is because he reports on the IRGC operations supporting the Iraqi Shia militias, especially Muqtad al Sadr. "

Will shook his head. "How can you trust him?"

Jamie smiled and intervened. "We don't really. Remember what Reagan said to Gorbachev. Trust but verify. We match up his reporting with other sources, technical collection and we lay traps for him all the time. So far, so good. But no one in station thinks that DUST-DEVIL is loyal to anyone but himself."

He turned back to Jamal who continued, "OK, so recently DUST-DEVIL's reporting has been focusing on weapons acquisitions for the Shia militia and the IRGC and Hizballah efforts to improve their IED capability and other weapons that are designed to send us packing. Last meeting, he says to me that he has information on material coming in from Damascus that will be used for some sort of special weapon. He gets very nervous, he says he can't probe too much because the delivery from Damascus will be through the desert in a convoy run by Russians. He starts to clam up. We convince him that it is ok and that we can live with whatever he can tell us — so long as he will continue to meet us."

Jamie interjected. "Sue, that's where you come in."

"Me?"

"DUSTDEVIL's scariest operations in the 1990s were handled by a female case officer who he believed was the single person who could keep him alive. She played the role of interrogator, sister, trainer, and encouraged him to do everything that he needed to do, mostly so that he did not lose face in front of his handler. "

Sue could feel her anger starting to form inside her skull. She hated it when men assumed that there was something special about female case officers that somehow they couldn't deliver themselves. "So you think that another woman case officer will do the trick? And, why me? There are plenty of female case officers in Baghdad station."

Jamie slid his chair away from the table and raised his arms in mock surrender. "Sure, Sue. Before you grab a chair leg and start to beat me with it, let me explain the two reasons why you are here. First, this debriefing will be focused on MACE and honestly, none of our other case officers in station are read into the project. Actually, you are looking at the only two who are read in. So, the COS tapped us to help you. "

Sue was hardly calmed. "And Jamal can't do the job because he is a man?"

"No, Sue. Jamal can't do the job because he isn't the daughter of DUSTDEVIL's best case officer. You are. Your mother was his handler for nearly six years. We could bring her out here, she is still on the books, but we thought we would try you first since you were already in country."

Once again, Sue realized her family legacy had a long reach both into the past running through to the present. Now she had to become like her mother and handle an agent who was not entirely certain he wanted to go on. Of course, at this point, Sue wasn't sure whether she wanted to run down the same path as her mother. "OK, I get it. We tell him I was sent by mom to help him. We get him to calm down, debrief him, and task him to get more on MACE while keeping his head attached to his shoulders."

"Exactly." Jamie's smile reminded her of Massoni just before he would give the S&R team some shit detail.

Barbara O'Connell waited outside the COS' office. His secretary, Norma, had already offered her coffee that Barbara has taken more out of politeness than need. It was the bottom of the pot that looked to have been on since Norma started her day at 0700hrs. She knew the protocol for tdyers, travelers on "temporary duty." After all, Peter was the COS in Baku right now and they hosted plenty of tdyers. Some to support the station, some to pursue a target that station knew nothing about, and some visitors just traveling in the region as, more or less, intelligence community tourists. She knew the drill. You arrived, you paid the courtesy call on the Chief, but before you met with the chief you met with either his deputy or his chief of operations and his secretary. All three were simply vetting you to see if you were serious and/or dangerous. Barb had completed step two of the three step process. She met with the deputy, Phil Barns, and Norma. They both went into the chief's office, did their report and now it was time for the meeting with the boss. She had real work to do in the United Arab Emirates and she didn't want to mess this up. It was a long flight from Baku to Istanbul to Abu Dhabi and she didn't want to have to turn around and fly home if the COS didn't agree to her plan.

Phil opened the chief's door and waved Barb in. The office was very familiar. Peter had one in the same style in the US Embassy in Baku. A couple of couches against the wall. A round table with four chairs and an L-shaped desk with a computer and piles of paper on its surface. On the walls were framed items that outlined the unclassified life of COS Brendan Miles. Barb already had the basic background for Miles, but she scanned the walls to see if there was anything important that she had missed or that she could use in the warm up conversation. She saw just the thing. Miles was a graduate of the University of Virginia Law School.

Miles walked over to Barb and shook hands. He was approaching 60, on his last assignment, and looked like many of the survivors of the Vietnam era. Miles was slightly taller than Barb, making him probably six feet. He had a slight paunch but carried himself well and moved with boxer precision from around the desk to her location. He had a crew cut and a "Pancho Villa" style mustache, both completely grey. He was wearing a safari suit in khaki. On his left wrist hung a heavy gold chain common to most of her father in law's partners from Laos. On his left, a gold Rolex GMT Master. In all, he looked like a character actor who just stepped out of a movie from 1975. The question was whether he was going to be a hero or a villain in this screenplay. Either way, you would not want to face him in a knife fight.

"Barb, good to meet you. I have heard plenty about you and Pete over the years. I worked for your father in law in Laos and in Bangkok. I think I met young Peter before he was recruited and went to the Farm in 1979 or 1980. Were you there then?"

"Chief, I hate to admit it, but yes, I was there in 1980. I suppose the years in the harness show."

"Hey, Barb, compared to me you are a kid. Of course, compared to Phil, I suppose you are a geezer, but geezer's have plenty to teach kids. I heard your work as a tandem couple in Islamabad and Nairobi was solid. Pete seems more of a Russia house sort of guy, but it appears that your work is more up my alley: terrorists, insurgents, and general villains."

"Chief, I confess. I'm more comfortable dealing with…well, let's say, less sophisticated guys than Peter handles."

"Hah, sounds more like you prefer to mix it up a bit rather than play chess with the Russians. I certainly understand that. Peter senior must be retired by now, right?"

"Yes, he still does some work for the historian working on old archives down at the Farm. Keeps fit by paddling a canoe up and down the Potomac."

Looking down at his own waist, Miles answered "He was always scary fit."

"I'm sure you heard Pete is chief in Baku and our son is at University of Virginia and our daughter is at William and Mary. We need that in-state tuition."

Miles smiled but didn't take the bait. "Good schools, both."

He shifted effortlessly to work. "Now, Phil says you would like to debrief one of our guys."

"DUSTDEVIL, chief. I realize he has been a very productive guy for you here and the folks from the Counterterrorism Center don't want to change that…"

"Like hell. CTC is famous for sending in cowboys to snatch our cases. We live in Arabia which means plenty of Sunni extremists and just across the Gulf from Iran which means plenty of Shia extremists in our town. The last two cases we decided to "share" with CTC ended up being met someplace else and we got shit from CTC."

Barb had expected the response. She had been a rover for CTC since Peter became COS in Baku. She couldn't work for him and her record on CT cases was strong enough that CTC simply put her on their books and she responded to their tasking. For the last year, she had been on the road throughout Eastern Europe and the Middle East. She heard the same monologue every time. It was simply an opening argument in the negotiations.

"Chief, I can't speak for the other cases or CTC for that matter. What I can say is my cable from Baku has no other agenda. I simply want to attend today's meeting with DUSTDEVIL, ask him what he knows about the IRGC Qods force, and hunt for a lead that I can use to get direct access to an IRGC source in Qods force. If that source is on your turf, we pursue it together and your case officer gets the recruitment. It's not like I need another scalp on my books."

Phil spoke up. "Chief, I talked to Barb for a while this morning. I think this can work for us and I am sure Sandy Baker will learn plenty from Barb if he takes her along to the DUSTDEVIL meeting." Barb was pleased. Her in-briefing with the deputy had been successful.

"OK, I'm not going to stand in the way. All traffic goes out through me, right?"

"Chief, whether it is CTC's protocol or not, it is definitely my protocol. You can check with the other station's I've visited."

"Already did before I gave you my approval to come here, Barb. Your rep is good across the region. Anything else?"

Barb knew that this meant "get out of my office," so she answered. "Nothing right now, Chief. I will get the needful from Phil and Sandy."

Miles turned to his deputy. "Phil, get Barb set up. She is going to need an encrypted radio and a weapon. I think we have the necessary kit, right?"

"Sure, chief. I'll make it so."

Miles raised both hands as if to push them away. "Get outta my office, go spy, steal secrets, find new sources, do your job!"

Barb and Phil walked down the hall toward a vaulted area where they kept the sensitive equipment.

"I didn't know you went armed to meetings here."

Phil opened the arms locker and said, "Generally, we don't. However, the Boss thinks anything that might go wrong could go wrong when you are dealing with Iraqis and Iranians. He was on a team during the Gulf War that hunted Iraqi sleeper agents in Europe. He knew he was in the right place but at the wrong time during one meeting when an Iraqi Mukhabarat agent tossed a grenade down the apartment building stairs toward him and followed it up with a few rounds from a Skorpion machine pistol. Ever since, he chooses to arm our case officers. Headquarters hates it, but he is on his retirement tour. So far, they haven't said much to stop him."

"OK. I'm not going to complain. Some of my cases recently have been more than a bit hairy and going in with just a switchblade or a collapsible baton means you have to stay real close if something goes sideways. A pistol is a nice luxury."

"We have some lightweight body armor here for our female case officers. It won't stop more than a 9mm or a knife, but it is not too beastly in our heat."

"Armor?"

"Barb, it works like this. If the chief says you get a gun, it means you also have to draw body armor. After all, it stands to reason that if you need a weapon, the odds are pretty good they are going to be trying to do you harm, no?"

"Sure."

"Last month, the IRGC kidnapped a UAE customs investigator — I guess he got too close to some smuggling they were doing. They wrapped him in a jute sack, took him by dhow over to Iran, opened the sack, told him to stop bothering them, put him back in the sack and returned him to Dubai harbor. He wasn't armed."

"Message delivered, Phil."

"Barb, we have Browning Hi Powers and some Model 10s. We checked to see if you are qualified on them and you are, so….?"

"Do you have a 2" or 2 1/2" Model 10? I like revolvers for lots of reasons — mostly because I shoot better with them."

"The chief will be pleased. He carries a 2" all the time. There's a match to his plus a small of the back holster. Work for you?"

"Perfect."

"Now, for the radio…"

They completed the sensitive items sign out and Barb walked down the hall to the ladies room to "armor up" so that she could leave whenever Sandy decided to roll. As she was using the Velcro straps to tighten the vest, a young case officer walked in.

"Welcome to Abu Dhabi! I guess you must be Barb O'Connell?"

Barb finished the strap, freed her right hand and shook the offered one from the young brunette. She was just barely 5 feet tall and probably weighed 110 pounds at best. Mid-twenties. Very fit. After she shook Barb's hand, the young brunette pulled off her shirt to reveal her own version of the same vest wrapped about a sports, bra. "Patty Dentmann. Sandy and I are the CT targets officers here. I just got in from an all-nighter with a Hizballah guy. Drove me crazy. He is a chain smoker and speaks Arabic with a lisp. I think he had a hair lip at some point and someone saved his face but messed up his teeth. Either that or some piece of shrapnel did a job in him some years ago. Anyhow, I had to ask him to repeat everything he said, all night long." Dentmann had finished taking off the vest and pulled the Browning out of a holster on her waist.

"Don't you think he might have wanted to spend more time with you?"

Dentmann cleared the Browning, checked it again to insure it was unloaded and put the Browning on the counter and loaded the previously chambered round back into the Browning magazine. She put the pistol and magazine in a padded case and put the case in the small duffel that she brought in to hold the vest and pistol while in station. "Could be, but I reckon he is gay, so his target might have been the CTC analyst who was with me. Either way, I'm dead on my feet. You staying here for a while?"

Barb had laced the holster into her belt, loaded the revolver and put it in the holster. She pulled her shirt back on and checked to see how it fit over the armor and whether the holster printed. She would need something back there — a vest or a scarf or something. Dentmann noticed her look.

"Hey, I have a cute little leather vest that might just fit you. You are taller than me, but it probably will work. Before you leave with Sandy, swing by my cubicle. Ciao for now."

"Ciao, Patty." Barb wondered what normal women talked about in bathrooms. It probably wasn't whether your weapon was peeking out of our shirt.

Phil walked back into the COS' office. "O'Connell is all set, chief. Sandy's meeting is at 1600 and I left them at his desk working out the specifics."

"Phil, what do you think?"

"She will be ok. I doubt she is interested in stealing DUSTDEVIL."

Miles exploded into laughter. "Phil, you were just talking to the best recruiting and handling officer in CTC if not the entire DO. She has recruited Palestinians and Lebanese and the occasional Libyan just for a little variety. Did you see how she tried to case officer me by inserting that her son is at UVa? I doubt she knew about my JD before she walked into the office, so that means she scanned the room in about five seconds. We don't have to worry about O'Connell taking our cases. You might check to see if she picked your pocket." Miles smiled his Cheshire cat smile that Phil had eventually gotten used to which meant the COS was working at several levels above him.

"What I meant was, do you think Sandy is going to learn anything from her?"

"Sandy can be a numbskull, chief."

"And if he stays a numbskull for the rest of this tour, he is done in this career. He is now your pet project, Phil. He has to start learning teamwork soon or he is done. As to riding with O'Connell, I suspect she will either teach him something or kill him and bury him in the desert. Either way is a win for the Agency."

Phil looked at Miles in a totally new light.

Miles continued, "Phil, let me tell you a little story about her father in law. It is instructive because I suspect she is cut from the same cloth even if she is only a relative by marriage."

Miles sat down at the round table and waved Phil into the chair across the table. He bellowed to Norma for more coffee — this was Brendan Miles at his most bombastic, but it usually meant he actually intended to teach Phil something. Norma came in with the pot, filled the Chief's mug. Phil declined.

"Peter O'Connell. OSS Jedburgh. Early Cold War veteran and the scariest case officer I ever met. We were in Laos together. In 1973, just after the rainy season and about five months after I got there, we got a job that came directly from Headquarters. He was on his second tour in Laos. He had the country wired. The mission was a stretch even for O'Connell, or at least that was what I thought. Get this, the mission is this simple.

We get to go 50 kilometers into North Vietnam and tap a land-line that was running from Hanoi to the DMZ. It was the primary landline between two headquarters of the NVA running along a rail line. Why? The idea was the tap would exfil the various teletype and voice comms and ship them directly back to Langley. Washington would know if, but more likely when, the NVA were going to cheat on the Paris Accords." Miles took a large drink from his coffee cup. Phil always assumed it was Irish coffee after 1000hrs, but he wasn't going to ask.

"Peter and I left our base with a dozen Chinese mercenaries that served as our muscle in case there was trouble. We took an Air America bird as close as we could to the border, then two unmarked helos right to the border. Then we walked in. It wasn't that much of a hump, so long as we weren't discovered."

"And if you were discovered?"

"We were screwed. But, I was young and a numbskull myself, so I didn't think much about it. Anyway, the Air America crews did their job and we walked in from there. Put in the tap, confirmed the exfil circuit between the tap and some military receiver either in Bangkok or in some ship at sea and walked out. A week of terror and they used two Bell 212s to get us out. We were eating steaks and drinking beer in Vientiane that night. Just that easy."

"Chief, the point of your story?"

"It was just that easy because two days before our insertion a local Soviet advisor at an NVA base near the tap location was murdered. There was enough evidence left behind that the NVA political commissar was blamed for the death. They hadn't been getting along. Everyone, including the Soviets and us, knew the NVA creep was a Chinese Commie spy. The NVA brass and the Soviets were so tied up with the investigation that there simply wasn't time for them to do anything else including protecting the rail line from infiltrators. Brilliant, no?"

"Bad news for the Soviet."

"True. But he was helping to kill Americans, so I reckon it was a righteous effort."

"I'm assuming your point is that O'Connell did it?"

"He never said. If he did, of course, he probably used another set of Chinese mercs that he kept on contract, but for all I know he went in there ahead of time and did the deed himself. He hated Soviets, especially Soviet spies. He blamed them for killing his wife in Berlin just before they built the Wall."

"Different times."

"Different times, but the same job, Phil. Sometimes, you got to get your hands dirty."

Phil realized as he left the office that Miles wasn't really joking even though he could hear the COS laughing as he walked down the hall.

They approached the second safe house in the neighborhood using a less conspicuous minibus. Six passengers filled the bus and they had removed all the possible hand holds so locals couldn't grab a ride as they wandered through the streets. This time there was no walled compound, no guards, no welcome. They just rolled up behind what appeared to be a bombed out warehouse, most probably from the 2003 bombing campaign. Neither Jamal nor Jamie offered an explanation. Once they were inside the ruined building, Jamie pulled down the garage door and locked it in place. Two of Jamie's locals were already waiting. They had checked the building an hour prior and would now disappear into covering positions on what was left of the roof.

Sue got out and walked along what was probably a machine shop some years ago. She saw an industrial sized lathe in the corner that had been bent in a u shape from the overpressure of whatever bomb hit this building. There was what appeared to be a lengthy tool bench where workers did their work, now filled with bird crap, rat droppings, dirt and scattered pieces of metal.

Jamie said, "The Air Force decided in February 2003 that this was a weapons manufacturing shop for those weapons of mass destruction we were here to capture. Put two smart bombs into the building at two in the morning — just to minimize casualties. It was a local machine shop for folks trying to keep their cars and consumer goods running. Ten old tool and die makers were killed while working on someone's refrigerator or old Fiat car; it did make an awful mess. When I came into the neighborhood in 2004 to set up the safe house, I decided that this would be a great place to have meetings. Half the locals have left and the other half are convinced the place is haunted by ghosts of the locals who died. "

Sue looked around at the debris and said, "Where do we hold the meeting?"

"You guys, follow me. Jamal is going to go out and get DUST-DEVIL and bring him in. We don't tell him where this is — he has to wear the sensory deprivation goggles for the last bit and then we bring him into the basement." Jamie pulled up a hatch in the floor and walked down a ladder into the basement. He turned on the lights and then shouted up to the four visitors. "Come on. No rats down here — well, not many. Hurry up."

Sue went down the ladder first. She didn't want anyone to see how difficult climbing a ladder was with her prosthetic. Jamie was waiting at the bottom.

"If you show me yours, I'll show you mine."

"Eh?"

"Scars. I got mine after a car bomb went off in Somalia. Nearly lost my left foot. Agency supported me from day one. They gave me the long term care, a bonus, the Intelligence Star, and then asked me if I wanted a desk job. Can you see me behind a desk?"

"Absolutely. Behind a desk, sitting on one of those pastel colored balance balls that is supposed to improve your balance. You would be giving advice to people who were half your age and not interested in anything you had to say."

"Yup. You captured it exactly."

The basement was actually a well-lighted bricked in hallway that led to a pair of rooms at the end of the hallway. The basement was just deep enough underground that it was close to the water table of the Tigris river and the first three inches of the walls were light green from mold.

Sue said, "Attractive."

"Hey, we aren't asking you to make baklava here, just debrief here." Jamie turned to the two Williams and Melissa. "Your room is to the left. The debriefing room is fully covered with mike and wire and a camera. You can do a commo check with Sue as soon as I get her wired up. "

Jamie and Sue walked through the door to the right. The room was paneled, had a wood floor and real furniture. If she didn't know where she was, Sue would have been convinced she was in a hotel room somewhere in a third world country. There was a desk, four living room chairs, two single beds and a small radio.

Jamie turned on the radio — it played an endless loop of Arab pop music. "The fridge has sodas and water. We don't let our visitors drink. The bathroom is to the right, it's just a simple shitter. No shower, no tub. The shitter is wired so the guys next door can watch to be sure DUSTDEVIL isn't getting ready to blow you or him or your both to kingdom come. You set here." He pointed to the chair with its back to the wall. "The radio loop for our comms is in the chair and you will get the best reception from the earpiece if you stay within arms-length of the chair. " Jamie pointed to a button on the upholstery. "Push there."

Sue pushed the button and the interior wall of the armrest opened up. There was a holster in the concealment. "Put your handgun in there. We tell him we don't allow firearms in the room. That's just in case you decide he hasn't obeyed instructions. Now, here's your ear-piece. I suspect you have used one of these before." Another Massoni smirk. Did he know Sue's background? Did it matter?

She put the earpiece in and as soon as it was fitted in place she heard Melissa's voice. "We can see you clearly and hear what is going on. Can you hear us?"

"Yes, kiddo. Technology is a wonderful thing."

Jamie said, "Until it stops working."

There were two clicks in both Jamie's and Sue's earpieces. Jamie said, "Jamal is back with DUSTDEVIL He takes him along a differ-ent path to get here. Too easy to kill an agent by forcing him to climb a ladder with goggles on. OK, Sue. Over to you."

"Thanks. I hope we get something useful."

"You better. This is supposed to be my bowling night." Jamie was out the door before Sue could think of a good response.

Sue had about five minutes to think about what she was going to say and how she was going to say it. Not a lot of time but it seemed like forever before she heard the knock on the door. "Come in."

Jamal walked in with DUSTDEVIL. Sue had no preconceived notion of what he would look like. His file photo was of a young 20 something photographed for the IRGC training program. Now he was a 40 something man who had lived through fifteen years of double agentry. He looked older than his age. When Jamal took off the goggles, DUSTDEVIL immediately put on tortoise shell glasses that were thick and looked like something from a British pop magazine from the 1960s. Sue stood up and reached out a hand. "Sir, it is good to see you."

"Do I know you?" His voice was strained — almost squeaky. His English was filled with an accent that could only be described as "Levantine." It was English filtered through a mix of Arabic, Turkish and Persian sounds. He took her hand and before she could close on it or shake it, he had it back in his pocket. He pulled out a pack of cigarettes and a plastic lighter. Before he said anything or did anything else, he lit a cigarette and took a deep drag. The smoke covered his face. The smell of the cigarette and fear filled the room as he exhaled. "I know you?"

"No, we have not met. But I know you."

"You look and sound so familiar. I have met you before. Anil said I would recognize you. Isn't that right, Anil?"

Sue breathed a sigh of relief. She and Jamal had forgotten to exchange throw away alias names before he left. Now she knew he was Anil. It was her turn to help him. "My name is Martha. You have not met me before, but you were very close to my mother, Anna."

DUSTDEVIL leaned forward to the point where he had to grab the top of the overstuffed chair in front of him to avoid falling over. The thick glasses made his eyes look nearly twice their normal size. "Anna. Of course, you look and sound like Anna. It has been so long and yet it seems like yesterday." He walked around the chair and sat down and took another drag from his cigarette and sighed through the smoke as it left his mouth and nose. Sue wasn't thrilled with the fact that the room was already filling with smoke, but that was inconsequential for now. Plenty of time later for commenting on how yucky it was.

Jamal looked at them. "I will make tea, yes?"

DUSTDEVIL spoke first. "Anil, that would be very nice. A big pot. We have much to talk about. First, though, I need to give you this. I know you want it, Anil, and I am pleased that you are learning patience." He handed Jamal his briefcase with his laptop.

"Thank you, uncle."

Jamal left the room for a minute to deliver the laptop to Melissa. He returned and started to assemble the tea. It was a mint tea — even over the smell of the strong tobacco, Sue could smell the tea brewing. Jamal made the pot, brought apple juice and sugar cubes as well as a small divided tray that had dates, almonds and pistachios. No one spoke while Jamal prepared apple tea for each of them and while each of them sipped their tea out of hot, clear glasses.

Once the glasses were empty, Jamal filled them and DUSTDEVIL started to speak. "Tell me about your mother. Is she well? And your father? I met him once in Germany. His name was August, correct?" Sue had no idea what name her father had used, so she nodded — hoping that this would serve either way as agreement or avoiding embarrassing an old friend.

"Mother is well. She doesn't travel as much anymore. My father died. Killed."

"The Russians, no doubt. They were always after both of them, you know."

"How so?"

"When we were working together on the Guards in Europe, I warned your mother over and over again. The Guards can do what they do because they are working with the Russian and Georgian gangs. Georgia was once part of Iran, you know?" He looked over his glasses — as a teacher to a student.

"Before the Great War, yes."

"So, they are used to working with each other — for centuries. They don't trust each other, but they work together."

In her earpiece, she heard William say "Exploit this! Get him to expand on…." Then there was a small gurgle and she heard Jamie's voice. "Pay no attention to the man behind the curtain, Dorothy. Just keep doing what you are doing. Sorry for the interruption."

DUSTDEVIL looked quizzically at Sue. "You don't believe me?"

"No, my friend. If there is one thing my mother said to me before I left for this meeting, it was to always trust in your judgment."

DUSTDEVIL beamed. He was clearly pleased by this remark. "Anna trusted me with her life — I know that to be true. I am so pleased she remembered."

"You were saying about my father."

"The Soviet Union collapsed and the Russians special services officers were suddenly out of work. They used their experience and their networks to build an enterprise that was very strong in Lebanon, Syria and Iraq. They provided assistance to the Guards…" He rubbed his left thumb and forefinger together and then took another deep drag from his cigarette. Before anything else was said, he lit a new cigarette from the stub of the old one. "They paid well and the Russians delivered — people, guns, intelligence, whatever would bring the highest price."

"You said you were convinced my father was killed by them?"

"Of course, little Martha. He and your mother were trying to break that chain between the two organizations. If he was killed, he was killed because he was going to succeed if they didn't stop him. I am sorry that they did."

"Sir, you need to know that I am here for two reasons. First, to stop the Russians from selling equipment to terrorists. Secondly, to avenge my father."

"Of course. It is what I thought. We can work together on these things. I have my own reasons for wanting to punish the Russians. "

In her earpiece, Melissa's voice came through. "We have persons, places and times of meetings between the Russians and the al-Sadr bunch. It's all here on his laptop along with a search for his brother. It looks like he was lost in Lebanon, he worked for Hizballah and then disappeared.

Sue spoke to DUSTDEVIL. "Your brother."

"How did you know?"

"My mother has been following your effort to find him. What do you know now?"

"Anna was always so caring. She told me she would never forget. " Through the smoke, Sue could see DUSTDEVIL's eyes filling with tears. "I think they killed him on a trip to Cyprus. He was trying to provide electronics for the Shia militia and they killed him. That is what I think."

"I will find out for you. I promise."

DUSTDEVIL reached out to Sue and touched her hand. His hand was cold.

"Thank you."

Now she was sure he was crying. It was time to push the conversation to the present. "What can you tell us now that can help us against the Russians here?"

"There are three Russians who have been talking to al-Sadr's militia as well as talking to Zarqawi's militia. They are offering bomb making material. I don't understand why anyone cares about this material. Most of the militias make bombs from the explosives taken from Saddam's artillery or tank shells. But they are excited. There is a bidding war going on right now between the two militias. It is a dangerous game and the Russians are living in Syria so that they can avoid being kidnapped by one or the other side and held hostage for the material. Al-Sadr's militia have been warned by their Hizballah and Guards trainers not to consider this. Hizballah kidnapped Russians in the 1980s and the Russian services hunted down family members, killed them, and delivered them one piece at a time to the families until their men were free. It was a lesson that Hizballah learned."

Another long drag on the cigarette. "I don't know anything about the Zarqawi militia other than they terrify everyone in my family and most everyone in the Iraqi government. They might be foolish enough to try a kidnapping."

"Do you know where the Russians are staying in Syria? How will they cross the border?"

"I do not know when they will cross, but we do know that they are living in Al-Malikiyah. It is a town where the Soviets used to have a compound, designed to spy on Turkey and Iraq at the same time."

"How do you know?"

DUSTDEVIL smiled through a cloud of smoke. "Just like Anna. Always the follow up question. I know this because my people have driven al Sadr's representative to Al-Malikiyah for meetings. As I said, the Russians will not come to Iraq."

"You could show me where in Al-Malikiyah?"

"Momken." Sue didn't know much Arabic, but she knew that comment. It could mean "perhaps" or "maybe" or "forget it" — better than "inshallah" but certainly not yes.

"Sir, we need to know. We can hurt the Russians there. We can end this part. What we do know is that Zarqawi has outbid al-Sadr and the Russians are going to sell the material to Zarqawi. We can't let this happen."

"Martha, daughter of Anna. I will find the place for you. I will ask my driver. He knows Al-Malikiyah."

Sue reached out with both of her hands and touched DUST-DEVIL. "Thank you, uncle." DUSTDEVIL broke down into tears.

Jamal took DUSTDEVIL out, handing him his computer on the way out the door. Sue assembled her notes, secured her pistol from the concealment, waited enough time for Jamal and DUSTDEVIL to clear the hallway and then walked out. She met Jamie in the hallway.

"That was brilliant. He will deliver on this requirement. I'm sure of it. Well done."

Sue leaned against the wall of the safe house. She realized she was shaking. "Jamie, you ever feel like you are giving up a piece of your soul when you do one of these?"

Jamie looked Sue in the eyes and said softly, "Every time you treat an asset like a human being, Sue. Every time. And the only way to do this job is to treat your asset like a human being, so I'm afraid the only proper answer is…get used to it."

"How did my mom do it for so many years?"

"Beats me, Sue. You probably don't realize but she is a legend in the counterterrorism world. She ran cases that no one else would or could. She always found the hook that made the asset deliver. Not so much different from you, kid."

"Except I feel like shit."

"Who said she didn't?"

S mith looked across the table at Sue. She was sitting with Flash on one side and Melissa on the other. Smith had to prevent himself from smirking. It had been a long time since he saw Flash in her Army Combat Uniform or ACUs. Smith hadn't said anything, but both Flash and Sue understood that if you were going to brief the Commanding General of SOF, you needed to look the part. Both uniforms were sterile of any identification, both had the USASOC shoulder patch on their left shoulder. Sue and Flash had a paired patch on the right shoulder identifying their combat tours. Smith knew Sue's tours were in Afghanistan and Flash had served as an analyst with the first SOF headquarters in Baghdad in 2003. As a civilian, Melissa didn't have a "duty uniform" but she seemed to understand the point and she was dressed in a classic Agency "in theatre" uniform of 5.11 cargo pants and a navy blue long sleeved polo shirt. It was probably the best she had in her bag and it would do nicely. Between the three of them, Smith was convinced they were going to crack the target wide open and succeed where plenty of others had failed in MACE. He had virtually all of 171 in theater at this point and was ready to deploy them to end the threat and, with a little bit of luck, recover Daniels alive. That would give him a chance to choke the dumb ass for taking tasking and not letting his chain of command know that he was operational.

They were waiting in the SOF commander's briefing room in Balad. Whether it was just the commander's style or budget issues, Smith noticed that this three star's briefing room was simply three folding tables set up in a U shape with 20 metal folding chairs. The open end of the U faced four plasma screens that were marked with duct tape and black lettering from left to right: Bragg, Mosul, Baghdad, Kabul. The senior SOF officers in each of these locations were already on the screen ready for a secure video teleconference with the Boss, CG/SOF. Kabul had dialed in simply because that was currently where the Deputy SOF commander was living and working with the SOF raid and S&R squadrons that were after al-Qaida in Afghanistan.

The SOF commander walked in, everyone stood up, he sat down at the head of the table with his brain trust including a senior Agency officer, a senior SOF analyst and his chief of staff. He was tall and thin with a high and tight haircut and a marathon runner's build. Sue thought he was about as different as the previous commander in style, shape and persona as she could imagine. The commander who visited her at Walter Reed nearly three years ago looked more like a lineman from a college football team.

The SOF commander started. "OK, we have lots to do and I wanted everyone to have the same situational awareness before we moved forward." He looked at Sue. "Chief, gives us the basics as we know them right now."

Sue had not expected this. During her previous experience with General Officers, they always looked to the most senior officer in the room to give them the briefing and she had provided a copy of her notes to Smith expecting the commander of 171 to do the talking. She looked over at Smith. He looked back as if to say "Well, get to work!" At this point, Sue realized that Smith knew all along the commander's style and knew in advance that he would look to the person with the most knowledge rather than the person with the highest rank.

"Sir, the most recent update on MACE is based on a meeting I had with an Agency asset code named DUSTDEVIL. He is an Iraqi Shia smuggler who has been working for the Agency for some time. I met him on 12 May in an Agency safe house in Baghdad," Sue paused and took a breath. She knew what she had to say, she just needed to take a moment to insure she said it in the right order. Based on his reputation, she knew that the SOF commander was not someone much interested in atmospherics.

The commander took that moment to turn to his CIA senior representative. "Please send our thanks to the Baghdad for making this happen."

"Yes, sir." The Agency representative was a senior paramilitary officer who had worked with the Special Operations community for his whole career. He might not like staff work, but he knew that this was probably the most important staff job in the Agency right now:

making sure that the CIA and SOF were operating as a single counterterrorism machine, the best machine of its kind in the world.

Sue continued. "DUSTDEVIL identified that the key meeting venue for the Russian mafia smuggling side of the MACE operations is in Al-Malikiyah. While we were debriefing him, my colleague, Melissa Nez, downloaded all of his files from a computer that he brought to the meeting." Sue decided if she was going to be in the spotlight, there was no reason why Melissa or, for the matter, Flash, would get to rest. She looked at Melissa.

Melissa looked down at her notes. She slowly looked up from her notes and made eye contact with the commander.

"Ms. Nez. Thank you for coming to the meeting. I understand from the Agency that you are the best and youngest technical specialist in their information operations group. I may have to ask your Director if I can get them to send you on TDY here so we can use your skills as we take apart AQ in Iraq." He smiled. Sue was certain it was the same smile that she had imagined as a child when her mother read here the story of the big bad wolf just before he devoured little red riding hood.

Melissa looked back down at her notes. "Thank you, sir." She shifted into her formal briefing mode and switched from staring at her briefing notes to staring at her computer. The image on the computer screen was displayed on the screen that previously had the image from Ft. Bragg. The secure video conference was set up so that whatever showed up on the Ft. Bragg screen was displayed simultaneously on the screens in the network. "Sir, we found about a dozen different email exchanges between DUSTDEVIL and the Shia militia leadership addressing the MACE threat and another five where DUSTDEVIL is included on emails between the Shia leadership and the Russian mafia connection. I won't focus on the texts right now. I have already forwarded them to your analysts. What I do want to point out that I was able to track down the internet service provider that the Russian end was using. It was a Wi-Fi hotspot at the following location."

Melissa clicked her mouse and a map of Eastern Syria appeared on the screen and then a more detailed satellite image of a specific part of Al-Malikiyah appeared. "The Syrian government is not very open to freelance Wi-Fi locations. They like to control all the ISPs in country, so I was surprised to find one that was not listed on the Agency programs tracking the various ISPs. It would appear that the hotspot used by the Russians is linked to a satellite phone. We were able to determine that it was a Thuraya phone which has the best coverage in the region. Once we had that sorted out, I passed this on to Flash." Melissa smiled a gentle smile and looked at Flash who had been following the story with no apparent expectation that she was going to be a participant. Flash jerked straight up in her chair as if someone had just stuck a pin in her back.

The CG looked puzzled, "Flash?"

This time Smith did come to their assistance. "Sir, Chief Warrant Officer Billings. She is the senior 171 analyst for this theater. She is my best analyst.

The SOF commander smiled. He looked at Flash. "And?"

"Sir, we have been working with your analysts for the past four years to build a network analysis for the Thuraya phone system used by Al Qaida, the Taliban and several other terrorist networks in the AOR. 171 has recruited several assets to support that analysis and we are working closely with the Fort to make sure we don't get crossways with NSA." Flash took a breath. "We have been able to geolocate the Thuraya being used in this operation. " Flash grabbed the laptop from Melissa and pulled up a second satellite map of Al-Malikiyah. In the middle of the map was a small, pulsating green dot."

"How current is that location, Chief."

"Sir, Ms. Nez and I have worked out a means to download a Trojan horse on that phone. This image and that location is live. Unless that phone is destroyed, we will have a live feed of its location for at least then next month until Thuraya downloads a new patch to their operating system."

The SOF commander smiled again. Sue was certain that it was the Big Bad Wolf smile. "Excellent. Mosul, you got that feed?"

The Army Major filling the screen spoke. "Sir, we got it and will work up an action plan to send to you in 30."

"Check, Barry. I need you to get this right. We are going to have to send this one to the White House for approval. It is Syria remember."

"Sir, we will have the plan to you soonest."

"Excellent. " He turned to Smith. "Jed, what else do you have in your bag of tricks?"

"Sir, my operator in Dohuk has another agent meeting set in Zakho tonight. He will have more details on the Syrian and AQ threats in and around Al-Malikiyah current as of this morning. I will make sure the feed goes directly to Barry in Mosul. This asset can get an advanced team into Al-Malikiyah by ground if that makes sense to you. I'm thinking one or two from 171 and an S&R team to put eyes on the target before Barry's team goes in."

The SOF commander looked at the screen. "Barry?"

"Sir, if we can get eyes on and an all clear from the ground before we send the little birds in, it would be great."

"OK, Jed, make it happen. Any alibi rounds from anyone at the table or on the screens?" No one said anything. "Let's get to work. I need something for Washington by 15 Zulu so that we can get it on the table at the White House when they wake up. That gives us four hours to turn this idea into a plan. Get to work."

The general stood up and left. The screens went blank and Sue, Melissa and Flash let out a deep sigh of relief. Melissa spoke first. "Working here is like being a particle in a linear accelerator. I thought Langley was fast, but this is wild."

Sue raised an eyebrow, "Eh? Linear accelerator? Remember, I was a liberal arts major."

Flash gave Sue a small dope slap on the side of the head. "Puhle-ase, don't give us that "I'm too stupid, I'm just a girl" routine. "

Smith walked over to the three of them. "You did great. Now, in case you are wondering, the CG was talking to you as well about planning. So, return to the MACE shed and get to work. Once again, we are expecting brilliance." They all left the room smiling.

They buried Max Creeter at Raleigh National Cemetery. He had all the credentials to be buried at Arlington, but the executor of his will, a retired command sergeant major from SOF, said that the will made it clear that Max wanted to be buried as close to Ft. Bragg as possible. He also wanted a cremation and a quick ceremony. They worked hard to make all of that happen. Barb was tied up with the Cleaners for several days as they worked with the federal authorities to make the shooting "disappear." The Cleaners were a joint operation with the FBI and it was efficient in ways that most government organizations would never dream of being efficient. Barb spent most of her time in a deep dive debriefing that most of the time felt like an interrogation. She held her own throughout, this wasn't her first hostile debriefing after all. The team left promising that this was the last time they would ask her to relive the story. Of course, these sorts of debriefings, much like any CI investigation always ended with the caveat "Of course, we will have to report to the seniors and they may wish to revisit the issues." Issues. Barb was unlikely to use that term for a gunfight where a SOF hero died, but she let that go because it wasn't worth the fight.

The burial was classic military protocol. Men in dress uniforms. An honor guard and a gun salute. The weather was perfect and the trees were in blossom after a cold winter. Barb stayed in the background in her formal black pantsuit. On her right was Bill in his FBI "testify" suit: black suit, white shirt, grey tie. On her left was Beth in her black dress and a black hat, a dress Barb had last seen her wear when Barb buried her husband and before that when Barb attended the graveside memorial the day Beth buried her husband. Beth's husband, Walter, was killed in the Khobar Towers bombing in 1996. Beth's husband was a retired ambassador working at the time on negotiations to formalize a US military presence in the Kingdom.

When it was over, they walked together through the cemetery. Bill said, "Mom, does Sue know?"

"Not yet, dear. She is "out of the net" working in Iraq somewhere. When she resurfaces, I will try my best to explain what happened."

"Are we going to get the ringleaders who ordered this hit."

"Count on it, Bill" This time coming from Beth who was behind them.

Barb said, "Bill, you need to return to DC. Beth and I have some work to do at the house and then we will get back in touch as soon as we return to the city. OK?"

Bill looked relieved. He had too many emotions running around in his head right now and a lonely drive back to DC would probably be the best way to sort them out. "Mom, please be careful."

"You too, dear."

As Bill walked away, Beth turned to Barb. "The house? I thought we were going to meet some folks here?"

"Beth, my son is an FBI agent. He doesn't need to know what we are going to do today because he might have to report it to his bosses. We don't want that, do we?"

Beth nodded. "No, we don't want that."

Barb and Beth were sitting in their hotel suite about ten miles from Ft. Bragg. They were waiting for a visitor.

"Barb, what do you know about this guy?"

"He was Max's team mate for nearly 10 years. He contacted me and asked if he could help. I checked with some of the folks from my old shop. He is legit and he definitely wants a piece of this action."

"OK. How about we open with my side and then see how this works. I don't want to waste our time with some geezer who is not going to work with us."

"Fine by me."

They waited another hour and were packing up to leave when there was a knock on the door. Barb when to the door. She had a 2" Smith and Wesson revolver in her left hand when she opened the door as far as the security lever would allow.

"Ms. O'Connell?"

"Mr. Longstreet? Thanks for coming. We have been waiting for you." Barb opened the door, stepped aside and quickly secured the revolver in a deep concealment holster in her jeans at the small of her back.

Beth started in before he could get too far into the room. "Mr. Longstreet, my name is Beth Parsons and I am a representative from an international investment firm Stearns and Mandeville. " She handed Longstreet her card.

Barb looked at Longstreet. He was about 5'10" and weighed about 190 pounds. His face looked every day of the 55 years old that Max had said he was, but his body looked to be as fit as any man Barb had seen at Max's funeral. Given his size and shape, Barb thought he looked like a retired NFL middle linebacker. His hair was cut in a longish style from the 1970s. He was wearing suede boots, jeans, a button-down collar shirt and a corduroy sports coat. He certainly had looked older when he served as a pallbearer at Max's funeral. Of course the black suit hadn't helped. Now he looked to be more at home as a gentleman farmer than a retired special operator, but then again, Max looked more like an academic than an operator, so Barb was not fooled by his outward appearance.

"Ms. Parsons, please don't think I'm trying to be rude, but I'm not here for a job interview, OK?" He looked over his shoulder at Barb who was standing in the kitchenette of the suite separated from Beth and Longstreet by a low kitchen bar.

"Also, Ms. O'Connell, if you really don't trust me, you shouldn't have let me in the room. I know and you know I can get across the bar before you can put two rounds from that .357 into me. So, let's just cut the crap and talk about why we are here."

Beth countered using her most serious professional voice, a voice that probably had previously made heads of state flinch and currently made her the primary negotiator at Stearns and Mandeville. "Mr. Longstreet, if you are so ready to get started, why are you a half hour late?"

Longstreet was not fazed by either the question or by Beth's tone. He actually looked pleased. "Ms. Parsons, I'm a half hour late because your background checks took that long to ferret out of my contacts in Washington. I do apologize for that, but I suspect you did the same, just quicker."

Beth smiled her Medici smile. She looked at Barb. "What precisely do you think you are here to talk about, Mr. Longstreet?"

"First, if you continue to call me by my last name, we are going to get nowhere. I'm Jake."

Barb finally stepped around the bar toward the two of them sitting in the living area of the suite. "Jake, I'm Barbara and this is Beth."

"A fair start. I understand that there are men out there who have tried to kill you and successfully killed Max. That means they are good and you have a good reason to be careful. I'm here to help you find them and finish them once and for all. I have a small number of Max's team mates who will do anything…" he paused and raised a blunt forefinger from his right hand "…but prison time to do this. We are assuming you need some help OCONUS and we are ready to do this for Max. "

"We need help with the finish part of the equation, Jake. I think we can find them easy enough. But…when it comes to the finish piece, we are going to need manpower."

"Given your background, I figured that was why we were talking. Just so you know, I am no mercenary and I don't have any connections that are going to deliver weapons to some location for the final act of this play. Two questions: Where is this going to end and are we going to need weapons to end it?"

Beth reentered the conversation. "We have been doing the research on this for a few weeks. I can't say for certain, but it looks like Salzburg, Austria is the venue." Beth looked to Barb.

Barb took up the conversation and said, "As to guns, Jake, I don't know if we are going to need them, so I can't answer your question, yet. However, if we need them and you are willing to carry guns in Austria, I am pretty confident I can find them when the time comes."

"How many men?"

"Probably five, maybe six. We will have to do some surveillance and with yourself and yours truly, we will be able to pull 24-hour coverage if need be. Just fyi, I will cover the costs, but I will eventually need to know your fee."

Now it was time for Jake to use his official voice. "Barbara, if you cover the costs and we get a chance to finish the people who killed

Max, no one that will be working with me will ask for money from either one of you. This is an obligation that we owe Max. There isn't a single one of us who doesn't owe his life to Max. This is just balancing the books. Anyhow, our other work is lucrative enough that we don't eat canned beans when we live here in North Carolina."

"I don't have enough information right now to give you even the beginning of a plan, Jake. I hope you know that. I have been focused on Max and, honestly, cleaning up the mess at the house on the Potomac."

"Understood, Barb. We have all agreed to stand down on any contract work until we get your call. There is plenty of work for guys like us, so we don't mind taking a little time off." Jake stood up and turned to Beth. "Ms. Parsons, here is my card. You and Barb can reach me anytime by email or on the mobile. Good night." He turned and walked out of the room.

Barb locked and bolted the door and sat down. She did two deep belly breaths to clear some of the adrenaline out of her system. Beth handed her the card Jake had dropped off. Across the top was an image of a 15th century pike. The card was very high quality and the printing was raised and lettered in a 19th century style script. It read:

James Peter Longstreet

Capitani di Ventura

Condottieri de Malatesta, LLC

PO Box 1200

Southern Pines, NC

jbl@malatesta.com

On the back he had written in neat pen a phone number that Barb immediately recognized as a satellite mobile phone number — most probably tied to a Thuraya phone which would forward the number to wherever Jake wanted it to go.

"Nice title." Beth passed Barb a glass of red wine which she had poured from a bottle that they had opened for the meeting. She poured herself a glass.

Sue was jammed into the back of the broken down van that doubled both as a local bus and, based on the smell, a goat transporter. Sue knew that for certain because on her lap was a lamb that they had bought this morning. Along with its smell, the lamb's voice added a certain degree of realism that Ginger had found amusing and Sue found annoying. Sue was in full hijab again, though this time the abaya was made of some sort of synthetic fabric purchased in the Dohuk market.

Sitting next to her in the last row of seats was Bill Jameson and next to him was Billy from Sue's old SOF unit, Surveillance and Reconnaissance (S&R). In the row in front of them was 171 officer Ginger, two SBS operators, George, Dozer, and a crate of chickens. They were all dressed in Kurdish garb. The driver was one of Ginger's smuggler assets named Mansour and two Peshmerga militiamen. While not obvious to the casual observer, including the sleepy Syrian border guards when they crossed the deserted border, all of the occupants of the van were armed with rifles and handguns. Under the crate of chickens was a bag with S&R surveillance gear and a set of infrared strobes that they would place at the designated landing zone for the SOF raid team that would come in a MH60 and a MH500 Little Bird. They arrived in Al-Malikiyah just after sunrise. Al-Malikiyah was simply a road crossing and market place for this remote section of Syria. Two dozen brick and stucco buildings, a road junction and a run-down village hall that also served as the phone exchange, headquarters for the mayor and police chief and the two policemen that also served as customs inspectors for trucks coming in from Turkey. The village market thrived on black market goods and, in the past, the hard currency that the Soviet contingent had paid to keep the villagers out of their compound. Since 2003, the village had enjoyed new profits as every side from the Iraq war had paid to either get into or get out from Iraq. The Soviet compound had become a Russian mafia compound profiting from weapons and explosives smuggled out of the Caucasus and into Iraq. It was one of the safer towns in Eastern Syria primarily because everyone in town was making a profit and no one wanted to upset the steady stream of money coming into town.

The safe house that Mansour had for his cigarette and refugee smuggling operation was a block away from the location where the Thuraya phone had been located at Balad. The satellite imagery suggested that they would have good visibility of the target location from the roof of the safe house. As soon as they pulled into the compound, Jameson and Billy headed up to the roof to confirm the sight line, George and Dozer worked with Ginger and Mansour regarding security for the compound and Sue, once free from the lamb, set up the SATCOM rig so that they could communicate with Balad and Mosul. A few minutes after Sue sent the first burst communications message confirming arrival, she sent a second message confirming the start of surveillance on the Russian compound. As expected, the safe house had excellent line of sight to the front and side of the building and the compound as well as excellent coverage of the Thuraya signal.

Before they left Dohuk, Balad had cleared their infiltration, but they were still waiting on approval from Washington regarding the raid itself. Sue understood that. After all, their mission was risky, but still arguably an intelligence operation. Once you brought in the raid team into Syria without telling the Syrians, it could be legitimately be argued the US had invaded Syria. With luck, the entire operation on this remote part of Syria would occur without anyone in Damascus knowing anything. With luck.

That afternoon, Mosul received the go signal from Balad and forwarded the same to Sue. As soon as the signal was sent, the team met in the main room of the house for a council of war. Based on his seniority, Jameson took the lead. "So far, we haven't seen much that tells us how many are in the compound. That's tough because we have about six more hours of daylight to get something useful. The team intends to hit the compound at 0330hrs. Not a lot of time after sunset to find anything useful for them. Let's go around the room. George and Dozer."

George was in black shorts and a tan t-shirt with his M4 in his lap. He was sitting in the corner of the room next to Dozer. They were both sitting on a white plastic chairs made in China and shipped to every third world country. It looked like it could barely hold Dozer's weight. "Dozer and I will go at midnight with one of Mansour's peshmerga and confirm the landing zone. We will set up the beacons and pull security for the LZ until the aircraft come in. We stay on sight until mission complete and board the number four aircraft on departure. Too easy."

Jameson nodded. "Ginger?"

"Mansour, another pesh and I will engage the police station at 0300hrs. First we cut the phone lines and then Mansour wakes up the mayor and the chief of police and offers them an opportunity to get rich. If they choose loyalty to the Russians, we resolve the problem whatever way we need to."

"We want to minimize your exposure and any unnecessary kinetics, ok?"

"Agreed and Mansour is on board with that because he wants to keep his smuggling operation here. He says the Mayor will play ball. The current batch of Russians have been cheap and arrogant. Not a good combination when you are out here. The cover story of a rival set of smugglers hitting the compound will work mostly because some Turkish smugglers are already planning to do so and have warned the mayor and the police to stay out of the way. Should work fine."

"Ginger, as soon as Mansour has control, you need to get to the LZ. Match up with George and Dozer. Check?"

"Got it, Boss. Believe me, I don't want any more time in Syria than necessary and the sooner we all leave, the better it is for Mansour."

Jameson continued. "Billy, Sue and I will use Mansour's van and his ten ton to move the raid team from the LZ to the compound and back. Sue joins the raid team because she is the only one of us who knows Daniels. If he is here, she will take control of Daniels and get back to the van. The raid team takes any rad material and individuals in the compound, bags and tags whatever material they can get on site and we all leave together. The team plus their haul go on the first three birds. We do a head count and board bird number four."

Jameson looked around the room. "Let's review. George and Dozer first: setting up the LZ and managing the LZ security. Ginger next: taking out the potential local threat, ideally with the bag of money. The rest of us pick up the raid team, make the delivery and return to the LZ. Remember, the raid team is going to come in on two Blackhawks and a little bird. They will depart on a Chinook and Blackhawk and a little bird. Once those aircraft have cleared the LZ, a final Blackhawk lands and takes us home. Check?"

Everyone nodded. Jameson turned to Sue. "Send the confirmation. I expect the folks at Balad to start jamming all SATCOM transmissions starting at midnight, so after that, take down the rig and secure it in the van. We will go line of sight commo after that." Jameson looked at his watch. "It is 1600hrs. Final equipment check at 2200hrs. Time for me to relieve Billy on the roof." Jameson got up and walked out.

Smith and the SOF chief of staff, Col. Joe Tennyson, were sitting with the raid team leader in Mosul, Major Barry Sanchez. Smith looked at his watch. It was 0100hrs which gave them plenty of time to get a final briefing before Sanchez and his operators left for the target. Smith knew Tennyson from his time in 10th Special Forces in Germany at the end of the Cold War and later when Yugoslavia started break up. Tennyson went to selection for SOF and Smith went to the Farm and eventually served as the creator of 171. Sanchez was a relative newcomer to the raid teams. He had 10 years in the Ranger Regiment. He had the reputation of a solid operator, a good leader, and a good raid team planner. Unlike Tennyson, however, his time in SOF had not included substantial focus on hostage rescue. Since 9/11, the raid teams had been the pointed end of the bayonet in the war on al Qaida. The SOF commander understood this and had sent Tennyson and Smith to Mosul simply as a double check that Sanchez understood his mission. After an hour with Sanchez, Smith was convinced that the CG shouldn't have worried. Sanchez understood all too well that this was a very different mission from the ones he had run in Iraq and before that it Afghanistan.

Sanchez was worrying over a cup of black coffee in what he pretended was his office in the hanger at Mosul which was a folding desk separated from the rest of the hanger by a stack of black plastic Pelican storage boxes. "So, the primary mission is to identify and snatch the nuclear material, right?"

"And capture the owners of the material." Tennyson added.

"And rescue Daniels if he is there."

"Not too much for 16 guys, right?"

Tennyson said, "Barry, we've looked at your plan and it is solid. You refuel at our base in Dohuk, make a quick run over the border, land at the LZ ready outside Al-Malikiyah, ride in the trucks to the compound and do the job. The little bird with your snipers provide top cover if needed. You return to the LZ, a Chinook picks you up and you come home. Ideally, no gunfire. You have drawn the TASERS to use on the occupants and you have two of the best in

SOF for the "render safe" mission regarding the material. It should be relatively quick and without complications. Jed's team has already reported the locals are secured and the S&R team has only seen three targets inside the building. The hardest part is we don't know how the building is configured. Remember, if it was easy, anyone could do it."

"Stand by, stand by." Dozer's voice invaded Sue's ear as she dozed on the ground floor of the safe house. "Shit" was all she could say as she raced up the stairs to the roof-top observation post. Ginger, Jameson, Billy and Mansour will right behind Sue as they came up to the roof, crouching to stay invisible to anyone from the various buildings. Each fell to their knees and then low crawled to the parapet where Dozer and George were in position. Sue looked at the night lumination on her dive watch. It was 0240hrs.

Jameson was the first to speak. "What's going on?"

"Activity inside the compound. It looks like they are loading to move out. Two very smart Mercedes GLKs. They are loading a fair bit of kit into the rear vehicle. I can't see much else."

Jameson turned to Billy. "Contact the raiders. Let them know that we have movement. We will have to intercept at some location other than this safe house." Billy scuttled back away from the parapet and headed down the ladder to the second floor where they had communications set up with Mosul. Jameson continued, "OK, here's how we play this. Sue, you and Dozer get down stairs, load up in the spare Land Rover that Ginger has in the garage. Drive out the back gate and set up a stakeout to the East of this block. We have to figure that if they are moving, they are going to move toward Iraq for a linkup with the Zarqawi's guys. Ginger, you and Mansour and your two heavies load back into the van, get out on the road to the West. As soon as both of you are in place, do a comms check with us. Got it?"

"How about you and I, boss?" George still looking through the night vision spotting scope as he asked. He had accepted that in this joint operation, Jameson was as close to his SBS chief as he was going to get in Syria.

"George, you and I are going to watch what happens and then pick up the trail. Ginger's guys have a third vehicle here — an old Russian Lada that his guys stole from some Russian base years ago. They guarantee it will run. We will take down the OP, Billy will take down the commo and we will load and depart in whatever direction is needed."

"Got it, chief." Sue and George were already down the ladder with Ginger and Mansour right behind them. They met Billy about to come back up. He looked over his shoulder as they passed.

"Alpha6 says keep eyes on and the intercept will take place as soon as they are loaded and on the way. If possible, intercept should be in Iraq. Alpha6 is starting the monitor our internals."

Sue realized Billy had come a long way from their time in Jalalabad. He was calm and working part of the job without drama. Also, he realized that it was critical that they know that the seniors in Mosul were now monitoring their communications. No stupid remarks or team jokes because if Mosul was monitoring their comms, then Balad was as well and that meant CG/SOF was listening.

It took Sue and Dozer twenty minutes to get loaded, get out of the compound and find a reasonable "layup" position that wouldn't look completely stupid. No one was out at this time of night and if they triggered any interest, it wouldn't be good. "Mike4 and Jack3 in place."

"Roger." Jameson had assumed his role as "Zero," the controller of the team. He also assumed what Sue recognized as his "zero voice" which was clear, concise and very calm. The only comparable voice she could think of was when she was a child and her folks made her and her brother watch "educational" videos on the US and USSR space programs. Jameson's zero voice was the same controlled voice used at NASA mission control.

Minutes later, Ginger came on line. "Echo2 and 3 in place with the heavies."

"Roger. "

Five minutes later, Jameson came back on line. "Stand By, Stand By. All call signs. Two Charlies are loaded. First Charlie — Charlie1 - has four pax — three Bravos and maybe our man in the seat behind the driver. Whoever is in that seat is handcuffed, so he is not one of them. All Bravos in first vehicle are Europeans. Bravo in the shotgun seat has a SMG slung in a chest mount. Back Bravo has an AK with the barrel hanging out the window. Break, Break." Jameson took a breath and said, "Second Charlie has four Bravos. Two Europeans, two locals. All armed with SMGs. This Charlie —Charlie2 — has a large cargo container in the back. It was heavy — it took all four of the Bravos to load the container. Alpha6, you copy?"

A voice distorted by the satellite feed replied. "Alpha6 copies. Charlie1 has our possible friendly, Charlie2 has our package."

"Roger, Alpha6." A slight pause. "Stand by, Stand by. Charlies are leaving the compound. One of the Bravos from Charlie2 has opened the gate, they are leaving. No sign of anyone else in the compound. Charlie 2 waiting to pick up their last Bravo. Vehicles are headed East repeat East toward Mike4. Copy?"

"Mike4, copy."

"Echo2 copy."

"Alpha6 copy."

"All call signs. Zero is breaking down comms and moving to our vehicle. Going exclusively to internal commo."

"Roger." All the players understood. Jameson would have intermittent radio capability until he was back in a vehicle.

The two Mercedes blasted by Sue and Dozer's layup position — accelerating well past 60 miles an hour as they headed out of town. "Stand by, Stand by. Mike4. Charlie 1 and 2 still together, heading East on main highway. We have."

"Roger, Mike4 has Charlie1 and 2." Alpha6 had taken over Jameson's role until he came on board.

"Echo2." Ginger acknowledged. He would be pulling onto the main road at this point and slowly getting into a trail position.

"Zero is back online. We will trail Echo2."

Dozer pulled the Land Rover out on the main highway, driving initially without any headlights until he was certain that the two Charlies had pulled well away. One of the advantages of this route was that there were approximately 20km of straight highway before any possible road turns and the road lead directly into Iraq and an international border which was unguarded. This meant that the raid team might be able to do the takedown in Iraq and, more importantly to Sue at the moment, they could follow at a distance and, assuming Dozer's night vision headset didn't run out of batteries, they could follow without any lights.

"Zero, Mike4. Charlies still accelerating. They have left the city and reached the main headed East, East toward Iraq."

"Roger. Mike4 reports two Charlies continuing to head east on the main." It wasn't entirely clear that Jameson needed to repeat all the messages since they were all on the same commo, but it was habit and it made everyone feel in synch.

"Zero, Alpha6. We have an airborne feed on the vehicles."

"Roger, Alpha6. New eyes on." There had been some discussion on whether a SOF drone or an Air Force reconnaissance bird could look far enough over the border to see into Syria. No one wanted to run the risk of a Syrian or a Russian radar system seeing any aircraft in Syrian airspace. Obviously, the answer was if you got high enough and had a good enough camera, you could look far enough.

"Mike4, Zero. Based on the new eyes on, I want you to stay back to just at the edge of cover. DO NOT LOSE THEM, but also don't spook them until we know Alpha team is on the way. Confirm."

"Zero, Mike4. Roger." Dozer looked briefly at Sue through his bug-eyed night vision headset. "I understand Zero's point, but do you really trust the airborne eyes?"

Sue had her own night vision goggles on. She knew that she looked at least as bug eyed to Dozer as he did to her. "Not at all, Dozer. If Tech can fail, it will fail. So, keep them just in sight, OK?"

"No dramas, Sue. We got them in our sights."

"Echo2, Zero. "

"Echo2."

"Close up to 250meters with Mike4. Lights off, but close enough to follow. We may need to pull Mike4 off if they decide to stop or slow down."

"Echo2, roger."

Alpha6's satellite voice came on — this time there was substantial background noise. "Zero, Alpha6."

"Alpha6, go."

"Zero, we are airborne headed your way. Expect TOT 15mikes. In Iraq, we hope. "

"All call signs. Alpha6 expects time on target in 15 minutes, confirm."

"Mike4"

"Echo2"

"Alpha6, you want us to intercept or are you going to set up?"

"Zero, stay in trail. We are going to drop off two snipers via a little bird. They will stop the vehicles. You serve as the blocking force. We engage, roger?"

"Roger, Alpha6. You will force the stop and engage, we will block."

"Stand by, stand by." Sue tried to use her own version of a zero voice, but she was sure it wasn't going to work. "Charlie1 has taken a left turn heading north repeat north. Charlie2 remained on the main and is heading East."

Jameson's voice remained calm. "All call signs. Mike4 reports Charlie1 is heading north, Charlie2 continuing East. Alpha6, your call. You can split the force or you do the intercept on Charlie2 and we do the takedown on Charlie1. From our perspective, Charlie2 and its package is the priority."

"Zero, Alpha6. Roger. We will do the takedown on Charlie2. As soon as the little bird drops off the snipers, it will move north to provide assistance on your operation. Check?"

"Check, Alpha6. All call signs, we take Charlie1 heading north. As soon as Alpha6 says they have Charlie2 secure, we take Charlie1. Confirm."

"Mike4."

"Echo2."

Sue turned to Dozer. "And you thought this was just going to be a standard follow."

"Sue, you know better. We never follow a target, we control a target."

Jameson came on the network. "Jack3, Zero." This was the first time he had spoken directly to Dozer.

"Jack3"

"I want you to turn on your lights, speed up and pass Charlie2. Do everything you can to make it look like a normal move — in fact, accelerate to pass them and continue to accelerate until I give you an update."

"Echo2, Zero." Now he spoke to Ginger. "Once you see Jack3 turn on his lights, I want you to close to a standard follow. Keep you lights off and make sure they don't see you. We need to be ready to act once Yankee6 has Charlie2 controlled."

"Wilco."

Sue and Dozer pulled off their NVGs and pulled up their scarves so that they covered their faces. Sue hoped that as they drove by, they might look like Arab smugglers running as fast as they could to into Iraqi Kurdistan. Like most of the SOF vehicles, the Land Rover looked like crap on the outside and was as close to being in prime mechanical condition as it could be given local watered fuel and weather extremes of 130F in the summer and 20F in the winter. Dozer waited until Charlie1 went around a bend in the road and then turned on the lights and accelerated. They were over a mile back from Charlie1, closing fast as the Land Rover topped out at 80mph. Dozer flashed his headlights, pulled into the left lane and passed the vehicle. Sue took a very quick look as they came up on Charlie1.

"Zero, Mike4" Sue waited until they were well past the target to send the message.

"Zero."

"I can confirm that we have our passenger in Charlie1. He is alive and looks weak, but it is our man."

"Roger, Mike4 confirms we have our missing man in Charlie1." Jameson paused. "Jack3, any evidence that Charlie1 was concerned when you passed."

"Negative. We went by like they were standing still and are now outside their visual range about two miles ahead."

"Roger. Keep your pace and stay out of headlight and visual. We will keep this set until we hear from Yankee6."

"Jack3, roger."

"Echo2, roger."

They followed the vehicle for about 20 minutes as it headed closer and closer to the Kurdistan border. The Charlie1 driver was clearly surveillance sensitive. He changed the pace of the vehicle several times in an effort to determine who was in front or behind him. Dozer and Ginger expected this and they responded accordingly as they noticed Charlie1 changing speeds. Given his experience in the raid squadrons, Ginger was very comfortable driving with NVGs, so he had no trouble. Dozer had switched to NVGs as soon as they passed Charlie1, so his job was slightly easier — as soon as he saw the faint glow of the headlights in his rear view mirror, he would speed up, as soon as they disappeared, he could slow down. Sue had seen this sort of front and back surveillance operation. S&R called it a "slinky" after the child's toy conducted before, but never at night and never with this much skill.

"Zero, Yankee6."

"Yankee6, Zero."

"We have finished Charlie2 as they entered Iraqi territory. Package acquired. It was as advertised. Engage Charlie1 at your earliest opportunity."

"Roger, Yankee6. Jack3, Mike4, Echo2. Confirm you heard Yankee6."

"Echo2."

"Jack3."

"Mike4"

"Jack3 and Mike4. Set up a blocking position immediately. If you can do it, try to do it in Iraq. Report when you are ready."

"Roger." Sue looked at the map. As near as she could tell from time and distance they had been in Iraqi Kurdistan for about 5 kilometers, but that was just a guess. She gave Dozer the thumbs up. Dozer drove until he found a right-hand curve in the road, as soon as he had negotiated the curve, he hit the brakes hard. The Land Rover responded as Dozer turned the wheel and slid to a halt across both lanes of the highway. They jumped out and searched the sides of the road with their IR flashlights. They had been traveling along two-lane blacktop built on a berm with irrigation canals from the Tigris River on either side. Even a GLK was going to have to stop or end up nose in the canal.

Dozer assumed his kneeling position behind the front right tire of the vehicle. Sue took a prone position to the rear and about five feet back from the Land Rover. "Zero, Mike4. We are in position."

"Roger, Echo2, close on Charlie1."

"Echo2" Sue could hear the whine of the engine in the Van as Ginger accelerated.

Sue looked over at Dozer. "For once, I wish we had a long gun."

"Why didn't you say so, mate?" He walked to the rear door of the Land Rover and pulled out a short gun case that looked like it could hold an M4 carbine. He pulled out a Remington500 taken down into two components. He locked the components into place and then clipped on the telescopic sight.

"You want it, or can I do the honors?"

"Very charming. I think you need to do the needful. I have seen how well you can shoot."

"Lovely."

They heard the Mercedes about a half mile away and saw the swath of the high beams cutting through the fields as the GLK made the curve. Sue and Dozer pulled off their NVGs and assumed their position. This time, Dozer was in the prone as well and had the Remington's bipod set up. As soon as the GLK made the turn and the headlights hit their Land Rover, Dozer fired his first shot. The front right tire of the GLK collapsed at the speed and the driver fought to keep control of the vehicle and prevent a quick visit to the irrigation canal. Dozer fired his second shot. The left rear tire collapsed. "Next time, invest in run flat tires." Dozer worked the bolt and put one round through the radiator and into the engine compartment. The noise of the German diesel tearing itself apart was clear, even from 50 yards away.

The doors of the GLK opened just as Ginger rammed the vehicle from behind. Not a full speed crash and just off the left bumper so that the GLK was spun 90 degrees. The door on the van opened up and two of Ginger's Peshmerga jumped out. The firefight was brief.

The three Europeans had jumped out of the vehicle with guns in their hands, but not up and ready to engage. The Peshmerga were ready to engage before they even left the van. Each of the men from the GLK was shot before they could bring their weapons into action. The Peshmerga then shot them again, this time to be sure that they were down for good and just in case they were wearing body armor.

Ginger worked his way cautiously along the left side of the vehicle, Glock at the ready and pulled open the left rear door.

Daniels fell out. He had been shot sometime before the crash. A torso wound that looked grim, but not deadly so long as they could get him evacuated sooner rather than later. Daniels looked tired, emaciated, and already suffering from shock. Ginger pulled a pressure dressing from a small triage pack on his left hip and a space blanket and put pressure on the wound and covered Daniels with the blanket.

Sue and Dozer closed from the front. "Zero and Yankee6, Mike4. We have secured our package from Charlie1. He is wounded and needs medevac as soon as you can get us help."

"Mike4, Yankee6. Little bird on the way. We have a medic onboard and will take your wounded immediately. Any Bravos that need evacuation?"

Sue looked at the three bodies on the road. "Negative, Yankee6. No other evacuation needed."

"Roger, Mike4. Zero, what do you need as help on your end?"

Jameson was walking up to the site with George. Billy had stayed in the van. "Yankee6, Zero. We can do cleanup here. No real damage to our capability. We will drive to the extraction site and call when we arrive. "

"Roger, Zero. Yankee6, out."

They heard the little bird just before it arrived. It had special exhaust fittings to make it very quiet and the charcoal paint job made it nearly invisible. The SOF pilot did one pass overhead and then put the bird down just north of the land rover. The medic came out of the aircraft with a collapsible stretcher. Ginger and the medic loaded Daniels on the stretcher and carried him to the bird. They locked the stretcher onto the left side rail that normally carried two raiders, snapped a plastic windscreen over Daniels head and launched. The medic continued to work on Daniels wound as the pilot pulled pitch and flew away.

"Cramped quarters, no?" Dozer was shaking his head.

Ginger spoke. "No dramas there, mate. The little bird will transfer Daniels to the Chinook that is waiting at a prepositioned LZ. They have a complete triage table there and will start work on Daniels before they reach Mosul. The Chinook will also carry any prisoners that the raiders took from Charlie2."

"And how many prisoners do you think that will be, Sue?"

"About the same number we have, Dozer."

"Exactly."

Jameson had conducted his walk around of the site. "OK, here's how we do this. Sue, you are responsible for site exploitation. When you are finished with SITEX, load the material in the Land Rover. Ginger, you check for any damage on your van. George, you and Dozer pull security to the North. Mansour, you and your fighters pull to the South. I doubt anyone else will come on the highway in the near term, but until we are done here, we do not want to be interrupted."

Sue reached into her shoulder bag which carried her full S&R kit and some of the kit provided at 171 including her lock pick, digital camera with an IR flash and a digital finger print device. She pulled out a pair of blue nitrite gloves, put them on and started on the three dead men. Finger prints first, then check the pockets for any ID or "pocket litter," the ephemera in the pockets that might prove of intelligence value. Once the Bravos were done, she started on the GLK. Front to back, first outside — left to right — then inside — left side then right side. Sue knew Jameson was not expecting her to do a full forensics job, but she also knew that he wanted everything of intelligence value. It took her a half hour working as fast as she could wearing her IR headlamp and NVGs.

She reported back to Jameson when she was done. "No pocket litter on the Bravos. Nothing. No ID, no paperwork. I did find a concealment cavity under the driver's seat. Four passports. Bagged and tagged. Cleared and bagged the weapons. One mobile and one laptop — bagged and tagged. The mobile is still on and has power for about another three hours. I figured the team in Balad can crack it open if the Mosul folks can't. Otherwise, the GLK looks like it just came out of the showroom in Istanbul which, in fact, is where it came from just a month ago. By the way, we assumed the vehicle was armored. It doesn't look that way from my initial check. Perhaps plates in the doors, but I would have to use a crowbar to sort it out."

"Good enough." Jameson spoke into his headset. "All, lets mount up, get this vehicle off the road and get out of here." Jameson put on his blue nitrite gloves. "Sue, help me get these guys into their vehicle."

They loaded the Bravos into Charlie1 and then used the Land Rover to push the GLK into the canal on the left side of the road. The GLK went nose into the water and sunk — leaving about a foot of the rear bumper exposed. Good enough for the near term. Smuggling routes were dangerous places.

They drove in convoy back to the road junction and then headed East. About ten kilometers along the road, as the sun was just coming up, they noticed a set of skid marks on the highway. Sue assumed that was the only sign of Charlie2 that they were going to find. George and Dozer were in the front seats of the Land Rover. Sue was in the back with the SITEX bags, her shoulder bag, and the long gun bag.

"Is that all we are going to see?" George seemed disappointed.

Sue said, "I suspect if you looked hard enough in the tree line to our South, you would eventually find Charlie2, but the guys from the raid squadron are good at cleaning up their messes."

"We mostly leave the mess behind when we leave."

Sue said, "So I've heard."

Dozer looked over his shoulder. "Just remember who had the long gun last night. If it had been up to you, they would have hit us."

"How do you know I didn't have a plan to stop them?"

"Just guessing."

They drove another half hour until they reached a dirt track that was designed for farm equipment and little more. Ginger was in the lead, then Jameson and finally the Land Rover. They pulled into a farm compound and unloaded. Mansour and his Peshmerga loaded back up in the vehicles and drove off — but not before bear hugs all around — except for Sue who received a formal handshake from Mansour and each of his minions.

They waited in the abandoned farm until dark. They pulled shifts watching from a position about 100 yards away from the farm. Sue pulled her shift with Ginger. It was the first time they had a chance to talk since her arrival in Dohuk.

"You doing ok?" Ginger sounded concerned.

"Yup, ok."

"First I heard about the business in Cyprus, and then about your grandfather and your brother. Sheesh, Sue. Are the O'Connell's bullet magnets?"

"Nothing but trouble, brother. Nothing but trouble."

"Remind me to stay clear." He was smiling.

"With your red hair, I will see you coming."

"I wonder how the debriefing with Daniels will go?"

"Smith and Massoni want to choke him, but I suppose a bullet wound to the torso will delay that effort."

"If I know Massoni, it won't delay him much." Sue was talking to Ginger while using the spotter scope to check the perimeter out to 1000 yards.

"This your safe house?"

"Well, it is Mansour's safe house. We built the network, just in case. No one was ever supposed to have to visit Syria, but the Zarqawi network doesn't follow the rules, so I had to put together a team that could make sure we had eyes on the target right up to the border. Mansour said he needed a staging area, so we bought this. It was a good farm at one point and Mansour intends this fall to make it look less abandoned and more productive. I know he is going to ask for a tractor and some farm machinery in his next paycheck."

"After what they did last night, I think they earned it, no?"

"Yes, indeed."

About an hour after dusk, they assembled out in the field just West of the farmstead. Jameson put down the IR strobe and they waited. They were back to back — six operators in two rows of three. Billy had set up the SATCOM with a small dish antenna about the size of a dinner plate.

"Hey mate, you sure you got the dish pointed in the right direction?"

"Dozer, he can't hear you anyhow with his headset on, so let it rest."

"I can to hear him, I'm just working hard to ignore him."

"Will you all keep quiet! I don't want some stray shepherd wandering over to see if there is someone here he can share his life story." Jameson had used the "zero voice" and everyone shut up.

"He always like that?" Ginger whispered to Sue.

Sue nodded. "As long as I have known him."

Billy touched Jameson on the shoulder. He raised his hand with fingers outstretched. 5 minutes. They shifted position so that they were in a long string with Jameson in the lead and George in trail. They pulled on their NVGs so that they could see their way to the bird depending on its approach. They heard the MH60 Blackhawk just before it arrived.

The grey-black bird hovered for a second about 20 feet from their position and then settled in. The left cargo door opened and one of the crew waved them on board while the second crewman manned the minigun on the left side covering their movement. They loaded on the floor, the crewman closed the door and the aircraft headed back to Mosul, full throttle, slightly nose down and about 30 feet off the ground. Jameson looked at his teammates. He gave them a thumbs up as he pulled on the spare crew headset the crewman handed to him.

LABYRINTH

Barbara O'Connell walked up to the rental car she had prepositioned in the eleventh district in the southeastern edge of the city. She had started from the Sacher Hotel, a room in the most expensive hotel in Vienna courtesy of Beth's company, and worked her way slowly out from the center of the city to the more industrial parts of Vienna. Barb hadn't been in the city for some years, but she had spent more than one night in Vienna in the 1990s for meetings with Iranians, Lebanese, Palestinians and anyone else that the Counterterrorism Center folks wanted her to meet and debrief. She also used the first district to hold developmental meetings with two of her best recruitments. While it just seemed appropriate to recruit spies at the Café Central, mentioned in dozens of spy novels and home to multiple sets of revolutionaries throughout the 20th century, CTC never agreed to allow her to spend a night in the Sacher.

This meeting, unlike the meetings in the first district of Vienna, was in a remote part of Vienna. The meeting was at least as important and far more complicated than any she had run before. Barb had arranged to meet a GRU spy under surveillance by at least two different services, perhaps more. Barbara O'Connell was going to hold a car meeting with Mary Sanderson.

Barb drove her planned route back into the City center. The traffic was light for the end of the week, the Viennese must be taking a long weekend in this beautiful May weather. Barb was, more or less, running against what little traffic there was of any commuters coming home after a late evening meal or a late night at the office. The rental car was a Skoda, a Czech copy of a Volkswagen Golf. Small, unobtrusive and with its dirty grey color, about as invisible as you could get in this town. This was also acquired by Beth or at least by Beth's investment firm which meant that Barb was also about as invisible as she had been for years.

She came upon the pickup site just as the local radio station provided the time hack for 22 hours, European Summer Time. She saw Mary walking up to the street corner just as she pulled up. A red light at the corner made the pickup seamless. Mary got in, Barb made a quick right turn, then a left and with little difficulty got onto the main motorway paralleling the Danube and heading Northwest out of the city. Both Barb and Mary had done this more times than they could count and they knew there is no real reason to have a conversation in a car until the driver is on a divided highway and can focus on the discussion.

"Long time, Barbara."

"Too long, kid. I wasn't sure you would come."

"It wasn't easy and, honestly, I wasn't sure it was going to be you. My FBI handlers have been pretty amusing in the various ways that they try to trick me into something so they can throw me into Supermax. The note in the newspaper was a nice touch. Very old school, especially leaving the newspaper at my coffee house and timing it so it was waiting for me. How long have you been surveilling me?"

"Only a couple of days. I figured you were either going to be very predictable or not predictable at all. Luckily, the answer was very predictable."

"I have to be predictable these days or my FBI surveillance team threatens me. I can walk from my apartment to my coffee shop. I can take a cab to the embassy. I can take a cab home. Pretty much sums up my life."

"Well, as you said, it is better than Supermax."

"Indeed. Now, let's get to business. I have about an hour before someone from the team decides they haven't disturbed me tonight and gives me a call on the home phone. I have forwarded it to my cell, but I suspect they will guess if that happens. So, what gives? After all, it has been years and it was your daughter who gave me up."

"She was just doing her job, Mary, you know that."

"Yes, but did she really have to break my leg?"

"Hard to say. I wasn't there. Here's my question to you: can you put me in touch with your GRU contact here?"

"Defection? I wouldn't put you in the frame for defection and anyhow, no offence, dear, but you are old and no one cares what you know anymore."

"Thanks for that reminder, lover. You will get there some day, if you are lucky. I want to talk to the GRU because I want some information on a Russian Mafia family called the Beroslavs, their location here in Austria and how much security they have."

"Barb, this is serious business. First, my GRU contacts are not the sort to give up information for nothing. You will need something to trade. Secondly, the Beroslavs may be considered rogue elements by the GRU. I just sent some information to Sue to help her disrupt one of their operations, but the Beroslavs are still Russians. If you think they are going to give them up, you are crazy."

"Mary, they killed Peter and his dad, they just killed my current lover while trying to kill me and they just tried to kill my son. I know all about how rogue they are. I want to end this once and for all and if the GRU will help, then I want their help."

"Barb, this is going to be very complicated. First, I have to figure out how to broach the subject. Then I have to avoid revealing this effort to my watchers who are very keen to know everything I do with the GRU. And, finally…" Barb realized Mary was trying to make a decision that would change everything. She had convinced enough men and women to commit espionage that she knew where this was going. Mary was trying to decide if she was going to cross a line. Barb knew that the only way to help her do that was to keep quiet and let silence in the car help Mary along. Barb looked at the car clock and realized she had very little time to get back into the city to get Mary back in time to meet her expected FBI phone call. Barb exited the motorway, crossed under and headed back to Vienna.

"Barb, what I am about to say may change your mind about all of this. I still think you need to know…" Barb saw Mary pause as if she was deciding if she really wanted to walk into a dark alley or jump into a pool not knowing if it was too cold. Barb simply forced herself to repeat over and over again in her head "wait, wait, wait."

"Barb, you need to know that I am part of LABYRINTH. Specifically, code name CLYTEMNESTRA which was the paired operation with your Peter's AGAMMENON. I have been working as part of an Agency double agent operation to penetrate the GRU. A dozen years."

Barb nearly drove off the road. First, was it true or was Mary simply building a rationale for not helping? Second, if it was true, why did she try to recruit Sue for the GRU? Finally, how much did Peter know of this and why didn't he tell her? "When?"

"Remember the Pole in Kenya?"

"Yes, you and I spent hours talking through why he was targeting you rather than dating you."

"He was targeting me, I was targeting him, and the Soviet handlers at station wanted me to keep it up. I couldn't tell you. I couldn't tell anyone at the time."

"And Peter?"

"He found out during one of his trips back to Headquarters. We were in one of those boxes in headquarters that look like where they keep children who have an auto-immune disorder. A box within a box within a box so that no one but the occupants can hear what is said. Very Dr. Strangelove, but I suppose they knew what they were doing. They briefed me on AGAMMENON and briefed Peter on CLYTEMNESTRA. It was in case we ever heard something that might protect the other and to be sure we knew we weren't alone. Honestly, I assumed you knew about the program. After all, Peter's father was the one who ran LABYRINTH. Surely you knew that."

"No, I didn't." Barbara was confused, hurt, and angry all at once.

"I know you were busy hunting terrorists across most of Europe and the Middle East, so it may have just been simpler not to tell you or it was a classic case of need to know. I worried about Peter and his dad. It was such a stressful program, far worse than working undercover because at least when you were working undercover, you had someone in station you could talk to about the operation. With us, it was just us…alone. I just assumed Peter survived it because he could share his secret with you." Mary paused. "It broke my heart when I heard Peter died of cancer."

"He died of polonium poisoning, Mary. The KGB or SVR or Russian mafia or all three did it. He was ordered to pull out after the fall of the USSR, did so, and then was poisoned." Barbara realized her comments were cold and her tone mean spirited. It had the right effect. Even in the dim light of the dashboard, Barb could see Mary's skin go pale.

"They killed him?"

"Yes, dear, they killed him. They killed him because he wouldn't play with the new Russian mafia. At least that is what I thought at the time. Now I think it was also mixed up in a vendetta that goes back to World War II. Worse still, it has to do with Peter's father and I can't ask him to explain it because they killed him just before Christmas this year. Now, you need to do some explaining. If you are a double agent, why did you pitch Sue last year?"

"We have always operated under the assumption that the GRU has their own targeting office and they select individuals for recruitment based on their own collection. I wasn't a talent spotter for them until I went to the Farm. I was instructed by the Agency and the FBI to play out the cases they told me to target. The assumption was that the GRU already had some line on the student and they wanted me to take the risk rather than one of their own. I only did this once with Sue. I had to play it out for lots of reasons, but in the case of Sue, the LABYRINTH team thought it might be an ops test that they were running against me. I didn't expect it to turn out quite like it happened."

"No broken leg planned, eh?" Barb couldn't help but smirk.

"Nope. Also, the grand entrance by the Agency seniors into the hotel room was not exactly as expected. It was not what LABYRINTH handlers intended and they were more than a little peeved."

"Took some work to put it back in the box, eh?"

"Hence my life as a semi-prisoner in lovely Vienna."

"Does anyone at the Embassy know?"

"The station chief. He was read in years ago. He has played along with the current plot line of Mary as an arrested spy being doubled back on the GRU because no one back in Headquarters can decide how to get me out of this. Back at Headquarters there are probably a dozen who know. That's it."

"And Sue?"

"I was instructed by Headquarters to play the role with Sue. The GRU really did want her as a recruit and the CI gurus in headquarters thought it was a good future operation for LABYRINTH. I have not told her that it is all part of a larger program."

"But, why was Sue a target to begin with?"

"I thought it was obvious. The GRU want Sue for precisely the same reason you want help from the GRU. They intend to use Sue as a guided missile tracking and destroying the Beroslav family network. I suspect they set up the meeting between Sue and the guy in Cyprus and, just so you know, I only found out just recently about Cyprus. They have great confidence in Sue's abilities and, more importantly, her determination to destroy that network. Once that mission is accomplished, they must figure Sue will be in too deep to refuse additional tasking. Of course, they haven't figured out yet that Sue is ELEKTRA in LABYRINTH." Mary paused and stared out the passenger window. Eventually, she said, "To give you a sense on how they are working, they were the ones that put the Army on the radiological waste program that the Beroslav's intended to sell to the Iraqis. They are determined to stop that effort. I suppose the whole nuclear material to terrorists crossed the line with Putin."

"What?"

"Sorry, I forget that you and Sue are not connected at the hip any more. Sue is currently involved in a program in Iraq to disrupt an effort by the Beroslav's to sell nuclear waste from either Russia or the FSU to either the Iraqi Sunni radicals or the Iraqi Shia radicals to attack the US forces there. I sent a message to Sue earlier this month on this. As far as I know from my Agency handlers, Sue closed that network down a couple of days ago."

"Anything else you want to tell me?"

"How about you tell me how I get out of this shit."

"Even if you are not a traitor, I'm ready to choke you right now for bringing my daughter into this game."

"Barbara, it's not like I have had a lot of choices here. Once inside LABYRINTH, I had to play the role as instructed. I don't know how to pull the plug on this whole thing and not end up either kidnapped, dead, or in a Supermax prison in Pueblo, Colorado. I am well and truly screwed."

"Shit. And here I come in to make it just that much worse. I'll bet you are ever so pleased to see me."

"Well, I would have preferred someone who might want to help me as opposed to someone who is trying to get me further involved in this vendetta. Yes."

"I'm sorry."

"Me too."

Sue was looking over Melissa's shoulder at a pair of computer screens. The left one was Melissa's — it was filled with computer code that she was typing at a breakneck speed. The right one was one of the computers taken from Charlie2 outside Al-Malikiyah. Between the two computers were a dozen different peripheral devices serving, as near as Sue could figure, as a means of preventing both computers from exploding. Sue was not a computer expert. She said, "Any luck?"

"Sue, that is the second time you asked that question in the last half hour. I told you, this is heavy duty encryption and I am working my way into the files as quickly and as carefully as I can. I still haven't determined for sure that they didn't build a hard drive scram into the program just in case something like this happened and someone like me was trying to access their shit."

"So, any luck?"

Melissa reached back and pinched Sue's ear — hard.

"Ow! What was that for?"

"To drive you away. Don't you have something you could be doing with your time? Don't you have spies you could be meeting? Reports to write? Men to chase? Anything other than annoying me?"

"OK, but you will miss me when I'm gone."

"Probably, but not right away. Shoo!"

Sue walked away from Melissa's work space and wandered down to the 171 section of the MACE tent. After the debriefing and after she worked with Ginger to bag and tag all the Russian and Iraqi material for shipment to the SOF and Agency experts, she had hoped to be part of the debriefing team for Daniels. Smith had vetoed that right away.

"O'Connell, you are too close to this problem. So am I, according to the intel shop at SOF. They are sending Daniels to a formal debriefing program based at the Navy facility in Norfolk. Don't ask me why we want the Navy involved, 'cause I don't know. All I know is that they have the lead on his debriefing. He also is not real healthy, so they need to keep him isolated and build up his strength after the ordeal. His first stop was the Army Medical Facility at Wiesbaden. He will be back in CONUS by next Wednesday."

"So, what do you want me to do?"

"How about you work with Flash and Melissa to see where the data takes us. We still don't have a good understanding of the origin of the nuclear material that we captured."

Sue's next stop was Flash. She was still not entirely comfortable seeing Flash in a military uniform. "What's the news, sister? Where did the nuclear waste captured in Syria come from? And while I'm asking questions, what's with the uniform?"

"Hey, don't you have a job?"

"Yup, but I need to get a lead to do my job. Since you are the brilliant one, I'm looking for some help."

"Ah, help. Well, if its help you need, then you've come to the right place. After all, I am Flash....super genius."

"And...?"

"Well, we have some of the details based on the analysis that we shipped back to DoE. They are the smart ones when it comes to nuclear material. Just as we predicted, it turns out that it was nuclear waste from an old Soviet research reactor. They don't have a location...yet...and don't know if they ever will. But, we can reduce the number of possibilities based on something else you captured in your adventure in Syria."

"Tell me that you have something that will get me out of Iraq and headed toward someplace where I won't have sand between my toes."

"Hey, if I found the location was the Bahamas, I doubt you would bitch."

"OK, so where did the stuff come from?"

"One of the Thuraya phones the raid team guys took from Charlie2 was still operational when they took down the vehicle. They kept it powered up and then handed it to...moi!" Flash raised her hand in a dramatic way.

"Because they knew you were a super genius."

"Well, either that or they have the hots for a chick who looks like me."

"Wins either way. What did the Thuraya tell us?"

"The great thing about a Thuraya satellite phone is that the software in the phone keeps 30 days of geolocation in memory. I'm sure the other phones will reveal more secrets once your pal Melissa cracks the passwords, but since this one was on, we could just scroll through the geo-coordinates and see where our little smuggler traveled in the past 30 days. It turns out, he started his travels in Sochi. From there, he took a boat along the coast to Batumi. Batumi to Istanbul, Istanbul to Diyarbakir, Diyarbakir to Al-Malikiyah. So, I looked up what research reactors might be in the Caucasus. Lots of possibilities. Actually, too many possibilities along his route of travel." Flash looked up at Sue. "Don't pout, O'Connell. It gives you wrinkles."

"I'm going to give you a dent in your head if you don't give me something to work on."

"OK, but it doesn't have anything to do with the nuclear material. It does have everything to do with the guys in Charlie2. Along with the 30 days of geolocation, the Thuraya has enough memory to store 30 days of phone calls. Interestingly enough, the owner of this phone called a number every day. The number is a residence in Greece. Thessaloniki to be exact. I did some research and found the residence has some peripheral links to a series of properties in the Balkans owned by expatriate Russians. It looks like the headquarters for this outfit is in the Balkans, or Greece, but not Russia or any of the other usual suspects," Flash paused. "By the way, I already passed the information to Smith. I think he is waiting to see you."

"Flash, you could have said that right away."

"And have you miss some of the brilliance of my work. No way. Also, I think he has some additional information for you and maybe even something he wants you to get done. One more thing…"

Sue was already on her way toward Smith's "office" at the end of the tent. She stopped and walked back.

"You could pick me up a nice Turkish bathrobe if you end up in Istanbul."

Sue looked for something to throw at Flash, but decided a chair or a computer would be too ungainly to launch at her. She walked away listening to Flash laugh maniacally.

Sue walked into what passed for Smith's office in the MACE tent.

It was a smaller folding table and chair surrounded on three sides by stacks of empty black PELICAN cases. She wrapped on one of the cases before entering.

"O'Connell, you got anything?"

"Boss, Flash told me to see you. She said you had something for me. "

"A couple of things. Let's start with the bad news first. It turns out that one of the Bravos in Charlie2 was a guy named Beroslav. Nice, right?"

"Shit."

"No foolin', shit. Now look at me, O'Connell. I got too much on my plate right now preventing a radiological weapon attack to get in the middle of the fight between the O'Connells and the Beroslavs. So, for now, we are going to let that one go. I reported it to your CIA Counterintelligence classmate. Your little project with the Agency and the FBI continues to intrude on our work. I don't want it to continue to do so. Check?"

Sue paused for a minute. It seemed like this all centered on this Russian mafia family, so how in the world could she let it go? "Boss, I understand, but…"

"O'Connell. I know the information points to the Balkans. I know the Beroslavs live in either Greece or the Balkans. I know the KGB front companies that the Russian mafia took over use banks in Central Europe. And, I KNOW THAT YOU ARE STILL WORKING FOR 171 WHICH MEANS, ME!" Smith paused and lowered his voice. "Check?"

"Check, Boss."

"OK, now we need to work on something right here in Iraq first. I understand from Baghdad station that you established a very close relationship with DUSTDEVIL. So, I want you to meet with him again and sort out some of the details of both the Shia militia and the Zarqawi guys involved in this search for a RAD weapon. I want to know everything you can squeeze out of him, nicely of course since he is a station asset. But, I need to know it now. SOF has a Blackhawk flying from here directly to the station compound in an hour and I want you on it. Take enough of your kit to spend a couple of days.

I want a long debriefing of DUSTDEVIL, as long as you can get. I have already cleared it with the COS and they said Jamie will be waiting at the LZ to take you directly to the safe house. Don't come back without something useful. Got it, O'Connell?"

"Check, Boss." Sue tried to sound as enthusiastic as possible. She understood that she had been involved in more "action hero" sort of work than the normal 171 case officer and she had to admit that Smith was right. A RAD weapon threat in theatre was substantially more important that the madness of the Beroslavs. Well, at least for now.

The flight from Balad to Baghdad was barely enough time to get anything done, but Sue used her field notebook to draw out some of the possible options for DUSTDEVIL's debriefing. It wasn't entirely a comfortable ride. The SOF MH60 bird had the regular set of sling seats common to all Blackhawks, but instead of flying at a comfortable 5,000 feet AGL, the pilots used this daylight "milk run" to sharpen their skills at terrain flying. SOF pilots rarely got a chance to fly in daylight just like the SOF raid teams rarely conduct daylight operations. Their specialty was night operations. So, a daylight flight from Balad to Baghdad station was a small bit of fun and they decided to enjoy it. After about five minutes aloft, Sue put the notebook away, put on the headphones for the onboard communications, sat back and decided to enjoy the fun as well. She knew that if she tried to read or write while the aircraft was following the terrain, she would be looking for a vomit bag quick enough and SOF aircraft crews hated it when you threw up on their airplane.

Both crewmen were sitting in their armored seats in front of Sue, ready to engage targets with the two miniguns mounted on either side of the aircraft. The slipstream along the skin of the aircraft was displaced just enough by the minigun barrels that the passenger compartment was filled with the smells of the agricultural fields below mixed with the smell of aviation fuel. Sue was wearing her flight suit over her running kit. She knew she would have to change into civilian clothes as soon as she arrived, but she was not about to give up her military rank quite yet. The copilot noticed she had put the headset on. His voice crackled through the headset — slightly distorted by the vibration of the aircraft and, she expected, by his effort to assume the "pilot's drawl" which they must teach in flight school. It seemed like every pilot she ever met was trying to sound like Chuck Yeager. Well, why not?

"Chief, we don't have a lot of time on the ground at the Klingon's LZ We are taking a station senior back to meet with the Boss."

"Roger, sir." Sue noticed both pilot and copilots were CW5s. As senior as you could get in the Warrant Officer rank structure and pretty consistent with the most senior pilots in SOF. "I didn't think this flight was scheduled just for my pleasure. The station seniors meet with the CG about once a week, right?"

"Sometimes more, Chief. We use the run as a training run for daylight low level operations. Please don't get sick in my bird, chief."

"No dramas, sir. I've run on worse."

"OK, we are about to enter some bad guy country in about five minutes, so we will be running fast, low and doing some juking about to keep from drawing any gunfire. In case there is any trouble, we are counting on your M4 as part of our punch."

"Sir, I doubt my 5.56 is much compared to a mini-gun, but I'm certainly ready to help." Sue had her weapon barrel down between her legs. It was locked and loaded, but on safe. She intended to keep it there unless there was serious trouble. One of the most import-ant things you did in SOF was always demonstrate you knew how to handle weapons, both when you were shooting them and when you were carrying them. When she was in the 18th Airborne Corps, she noticed how the pilots and crew chief got seriously nervous when troops loaded on the bird with weapons pointing every which way. Even when there were no seats on SOF birds, you could count on the fact that not one weapon faced anywhere but down or out of the bird.

The rest of the flight was filled with hard turns, rapid altitude changes and low-level flight along the river from Balad to Baghdad. Sue wasn't sure whether it was really necessary or simply an opportu-nity for the pilots to play. Probably a bit of both. The aircraft eventually flared up about treetop level about 50 yards from the Baghdad station LZ inside the Green Zone. Sue saw an armored Land Cruiser waiting at the end of the LZ. Two men were waiting next to the aircraft. One was in khakis, a dress shirt and a nylon jacket, the other was in jeans and a polo shirt. She recognized Jamie as the latter, the station senior must be the former. The pilot brought the bird down as if he was landing at some airfield in CONUS, light as a feather. "Thanks, sir. It was a great ride and I'm glad we didn't have to count on my shooting skills. See you on the other side. "

"Right, Chief. See ya."

Sue took off the headset and grabbed the pull handle of the main door and slid the door open. The crew chief on that side of the aircraft hopped out first. He was tethered to the aircraft by a long cable linking his flight helmet to the onboard communications. He had his visor down to avoid any dust from the rotor blades. Sue knew the protocol and let him pass in front of her before she picked up her ruck from the floor and headed directly out from the door. Sue had her blade sunglasses and a set of quiet ears that she used for range training. After years of working with Army aviation, Sue also knew that protecting her hearing was something that she had to do every time. She passed the station senior on the way, he nodded to her, it was too loud to say anything, and loaded on the aircraft. The crew chief made sure that the area around the aircraft was secure, jumped on board, closed the door and the aircraft engines accelerated and the Blackhawk was gone in a few seconds.

Sue pulled her quiet ears off and walked toward the Land Cruiser. "Nice to see you again, Jamie."

"Likewise, Sue. Sounds like you had some fun on the border."

"Jamie, you know the US government doesn't do combat operations close to Syria."

"Right."

Sue walked over to the small building on the compound that served as the flight ops office and walked into the bathroom. She slipped off her jungle boots and the flight suit and then completed "rule number one" for TDYers which was always pee when you can. After that, she pulled on a pair of jeans and a long sleeve polo shirt. Boots next.

Then her paddle holster with the Glock. Finally, a tan ball cap. Sue had brought full up abaya and an Arab woman's clothing if needed, but she figured if Jamie was in western clothes, she could be as well.

"Ready to rock and roll, Sue?" Jamie greeted her as she left the Base Ops building, rucksack in one hand, M4 in the other.

"Let's go." They loaded into the armored Land Cruiser. Jamie turned the key, put the vehicle in gear and headed to the closest vehicle control point in the Green Zone. He called into the station ops center at the VCP and by the time they got there, the soldiers and civilian contractors at the gate had cleared the obstacles and they blasted out of the Green zone at nearly 40 miles per hour.

"Hey, what happened to the low-profile stuff?"

"Oh, that was important last time for lots of reasons, mostly because we had the eggheads on board and we didn't want any trouble. It's just you and me this time. Just two case officers in a truck. So, we are going to do what we normally due, blast out and then do an anti-surveillance run and that will be that. Time for the soundtrack." Jamie turned on the sound system. The inside of the Land Cruiser filled with the 70s rock music. Sue was not entirely certain, but it sounded like the CD was a mix of songs by The Who and Jethro Tull.

"Soundtrack?"

"Sue, how long have you been a case officer?"

"About six months. "

"OK, there are some case officer rules. One is: always have a soundtrack."

"Really?"

"Nope. I just made that up. But if you are going to be driving for hours alone making sure you are not being followed and especially if you are driving at night, a soundtrack makes it slightly less annoying. At least, that's what I think."

"OK, any other Jamie rules?"

"You already demonstrated a couple of other rules when you got in. Make sure your weapons are ready, but not so ready that if we get into an accident they fly all over the inside of the truck. Good show that you didn't flash me with the barrel of your M4 as you loaded in the vehicle and the muzzle is still pointing down but your hand is on the pistol grip. Another rule that you followed: I noticed you have a knife in the neck sheath. That's critical because you might have to cut your seatbelt off if we get in an accident or an IED hits us."

"An IED? Really? Like we are going to survive an IED and cut our way out of the truck?"

"Actually, the Agency up armored vehicles can and do survive IEDs. I was in a vehicle in Qandahar. The entire skin of the vehicle was peeled off the vehicle and it was flipped upside down, but none of us was hurt by the concussion or by any shrapnel. I suspect the Taliban didn't think so since the entire outside of the vehicle was melted. We did cut ourselves out of that one and stayed in the fight."

"OK, next."

"Passenger is responsible for helping the driver sort out surveillance. I have moved the right side mirror so you can watch my right rear quarter panel and the sidewalk on your side. Let me know if you see anything useful."

"Check."

"Finally, passengers are not allowed to bitch about the sound track. I drive, I choose. OK?"

"Drive on, Jamie. I will do my best on the last rule."

They had moved from a main highway to a secondary road in the opposite direction of the safe house but heading toward the river. Sue watched as Jamie drove carefully but fast through a market area and then out again to another main highway paralleling the river. He knew this city. Thirty-five minutes into the route, Jamie started the conversation again. "The techs set up a front and rear camera system so we are capturing the entire route. We will review it when we get to the safe house to see if there is anything we missed on the route today. Right now, we are clean so I am going to work our way back to the safe house. You good with that?"

"Sounds good to me, even though I'm a little worn out with the 70s bands."

"Remember, I drive, I control the soundtrack." Sue had to smile.

It was 1900hrs and Sue had been debriefing DUSTDEVIL for nearly two hours. They had started with what he knew about Muqtad al Sadr's militia, what he knew about the militia element building IEDs and eventually how they heard about radiological material up for sale. She had worked him slowly and gently along this path accepting small detours, sometimes complete non-sequiturs. As a result, he provided what he knew and isolated that from what he suspected. Sue was surprised how good an agent DUSTDEVIL was and how lucky station was to have him. Eventually, she said so.

"You are so helpful. I just want to thank you again."

"Martha, you are like my family. Anil has been so kind. He brought a doctor to see me last month. He was worried for me. I told him that I was dying and the doctor told him the same thing. He made sure we had medicine to make me feel better, he is working to help my family when I am gone. And it all started when I worked with your mother, little Martha. Before that, I was just giving the man little crumbs and he paid me. After Anna, I realized that I was a part of a family that stretched all the way to America. She saved my son's life by bringing in a doctor to save him when the Iraqi doctors said he was going to die. We had to go to Europe for the operation. She arranged that. Then ten years ago, she flew me and my wife to Washington and I met your leaders. They gave me a medal. Anna took us on a tour of the Lincoln and Washington monuments. It was wonderful."

Sue realized that this was one part of being a case officer that they rarely talked about at the Farm. You became family. You were the person that the agent trusted over anyone else. That trust had to be earned. Not through money, but through actions. Her mother had never said anything about DUSTDEVIL or how she handled her cases for CTC. Sue had assumed they were terrorists and therefore were simply motivated by either money or revenge or both. Not so much.

"Martha, what do you want from me? I am old, I am dying and my family is all out of Iraq or like my lovely wife, they are dead. What do you need?"

Sue looked over at Jamal. He looked back and nodded. "We need your help in finding who in the Shia militia thought it was a good idea to buy the material from the Russians. Did the leadership know? Did the Iranian Rev Guard know? We need to stop them before they try again."

"I may not be able to answer these questions, Martha. I don't know if there is anyone I know who will be able to help."

Sue reached over and touched DUSTDEVIL's cold hand. "We need your help."

In Sue's ear bud, she heard Jamie transmitting to both her and Jamal. "We are not about to send an agent on a suicide mission. You can continue to task him but only if both of you are confident he can complete the job. I will not be the one authorizing DUSTDEVIL's insurance payout to his family."

Sue looked at Jamal and then looked DUSTDEVIL in the eyes. "I have to be sure that you will be safe if you try to help us. I need to know that you can do this safely."

DUSTDEVIL laughed and his laugh ended with a coughing fit and then a slight croak which seemed to come from deep in his chest. "Martha, I have been staying alive in this fight since you were a child. I have no interest in dying at the hands of an Iraqi torturer, Sunni or Shia. I will only do this if I can be sure that I can get out." He paused. "It may be the last thing that I can ever do for you. Are you willing to have me end my work with you for this job?"

This was the first time Sue had ever thought about the seriousness of "the game." She was about to task a man to risk his life for the greater good of saving US soldiers lives, but those soldiers were not known to her. She was looking at the man that she was sending into danger. She looked up at Jamal. He nodded. Jamie did not add anything through her ear bud. "Yes, we accept that if you do this, you will be retired and we will keep you safe. That is a promise that I make to you."

DUSTDEVIL smiled and nodded. "Then I will do this for you, Martha, for you, Anil and for Anna."

On the return trip from the safe house to the Green Zone, the Land Cruiser was completely quiet. Jamal and Jamie were in the front seats, Sue in the back. It was near dawn and the amber light on the horizon reflected into the vehicle. It was a grim ride home. Finally, Jamie spoke. "I know MACE is critical. I hope DUSTDEVIL can help us. I also hope he doesn't end up in a ditch someplace between here and Ramadi. This was a tough one, you guys. I think you played it as well as can be expected. I'm still not entirely certain it is going to…." Jamie never got a chance to finish his sentence because the car bomb went off next to the Land Cruiser.

The bomber hadn't considered where to place the bomb as it was being assembled. The force of the explosion lifted a parked car up from its front and tipped the car over onto its back. If the bomb had been placed on the driver's side and if it had been properly triggered, no one in the Agency vehicle would have survived. If it had been placed on the gas tank, the explosion would have started fires across the street and blocked any hope of escape. Instead, the concussive force from the explosion stripped the outer metal from the passenger side of the Land Cruiser revealing the inner, silver cocoon of armor that encased the passenger compartment. It was tipped on its side and pushed into the oncoming lane of traffic and slid on its side until it was stopped by the row of parked cars in the opposite lane.

Sue was the first one to recover from being tumbled inside the vehicle. The multiple airbags had deployed and she had to use her small chest knife to cut her bag that had deployed from the ceiling and deflate it. She unbuckled her seat belt and crawled over to Jamal and Jamie. They were both alive and slowly returning to consciousness. She used the knife to deflate their airbags as well. Jamie's right arm was twisted in what was clearly a direction that no arm should go. Either a broken arm or a dislocated elbow. Hard to say from her position. Jamal had a few cuts and bruises, but he seemed generally ok.

Jamal reached up to the dash and hit a red button on the top of their radio tracking system. Assuming the antenna was still intact, it would immediately warn the station that they were in trouble.

He pulled his headset back on his head and keyed the microphone. "Zero, this is Nestor. Hurricane. Do you read me?"

The onboard radio appeared to be working. The speaker was clear. "Nestor, read you. Hurricane. Tracker has identified your location. Support team is on the way. Are you under fire?"

"Zero, we are in the vehicle and do not appear to be under fire at this time. Augustine is injured and will need Medevac. Our visitor is fine."

"Roger, Nestor. Support team is leaving from the Green Zone at this time. They should be in place in 5, stay in place."

Jamie looked up from his position — held in place by the seat belt harness and tipped slightly into the console. "Tell them we aren't going anywhere."

"Zero, we will stay in place."

Jamie looked back at Sue. "Aren't you glad you are riding in an Agency vehicle? Highest level of armor possible. Not that it made all that much difference in the ride, but we are going to walk away. Sorry, but it appears my soundtrack is crushed in the vehicle. I was going to loan it to you for your next visit."

"Thanks, but I'm not sure I can stand any more 70s music."

"Barbarian," was all Jamie said.

Five minutes later, four armored Suburbans pulled into the area and blocked off the street. The team in the first vehicle set up a security perimeter while a tech officer in modified armored suit worked the area looking for additional IEDs. Along the route from Baghdad to Baghdad International, the most common IED tactic was to have one bomb go off drawing a response team and then a second bomb go off killing that team. The Station officers weren't going to take that chance. The second team from the Station security element came over and used pneumatic jaws to pull open the compartment. The smell of burned tires and gasoline filled the vehicle compartment as the door frame was pulled apart. A bearded man looked into the hole made by the jaws. "Hey, Jamie. You sure know how to give a TDYer a taste of the real Baghdad."

"Duke, you always know how to make a guy feel great."

"Just happy to be talking to you."

"Likewise." Jamie winced as they pulled him out of the vehicle and put him on a portable backboard. The medic placed a neck brace on Jamie, did a 100% check to make sure his arm was the only injury and two more of the security element carried him to the back of one of the Suburbans and they left with lights one and a siren which cleared the street.

Duke grabbed Jamal's outstretched arms and levered him out of the wrecked vehicle. "This is going to be one serious insurance claim."

"I think we got this covered on our rider against car bombs."

"Nice."

Finally, Duke pulled Sue out of the vehicle. The concussion from the blast had shifted her prosthetic so that when she dropped to the ground, her left foot was pointed 90 degrees out from her body. Duke looked at it and waved another medic over. The Agency medic used a calm, first responder voice when he said, "Take your weight off this leg and sit down. It looks like you have a serious knee or foot injury."

"Looks can be deceiving, Doc. " Sue reached down and with a quick, and honestly, painful, twist she reset the prosthetic. "All good now."

Both Duke and the medic turned white.

"Boys, it is going to be fine. Watch." Sue jumped up and down and then walked over to the Suburban where Jamal was being treated for his superficial wounds.

"You going to be ok?"

"As good as you can be after you have been blown up."

"Let's get back to station, eh?"

Jamal nodded and walked with Sue back to Duke. He said to Duke, "Can we get outta here?"

"Just waiting for you and superwoman to get in my Sub."

Barbara called Beth on her cellphone. She hoped to catch her before she was involved in some downtown soiree.

"Parsons."

"Beth, just wanted to let you know that I'm having a wonderful time here in the Sacher. " They had arranged an open code before Barb left and Barb's opening meant that it was time to assemble. She just needed to know where.

"I'm glad you are enjoying it. It is the least we can do for you for your recent consulting work. I haven't been to Vienna in years. I suppose it's changed."

"Not especially. Still the wonderful city it always was. Any suggestions for my next stop on the vacation?"

"Someplace warm, on the Med coast would be my recommendation. You ever been to Greece?" Beth's job was to narrow down the options for the Beroslav headquarters. It appeared to be Greece.

"Beach?"

"Beach is nice. Try someplace near Halkidiki. It is quieter, fewer tourists, more beach." OK, so the next stop was Eastern Greece. She would fly from Vienna to Thessaloniki.

"Any suggestions?"

"Sorry, nothing at this time. Good luck and enjoy!"

Beth had promised to arrange a month-long rental in whatever area that she identified. They had arranged to pass the details via a map reference she would send to Barb through an email or text. Beth would arrange the car rental at the airport and Barb would simply drive to the reference location.

"Have a great time and we have to get together as soon as you return."

"Thanks again. Ciao bella."

"Ciao."

The knock on her hotel door twenty minutes later was unexpected. The Sacher Hotel was a very "old Austria" gem and it wasn't "proper" for anyone to just visit a hotel room. Barb hadn't ordered room service, so this was definitely not a welcome visitor. Earlier, she had switched into a nylon track suit that doubled on her trips as her "lounge wear." Before she answered the door, Barbara reached into her suitcase and removed the interior lining from the handle side of her roller bag. She released a small Velcro clip and pulled out a very thin, very flexible, eight-inch rubber handled weapon. It looked, more or less, like a very thin nightstick. It was called a cosh and it was courtesy of the OSS collection of weapons that Peter senior had squirreled away in the Potomac River house. Thin enough to look in the x-ray to be part of the stiffener of her roller board, heavy enough to deliver a disabling blow if the target was not expecting an attack. Barb also pulled out from the roller board a three-inch piece of plastic stiffener which had been sharpened to an edge on one side. She placed this piece of plastic inside the track suit pants in the middle of her back. It could be used as a weapon or a tool, depending on what she needed. Either way, it would be concealed until needed. The cosh on the other hand needed to be out and ready when she opened the door.

Barb approached the door and pressed a small button on a screen at the left side of the door frame. The Sacher might be old fashioned, but they understood security. This was far better than a small lens in the door. The screen illuminated and an image of the visitor appeared. A young, fit man dressed in North American not European cut clothes. Military haircut. Friend or foe? Still too early to tell. Barb pressed the button on the front of the screen. "Yes?"

"Mrs. O'Connell? The name is Stan Cyzneski. Mary told me you had met her."

"Mr. Cyzneski, let's see some identification."

In the screen, the man reached into his jacket pocket and pulled out a lanyard with a laminated photo ID. He put the photo ID to the lens showing a Vienna US embassy identification. So far, so good was all Barbara could think.

"I am going to open the door now." Barbara continued to watch as she started to work the door handle. If he made any move to pull a weapon, he would meet "Mr. Cosh" rather quickly when the door opened. He did not move in any way, so she opened the door while remaining to the left of the door with the cosh hidden in her right hand behind her back. She could easily drop to one knee and crush a kneecap before he could pull any weapon. Stan walked in and closed the door behind him.

"I'm used to seeing Sue meet me at the door with a pistol. I suspect the weapon in your hand isn't a pistol, but I would be more comfortable if you would let me see what you do have in your hand."

"And I would be more comfortable if you would take off your coat and let me see if you are carrying a weapon on your hip."

"Touché." Stan pulled off his suit jacket coat and attempted a quick 360degree pivot. Barb caught him by the belt as he turned his back to her and introduced him to the wall. She ran the cosh along the inside of his pants from knee to ankle. No weapon on the belt, no weapon in an ankle holster. Again, so far, so good.

"Mr. Cyzneski, please have a seat." As he moved to the small seating area in the room, Barb returned to the door, locked it and pulled out a small steel chock from her track suit pocket and jammed it into the door. It would be hard to have additional visitors at this point unless they intended to use a shotgun to blow through the hinges. Shotguns were definitely not allowed in the Sacher.

"Mr. Cyzneski, what are you doing here?"

"Mrs. O'Connell, I might ask the same question."

"I am a lonely widow on holiday in Europe courtesy of an old friend who happens to be a very rich lawyer in DC."

"And I am the Akhund of Swat."

Barbara had to smile. She wasn't expecting a visitor from the Embassy with a sense of humor or a familiarity with the Edward Lear poem. "Now that we have determined you are an erudite intruder, how about you tell me why you are in my hotel room."

"I heard you talked to Mary. I wasn't too pleased and before I tell headquarters, I thought I would ask you why."

"Mr. Cyzneski,"

"Please call me, Stan…"

"Please let me finish. Mr. Cyzneski, I have known Mary probably longer than you have been the literate person that you seem to be. I heard she was assigned to Vienna and I thought it would be nice to have a chat."

"A clandestine chat?"

"I'm a private sort of person."

"A car meeting?"

"Viennese coffee houses get so crowded at night."

"I'm not going to get anywhere, am I?"

"Let's think about this for a second. You are a representative of the Federal Government. I am a mere, wretched federal pensioner who has had her father in law and her husband killed by the Russians. I believe you and your crew have asked my daughter to work as a double agent. What do you think?"

"I might try a different approach?" Stan looked down at the floor and tried his best not to smile.

"OK, let's see the next approach. Remember, I'm the one with the cosh and I could just say you broke into my room. I speak excellent, Austrian accented, German, so I suspect the Sacher security folks might just believe me over you. Especially since you look like a movie version of a well-dressed thug."

"I have to live on my federal paycheck, so my suits are an unfair criticism."

"But your shoes, my boy, are simply giveaways that you are not someone who understands the gemutlich ways of Vienna."

Stan looked down at his shoes. "This is going nowhere."

"Feel free to leave any time you like. Or, you could be polite and ask me what you want to ask me. Nicely, bitte."

Stan sighed, raised his hands slowly to avoid a cosh on the side of his head, and surrendered.

"So here is my question. Are you here to screw up ELEKTRA?"

"A fair question indeed. The answer is no. I don't have any interest in ELEKTRA other than that you and your brain trust in Washington don't kill my daughter. My conversation with Mary had nothing to do with Sue."

"Will you tell me what you are doing in Austria?"

"If I do, will you tell your headquarters?"

"Will I have to?"

"Now we are heading toward philosophical questions of free will and I've always been an existentialist. I think free will is the only moral imperative. So, I don't know the answer to your question. Sorry." Barbara smiled her most charming smile.

"If I said I wouldn't be a fink to headquarters, would you tell me then?"

"If I tell you a story, will you believe it?"

"This is starting to sound like Alice's discussions with members of the Mad Hatter's tea party."

"Lewis Carroll was a mathematician, you know. All the dialogues were filled with double meanings. All puzzles. This is why Lewis Carroll is so popular with spies. There is no single meaning to anything."

"And…"

"And, I think you are ready for a little history lesson." Barbara started at the beginning or at least as close to the beginning as she understood the story to be. She left out some of the details simply because they were too painful and offered plenty of details that she was sure Stan already knew. When she was finished, she had given Stan a story that would answer his questions and not risk her real plan. That way, he would not get involved in an effort to find and kill whoever was in charge of the Beroslav side of the vendetta.

Sue was still more than a little sore from being thrown around the Suburban, but the doctors at the SOF field clinic in Balad had cleared her for light duty, so she figured it was time to get back to work. Her head still hurt when she moved too fast or raised her blood pressure. A "slight concussion" was the medical analysis. Otherwise, she was ready to sort out the next steps.

Her first greeting was a surprise. Jamie was sitting at her desk, right arm in a cast that pushed his arm away from his body at a 90 degree angle. The right side of his head had been shaved and there were a couple of stitches that might have been designed to keep his right ear attached to his head. He said, "I was wondering when you were going to get back to work."

"Hey, the SOF doctors barely let me out today. What are you doing here? Don't you work for station?"

"I just got out today as well. Station has no work for a cripple like me right now, so I'm just hanging out with the cool guys figuring there might be something we can do together." Jamie turned serious. "I heard today that DUSTDEVIL turned up dead last night inside the Green Zone. He was shot in the head with a small caliber round. A note in Russian pinned to his chest. Just one word in Russian: прекрати! I have no Russian, but the gurus at the station say it just means "Stop.""

"One more reason to hate them."

"You have more than one reason? Do tell."

"It is a long, family history and I doubt you would believe me if I told you."

"Well, the point seems to be that they intended to blow us up and kill DUSTDEVIL. I figure that is enough for me to hate the guys who are doing this."

"Just sit there for a bit and hate them and I will get back as soon as I check in with my boss."

"Don't worry, it's not like I have a lot of options."

As Sue walked toward the 171 section inside MACE, she passed Flash and Melissa working side by side on something that looked enormously complicated. "Hey, could one of you two go entertain Jamie for me. He's the guy with the cast on his arm and half his head shaved. Pretty hard to miss. Good guy, funny and probably going through my desk drawers looking for something to steal. "

"My kind of guy!" Flash got up and headed toward the coffee pot. She filled her mega-mug and one of the plain ceramics next to the pot, filled it and headed in his direction.

"Be careful."

"I'm always careful, Sue. Count on it."

Sue heard Flash approach Jamie and say, "Hey, Klingon. Nice ear."

Sue turned to Melissa.

"Any luck in sorting out another lead?"

"Russian or Iraqi?"

"Do I get a choice?"

"You always get a choice, but if you choose Russian, you are out of luck."

"OK, then Iraqi."

"The al Qaida in Iraq shitbirds have a link to another AQ network that seems to be working out of Turkey. I am tracking the internet linkage right now and hope to have something soon. Flash was giving me a hand on the intel side. It seems that SOF has its own networks in Turkey and, surprise, the intel isn't in the Agency databases."

"Imagine that." Sue headed toward Smith's cubicle. She figured it was time to get her daily dose of ass chewing from her boss. She wasn't disappointed.

Smith looked up at Sue as she walked in. He looked as if he hadn't slept in days. Sue was surprised to see Massoni sitting next to Smith. Massoni spoke up as soon as she walked in the space. "What, you thought I was going to miss all the fun?" Once again, Smith gave Massoni the stink eye, but it was only at 50 percent stink, so it probably wasn't all that serious.

Smith turned to Sue. "Hey, O'Connell. How are you doing?"

"As well as can be expected given the fact that I was the target of a car bomb and the assholes just killed my only source to who did it."

"For once, O'Connell, I can't think of any reason to blame you for this operational catastrophe. It was a Klingon safe house, a Klingon source, and the Klingon's got you there and drove you back. I'm thinkin' the security problem was probably with the Klingons."

"Boss, I am beginning to think the bad guys have a line inside MACE or Baghdad station. They seem almost always one step ahead of us."

"Now, there you go with the negative vibes, O'Connell. You start talking like that and the Klingons aren't going to work with 171 anymore." Massoni was only half kidding.

"Seriously, Sue, you can be certain that the Agency is doing a full scrub of what is going on. DUSTDEVIL was a long-standing source. Likely a decade plus. He survived living under Sadaam. As an Iraqi Shia, you can believe that wasn't easy. So, they have to think about their current operational patterns and that safe house. I would be very careful about suggesting there is a more perfidious reason for this shit. I know you are steeped in double agent mumbo jumbo at this point, but not everyone is a fink, Sue."

"Not entirely everyone, that's for sure."

Massoni said, "I'm not!" Smith gave Massoni another dose of the stink eye.

"OK, now Flash and your pal Nez are out there working hard to find you a target to pursue. In the meantime, I have some notes from Energy saying that they have tracked the radiological material to an old research reactor in Georgia."

"Boss, no offense, but what city in Georgia?"

Massoni was showing off when he said, "Keep up, O'Connell. Georgia, the former Soviet Union republic and now an independent country. Seems to me that Flash already told you that there was a Thuraya track in Batumi."

"How in the world can they sort out where it came from?"

Smith looked down at the report he was reading. "This reads like a bed time story, O'Connell, so I will give you a brief and then assign it to you to read overnight and give me a more thorough briefing in the morning." Smith looked up, smiled and continued, "You didn't expect it to be all roses as you recuperated did you?"

"No, Boss."

"OK, the abridged edition is that after the fall of the USSR, the USG worked hard to track down all the nuclear material that was available in the newly formed states. They took samples of all the material from research reactors and data and it was collected at the Department of Energy. Sometimes it was done in partnership with the new governments, sometimes not."

"That's where we and the Klingons came in?"

"Good Guess."

"And?"

"Well, I think we need to see how in the world material from Georgia made it to Syria, don't you?"

"Roger, boss."

"Basic outline: Get smart. Engage Flash and Melissa on what they already know from the collection. Take the first aircraft you can find to Turkey. There is a daily cargo run to Incirlik. Use the MACE connections to sort out who you are going to work with in Turkey. I suspect the Klingon base in Istanbul or the Navy attaché there, but that would be telling. Istanbul is the most likely intel base following smuggling out of the Black Sea. After that, write and let me know what you find. Oh, try to not to get blown up in Istanbul, ok?"

"Trust me, boss. It is high on my list of things not to do."

"Excellent. Now, get outta here." Sue turned to walk away.

"Wait a minute. You forgot your homework." Smith tossed her the bound copy of the Department of Energy report.

"Thanks, boss."

"If you need help with the big words, you can always call Massoni."

Massoni pulled his best caveman face. "Me like science." Sue had turned away before Smith dope slapped his sergeant major.

Barbara pulled into the neighborhood where Beth's office had rented a house. Not exactly low profile. The houses looked old, expensive and filled with wealthy old Europeans looking for sun. Barbara was pleased that Beth's office had also rented her car at the airport, a gray Mercedes E class. It was fast but boring to look at and just the thing to be another European. The house sat on a ridge line overlooking the port. It was surrounded by a six-foot high wall and accessed through a gate with a PIN code. Barbara used the code and drove inside.

The house was even more impressive once you entered into the small enclosed garden in the front. A pair of pines served as sentries to the garden with roses in the middle. It was beautiful. Barbara walked up to the door with her suitcase. It opened well before she got there.

Jake Longstreet was at the door and said, "Seems you had no problem getting here."

"Nope. Too easy. The hard parts start soon enough."

"Maybe not. We'll see what Beth says, but it doesn't look like any of the targets are here. Come inside and I will explain."

Barbara grabbed her bag from the Mercedes, locked the car, and walked inside. She was not happy that there might not be any reason to be in Greece other than the weather and the food. She found Beth and Longstreet's team on an upstairs patio overlooking the port. The patio had a twenty foot blue striped awning with two tables, eight chairs and five chaise loungers. On the table to her left was a large ice bucket with an open bottle of wine, two bottles of German mineral water and four bottles of Munich Pilsner. Longstreet's team were in khakis and t-shirts, Beth was dressed in a lightweight track suit that had "designer" writing in its lines. They looked like any other holiday makers in Greece.

Beth turned her Ray Ban Wayfarers in Barbara's direction. "Before you chastise us too much you need to know we have been pulling 8 hour shifts on Schloss Beroslav for the past three days. Once we realized they were gone and all we were surveilling was the cleaning staff in both the offices and the house, we decided for a good night's sleep and wait for you on the patio."

"A glass of wine would be nice."

"Just the ticket." One of Longstreet's team introduced himself as Mutt and poured Barbara a glass. It was an ice-cold Riesling.

"So?"

Longstreet took over. "Beth found the house registered to one of the Beroslav front companies. It was a villa in the old Ottoman part of the city. Pretty easy to set up on, so we worked out shifts. Beth and Mutt took the day shift at a café on the cornice. Duke and Joe…" Two other fit 60 year olds raised their hands. "took the mid shift and I took the night shift with Mark." Longstreet pointed to a less fit, more academic looking man with a gray beard and reading glasses sitting at one of the loungers working a crossword puzzle from the London Times. "After two days of this with no sign of life, we decided to do an entry. Mark is our guy for locks, alarms and any other sneaky stuff."

"Sneaky?" Mark's voice was higher pitched than Barb expected. Hard to imagine a professor with that voice.

Longstreet continued as if he hadn't even heard Mark. "Nice villa. Lots of electronic surveillance, alarms and some 19th century locks as well. No challenge for Mark."

"None whatsoever." Mark returned to his crossword.

"It does seem they cleared out in a hurry. Computers were gone. Safe left open. No desk calendars, notebooks or any other material we could exploit."

"That's where I come back into the story," Beth was clearly enjoying this adventure. "It turns out the shell company that owns the office and the house also owns a small inter-coastal cargo ship. Not a lot of tonnage, but enough to make a profit in the Adriatic and the Eastern Med. It left port the day we arrived on 28 May. The ship is called The Minotaur."

Barbara thought about the date and the name of the ship. It was as if they were playing with her. "So, a complete bust."

Mutt finally spoke up. His voice matched his age and physique and the USMC Globe and Anchor tattoo on his bicep. "Not exactly. First, we got a chance to spend a few days here."

Barbara scowled. "And…"

"Mutt, since this is my party, I think I get to talk about the second point."

"Right, Beth. We will be inside." Longstreet nodded to his men and they all walked back into the villa.

"And?" At this point, Barbara was not thrilled with the cat and mouse taking place on the patio.

"And, we did find this in the house. It was addressed to you."

Beth handed her an envelope. Very high-end stationery, embossed with a gothic script B. Addressed in emerald green ink, in old style German or Eastern European handwriting that belonged in the 1940s. Addressed to Mrs. Barbara O'Connell nee' Banfield. It was sealed with green sealing wax with the sword and the shield of the old KGB.

"You already read it?"

"You can see that its sealed."

"And I suspect Mark could and did open it. Among other skills, he looks like a "flaps and seals" sort of guy."

"OK, we are guilty as charged."

"I thought lawyers were tough under interrogation."

"You are my client and my friend, not my interrogator. Plus, we thought it just might be a letter bomb."

"Right."

"Will any other excuse work better?"

"Nope."

"You going to open it?"

"Worth it?"

"We all think so."

Barbara opened the note carefully in an attempt to save the seal. It cracked into a dozen pieces and fell to the ground. Inside was a single sheet of embossed stationery. A hand-written letter in green ink.

Dearest Barbara,

I am sorry I can't be here to meet you in person. We have so much to discuss and so little time left to do so. However, events in Syria have forced me to change my plans and return to Abkhazia. Your daughter played no small part in my problems. I fear my nephews were a bit over zealous when they kidnapped an Army intelligence officer and this led to their demise. They never served with our special services, so patience and forethought were not their strengths.

Now, Barbara, I want you to consider this note a request for an armistice. I have accomplished my vow to avenge my father-in-law by arranging the death of his murderer, your father-in-law. Your husband was a tragic loss that had nothing to do with me and your son's wounds were not the result of any action on the part of the Beroslavs. Mr. Creeter's death was a decision by my nephews who have now paid the ultimate price in Syria. I suspect you will not believe me, but the game we have played is over and any further effort on your part will put us all at risk from more than one set of enemies.

Do we really need to continue?

Yours very sincerely,

Anastasia Beroslav

Barbara looked up from the letter. Beth was watching her. "What do you think?"

"I think we missed a chance to end this once and for all."

"And her story that she was not part of Peter's murder?"

"One of the risks we take in this game is assuming we can make sense of a random world that is filled with villains. They killed Peter's dad and they killed Max. She says they didn't kill Peter. I don't believe her, but even if it was true, I am not about to let it go with a simple letter saying she is done and I should accept it." Barbara paused and then said, "Beth, this wasn't cheap and we got nothing out of it. I'm sorry I asked for your help."

"Well, my firm ended up learning more about the Russian mafia in the Eastern Med and I got to hang out with Longstreet and his gang of action heroes. Consider a break even from my side."

"Thanks."

"Can we at least have a day or so here before we return to your Cold War?"

"It's going to take me that long to figure out what to do next."

"Excellent, then let's bring the boys back and continue to enjoy Greece."

Barbara knew Beth was irrepressible particularly when it came to men, good food and wine. She raised her hands in surrender.

The Minotaur gently rocked at anchor. Anastasia Beraslov was on the bridge with the ship' captain. "I don't remember us needing a pilot from the port authorities last time when we went through the Dardanelles and anchored in the Sea of Marmara." Anastasia was speaking English to the Greek captain. It was their only common language.

"Madam, I just follow orders. We received a radio message from the Istanbul port authority. They said anchor and wait. Something about the anchorage in the Sea of Marmara. Too many cargo ships and our tonnage makes us vulnerable. We are running empty and that means we get the last anchorage. I suspect it also means we must be prepared to bribe the pilot from the port authority when he comes on board. Otherwise, we will sit here until we decide to bribe him."

"Do what you must. I will be below in my cabin. I will send up the money with Dimitri." Anastasia turned and walked out of the bridge.

"Thank you, madam." Captain Scaros hadn't lied too often to the Beraslovs. He often carried some of his own cargo along with their goods, but he expected they knew that he was committing that small sin. Sometimes a few drugs, gems from Lebanon, a few guns to friends in Europe. This time he realized it was the last time he would ever lie to this family who treated him like a chauffeur rather than the captain of a ship.

The pilot boat pulled up at 1800hrs. The pilot stepped off the bright orange pilot tug and on to the gangway on the starboard side of The Minotaur. Dressed in the uniform of the Istanbul port authority, the pilot climbed the stairs and met the captain at the rail. "Permission to come aboard, captain?"

"Permission granted, lieutenant." Scaros had to admit his new client was much more polite that the Beroslavs.

"Is everything prepared for departure?"

"Yes, sir. We are ready to enter the Dardanelles."

"Excellent." Scaros never saw or heard the suppressed round from the MSP Grozha silenced pistol that entered under his chin and killed him.

The "Istanbul pilot" keyed the concealed mike. He spoke Russian. "All clear, come aboard."

Five Russian Navy special forces operators climbed from the pilot boat to the deck. They were dressed in gray jump suits, black high-top trainers and grey balaclavas. As they moved, the equipment attached to their load bearing vests made no noise at all. Two were armed with suppressed OTS-14 carbines and two were armed with suppressed MP-442 Grach pistols.

"One crewmember. Four principal targets — most likely in the cabins aft," the officer in the pilot uniform said. The lead operator nodded. He waved his right hand and two of the operators moved toward the bridge and forward and he and the two remaining operators moved to aft, found a hatch and entered. The "pilot" moved behind the two headed to the bridge. There they found a very puzzled Dimitri with a pouch carrying $1000 in twenty-dollar bills. The first operator shot Dimitri — one in the head, two in the chest. The rounds made less noise coming out the pistol than Dimitri's final exclamation.

"Which of you can run this tub?"

"That's my job, sir." The operator with the carbine spoke.

"Once we have finished all the targets, weigh anchor and head into the channel."

"Yes, sir."

The man in the pilot uniform moved back on the deck and waited. Five minutes later, the senior operator returned to the deck.

"Principals eliminated. We didn't find the crew member."

"We got him on the bridge. Move all the bodies into the hold."

"Yes, sir."

"Did you find the Thuraya phone?"

"Sir." The operator handed the phone to the officer in the pilot's uniform.

He pocketed the Thuraya and walked down the gangway and jumped back on the pilot boat. He turned to the senior Navy commando waiting on the deck. "Take the charges and the special material up to Mikhail. He knows what to do with it. Also, take the bag with the civilian clothes up to the team. It won't look right if you pull into Istanbul dressed in raid uniforms."

"Yes, sir."

"And weigh anchor and sail into the Sea of Marmara. Anchor in the agreed position and wait until you hear from me."

"Yes, sir."

The man in the pilot's uniform walked down the gangway and returned to the small bridge of the pilot tug.

"Please take us back to Istanbul."

"Yes, sir."

Once the tug was underway, he walked out to the uncovered deck and turned on the Thuraya phone. He dialed a number in Thessaloniki.

"Yes?" The voice spoke in German.

The man in the pilot's uniform responded back in German. "Close the deal."

"As you wish."

He hung up and checked the power on the Thuraya. He was instructed to keep it on and charged. He needed the signal to continue to run for several days while they were all in the Sea of Marmara.

On The Minotaur, Captain Mikhail Polostov was on the bridge with his senior NCO, Ivan Savaroff. Ivan was at the controls and weighed anchor. In the engine room, Boris, another of the team, responded to the electronic commands from the bridge. Lieutenant Sasha Wegmann entered the bridge and said, "Mikhail Mikhailovich, what was that accent?"

"Sasha, I have been thinking about this since we started working with this contact. Sometimes, he seems to pronounce words like a Pole speaking Russian, sometimes like an American speaking Russian. I can't quite figure it out."

"Mikhail Mikhailovich, why do we put up with that outsider?" Ivan looked out from the bridge as the ship started to move.

"Ivan, my friend. He is certainly a foreigner, but he is most certainly from the Special Services. If we don't obey his commands, we can end up like the passengers on this ship. This is a long running operation and our job is to make it happen." Polostov paused. "All I know and all I want to know is he is sleeper agent working deep inside the intelligence services of the Main Enemy, and he talks directly to the seniors at the Aquarium."

Both Polostov and Savaroff were just old enough to remember the days of the USSR when the GRU headquarters was referred to as the Aquarium while Wegmann was a newcomer to the unit. All three had fathers who were Navy special forces during the Cold War and all three knew that like it or not sometimes they worked as the action arm of the Soviet military intelligence headquarters of the GRU and sometimes for the KGB.

Little had changed with the end of the USSR and the rise of the Russian Federation. Polostov thought of an Afghan phrase he learned while serving with a deep cover unit assigned to the International Security Assistance Force. When speaking about the dozens of changes in government in Kabul, the Afghans said, "The donkey is still a donkey, they just changed the saddle." Polotsov felt that way about the various changes in the GRU as the FSB rose to prominence under President Putin. Still, life as a special purpose troop commander was pleasant enough. "Sasha, if we have to occasionally work directly for these cloak and dagger types, it is a small price to pay, no?"

Sasha and Ivan nodded as Polotsov felt The Minotaur go underway headed into the Dardanelles.

Sue walked over to Flash's work station. They were both in their workout gear. Flash was wearing a black Under Armour T-shirt 2 sizes too big and a pair of black sweat pants. Sue was in similar kit except in Navy. Sue thought they looked like a pair of dancers instead of a pair of Special Operators. She gave Flash a cup of coffee.

"So, what do we know?"

"Jamie is not married and he is a pretty interesting guy for a guy and...for a Klingon."

"About work, Flash."

"Ah, well, work. OK, we know the Thuraya signals point to a smuggling route that is conducted by ship. Looks like the network sometimes runs from Sochi in Russia to Batumi in Georgia to northern Turkey and then into Iraq and sometimes from Georgia through Istanbul to Beirut. I can't say why there are two routes. One interesting point is there is a parallel signal that runs almost directly from Thessaloniki to Sochi."

"Parallel?"

"Two Thuraya phones, purchased and managed over the last year by the same bank account. Melissa and I agree it can't be a coincidence. No name attached to it. Just a simple name - Black Sea - Dardanelles Cargo GMBH. It is registered out of Hamburg. The Euro account is in Hamburg and Thessaloniki."

"And that helps me...how?"

"Might be interesting that the primary phone is on a ship right now anchored in the Sea of Marmara off Istanbul, no?"

"Yes. Any chance of a picture?"

"Already requested. It turns out there is a Royal Navy Orion flying back from Incirlik to RAF Akrotiri right now. Our Brit cousins did the tasking. We should have something soon if it works out."

"Flash, you deserve another cup of coffee."

"I deserve more than that, girl, after sweet talking the Brits but coffee will serve for now."

An hour later, the digital photos arrived. They showed multiple shots of a short haul cargo ship at anchor in the Sea of Marmara with an Istanbul Port Authority tug anchored next to it. Flash and Melissa walked over to Sue with the photos and a write up from a mix of intelligence sources and maritime registries. Flash hadn't changed clothes. Melissa was in khakis and a t-shirt and OD green crocs.

Flash offered Sue a folder and said, "Here's the photos and information on the ship - called The Minotaur. Registered out of Beirut though not flagged as a Lebanese ship. I think it is Liberian flagged, but honestly that's a little murky. As expected, owned by Black Sea - Dardanelles Cargo. Temporarily anchored in Istanbul awaiting cargo. Next port registered on the shipping manifest is Batumi. Three days in Istanbul and then she sails through the Bosporus and into the Black Sea. The Thuraya still in use on the ship. Registered crew of five with four registered passengers - the owners of the company."

Melissa started in as if cue. "This cargo company was created back in the 1980s. It has been listed in the community since 1990 as either a KGB or SVR front company or a Russian mafia front company or sometimes both. Nobody in the IC ever wanted to give up the intelligence to get an Interpol investigation going..."

"Figures." Flash was no fan of Big IC as she called it, but in this case she appeared to be pulling Melissa's chain. Melissa responded by sticking her tongue out at Flash.

"So now we have an interesting challenge. We now know from all our intelligence that this outfit has been smuggling weapons and equipment and now radiological material to terrorists. That doesn't mean we can prove any of this in a NATO country court unless we give up our sources. So, what do we do?"

Sue took a few seconds to assemble the right answer. "Melissa, we aren't going to arrest these guys. We are going to either capture them or kill them. We might even sink the ship. They fall into the category of enemy combatants as far as I'm concerned."

"And Smith will agree?" Flash looked a bit worried about the blunt response.

"I guess we will have to send this up the MACE chain of command, but I'm thinkin' there will be no love lost after what we saw in Syria."

"We better get hopping then because we have three days before that ship moves again."

"Well, I don't know about you girls, but before we do anything I'm hitting the showers. No need to smell up the office when you are trying to pitch an idea."

Flash turned to Melissa. "You might want to put on shoes."

Barbara sat on the patio looking out on the harbor. It was mid-morning and already hot in the direct sun, but under the patio awning, it was still cool. She was sitting alone trying to put together a plan that made sense. Pursuing the Beroslavs from here didn't make any sense, but returning home wasn't satisfying after coming this far.

"Deep in thought?" Longstreet hadn't made any noise as he approached. Barbara thought she was aware of her surroundings and then - poof - Longstreet was there.

"Trying to figure out what we do next."

"Want a suggestion?"

"Right now, any idea would be more than I have in my head."

"Have you sorted out why the target knew we were coming?"

"I have a couple of thoughts..."

"Care to share?" The sarcasm was pretty thick.

"It seems that every time I am close to forward progress, something bad happens. My father in law, my son, Max, and now this. Hard to imagine it is chance."

"Or you have the worst luck I've ever seen."

"There is that..."

"So?"

"So, there is a Russian mole in the system that either I or my daughter or my son knows."

"Not on my end."

"That's certain. Not because I think you are a good guy...."

"Though I am..."

"But because you weren't part of this at the front end of our bad luck."

"Thanks for the vote of confidence."

"You're welcome. Anyhow, what would be the point? Even I don't think the Russian mob or the SVR think I'm so important that they would surround me with their sources."

"Good to hear you have a reasonable sized ego for a Klingon."

"Thanks."

"On your trip to Vienna, who did you meet?"

"A colleague who is playing a very dangerous game."

"Spy?"

"Yes."

"Trust him?"

"Her. I don't know."

"Great."

"Anyone else?"

"An Agency guy from the CI shop."

"Worse."

"Careful. My son is a Bureau guy working in a CI shop."

"But we can eliminate him from the suspects because he was shot."

"Not because he is my son?"

"Just sayin' that being shot is a clue he isn't part of the problem."

"So, Mr. smarty pants, what is your suggestion?"

"First, you need to know right now we are the hunted not the hunters."

"Evidence?"

"While you were whooping it up with Beth and the mates..."

"So unfair a characterization..."

Longstreet continued as if not interrupted. "I did a bit of a recce last night. Mark was convinced we were under surveillance. He is a paranoid bugger, but he has technology on his side and he was right. The house is under surveillance. First time since we arrived. At least a four-man team per shift. Four new ones out there this morning. Not Americans, not Greek. Russian speakers though they look Turkish or Central Asian. They didn't see me during their shift change. Sloppy. But if they had been careful, Mark wouldn't have captured their cell-phones with his magic box."

"Suggestion?"

"We get out of here as soon as possible. Definitely before tonight. They may be just surveillance or..."

"Yeah. I get the picture."

"I recommend going home, but if you have another suggestion, I'm open."

"I don't think there is much sense in going after the Beroslavs in the ship."

"Beth may have dough, but I think a yacht might be a bit over the top. If you want to know more about these guys, we could drive for a bit before we catch a flight."

"Why not?"

They had a quick meeting of the team and all agreed that it was time to leave. They would drive north into Macedonia, keep going north to Vienna and fly home from there. They split up, packed and loaded the cars. Barbara, Beth and Duke were the drivers. Longstreet paired with Barbara, Mutt with Beth, and Duke, Mark and Joe were the trail team. Just before they left, Beth handed Longstreet and Joe a small canvas bag that matched one in her own hand.

"Don't ask how. Also, don't worry if you have to throw it in a river or over a cliff."

Joe opened his like he was a kid on Christmas. "Beth, you shouldn't have! My very own Browning High Power from Nazi occupied Belgium. Fifty plus years old. Will it work or do I expect it to blow up in my face?"

"It's not older than you and I tested them myself before I paid for them. They have been around a while."

"No doubt." Longstreet looked at the weapon - it had been recently oiled. He did a quick function check, loaded it, chambered a round and carefully dropped the hammer and put the safety on. "Condition two, gents." Mutt and Joe followed Longstreet's instructions and placed their weapons in the same condition.

"Please wipe the weapons..."

"Before we ditch them," Mutt put on his best example of I'm hurt face. "Beth, we know how this works."

"We know how this works." It was all Mark said as he climbed into the back seat of the black four door Skoda. Barbara noticed he carried a small duffle with him into the back.

"Tools of the trade." Longstreet said to Barbara as they loaded into the Mercedes.

They left shortly after noon. Beth and Mutt in the sky blue Audi

A6, followed by Barb and Longstreet in the Mercedes and Duke driving Mark and Joe in the Skoda. They didn't need a complicated route to reveal surveillance. The 19th century roads headed north out of Thessaloniki did all the work for them. It was a half an hour before Longstreet dialed Mutt and Joe and set up a conference call.

"2, 4 this is 6."

"Check." Their two voices digitized and passed through the speaker phone sounded like robots to Barb.

"What are we seeing?"

"Black Merc. C class. Euro plates. Four Bravos." Joe's voice.

"I caught another Charlie pull in as we left the town. Silver BMW 5 series. Euro plates. Three Bravos." Mutt's voice.

"OK. Let's stretch them out a bit. 2, let's pick up the pace."

Mutt obviously told Beth to move out because she shot forward moving from 100 KPH to 150 in a few seconds. Longstreet turned to Barbara. "Close the gap to one half car length." Barbara did as asked and saw Duke in her rear view mirror do the same. "2, keep that speed for the next 20 kilometers."

"Check, Boss."

Barbara thought of herself as a good driver, but the pace and the distance between the cars was nerve wracking. Five minutes later, the BMW moved into the left lane to pass Duke.

"4, let this one go. You handle the Merc."

"Check."

Barbara watched the ballet as the BMW worked to pass the three cars with Beth speeding up to 200 KPH at the instruction of Mutt. In the side mirror, Barb saw the Mercedes begin to close on Duke. She could see Mark doing something in the back seat.

"Eyes on the road, O'Connell. They have their job. We have ours."

Barbara refocused her attention on the BMW as it passed them. Three very rough customers in black suits and white open collared shirts. Given their neck sizes, Barbara was not entirely sure they could wear neck ties. She heard tires squeal and watched in her rear view mirror as the Mercedes spin off the road.

"Road nails. Easy to make. Mark whipped together about fifty while we were waiting for you to arrive. Part of what he had in the bag." Barbara checked the mirror and saw Duke closing in again.

Longstreet said, "Pull behind the BMW." She followed the instructions and pulled into the left lane behind the BMW as she watched Duke pull into her former position in the right lane behind Beth. There were now four cars racing down the road at 200 plus kilometers per hour. The passengers in the BMW didn't know for sure what was happening, but they looked worried.

"2, accelerate on my signal. 4, you know the drill."

"Check." Two digitized voices.

"Now."

Beth floored the Audi and it shot down the road at well over 250 KPH. Longstreet turned to Barbara and said, "Aim at his right rear tail light. Hit him just below the light. Just a tap."

"We will hit Duke."

"No, we won't if you pay attention. Duke is watching you. Do it now."

Barbara hit the Mercedes. At the same time, Duke angled in and hit the Mercedes on the right front wheel. The two actions sent the Mercedes in a spin that ended when the driver tried to correct, over corrected instead, and the BMW rolled and ended upside down in the ditch on the side of the road. Barbara kept the car on the angle they used to hit the car and she returned to her place behind Beth. Duke kept the Skoda on the angle he used to hit the BMW and ended up in the left lane just slightly ahead of Barbara.

"Generally, I'm not a proponent of hit and run, but in this case, I think it makes sense." Longstreet spoke into the phone, "Ok, let's return to legal speed and distances. 4, slow down and get into the formation. Also, keep a watch for more Charlie's but I think we are good for a while."

Barbara realized she had been holding her breath. She exhaled and took two quick breaths.

Longstreet looked at her. "Now, wasn't that fun?"

"A bit dramatic, but satisfying. I think it's clear that the Beroslavs really didn't intend to let this go."

"Thank you, Dr. Science." Barb reached over and punched Long-street in the shoulder. "Now we have to figure out who was running the operation against us. I do have a couple of ideas, but I have to make a couple of calls first."

"Let me know when you figure it out. I want to meet him personally and have a...conversation."

"I'm not sure I want to see that conversation."

"Count on it."

The local supply boat pulled up next to The Minotaur. The Russian Special Services agent and another member of the Russian Navy team walked up the gangway on to the deck. Polotsov shook the agent's hand and welcomed back his team member. Ivan and Boris were working the deck crane to lift the aluminum container from the supply boat to The Minotaur.

"It was just as you said. We have been under surveillance and I think they put a limpet tag on the ship last night."

"Excellent. The lions have found their prey."

"Sir?"

"This is all part of a larger plan, Captain. We are simply setting up an ambush for a team that has been disrupting our operations for the better part of a year. They think they are hunting us. Actually, we are hunting them. The container has your zodiac and the automatic pilot software for the bridge. You need to leave tonight at 2100hrs and head to the Black Sea. Before you leave the Bosporus, engage the autopilot, set the timers on the scuttling explosives for 0300hrs. Set the intrusion alarms so that they initiate the scuttling charges if tampered with before 0300hrs and then leave the ship. The Minotaur will do the rest on its own."

"Sir, you don't have to encourage us to leave the boat. The cadavers down below are starting to smell."

"No doubt, Captain, no doubt." The agent walked over to one of the radio masts on the deck. He pulled out the Thuraya phone that he had taken from the Captain, turned it on, insured it had a good satellite link and then taped it to the mast with black duct tape. "This is our final scent mark for the lions. They have already nibbled at the bait by placing the tracking device. With this on, they will know they have the right ship and the right people on board. The rest is up to you and your team. Good luck." The agent offered his hand, shook Polotsov's hand, turned and walked back down the gangway to the local cargo hauler.

Ivan returned to the bridge. "The zodiac is in good shape. I checked it twice. I was afraid our boss might have tampered with it to make sure we ended up at the bottom of the Black Sea."

"Still a possibility, Ivan. Have Boris do a double check on the explosive charges to make sure they have good timers and won't explode as soon as we set them. Also, when we disembark and head to shore for pickup, make sure everyone is prepared for a fight when we land. He might not want us to end up on the bottom of the Black Sea, but he might want to stage an accident on the Turkish Coast."

"How did we get such a lucky opportunity?"

"Kismet, Ivan."

"Eh?"

"OK, destiny."

"My mother still lights candles for me."

"When we are done, we both need to go to the Cathedral in St. Petersburg and light our own candles."

"Too true."

Sue walked down the lower level of the Galatea bridge. It was just afternoon and moored next to the fishing boats was an old cruiser. All wood. Open cabin. Inboard/outboard motors. Something from Istanbul of the 1960s. Standing on the dock, a man in his 50s, dressed like the rest of the fishermen.

"Madame wishes a ride to the Princes' Islands perhaps?"

"Yes. I have some friends."

"Of course. A picnic on the island! Fantastic!"

"The price?"

"Negotiable, of course." He smiled what would be described in novels as a wicked smile.

Sue looked up to the bridge and waved to Melissa and Flash. They nodded and walked down the stone stairs followed three men carrying wicker picnic baskets. No matter how he dressed Dozer always looked menacing even when carrying a picnic basket. Behind him were two American SOF members from the MACE team. Smaller than Dozer, but Sue suspected just as deadly. The last in line cast off and the boat was underway.

Sue stood next to the owner at the wheel. "When they told me we would work with an Istanbul base officer, I didn't expect.."

"Someone this good looking?" Another wicked smile revealed yellowed teeth and three weeks of beard.

"Not exactly."

"This young?"

"Not exactly..."

"OK, someone who looks like me?"

"Exactly."

"Disguise team plus time on target. I really look like Cary Grant."

"Who?" Flash stuck her head between them. "Dude, you smell like dead fish."

"Cover."

"Remind me never to volunteer for a Klingon undercover assignment."

"And you are...?"

"Flash at your service, mon Capitan." Flash did her worst possible salute.

"Doug." He held out a wrinkled, dirty paw. No one took it. "So, we run up to our safe house at the East end of the Bosporus and wait until dark. I expect The Minotaur to clear Istanbul tonight and then we get to work. Everyone agreed they need to be in international waters before we do our pirate routine so we will track them for couple of hours and intercept them around 0300 tomorrow."

"Aye aye, Captain." Flash was obviously having a too much fun. The two SOF operators in the back shook their heads and then laid down in aft cargo deck of the speed boat. Melissa was sitting close to Dozer using for his bulk to block the wind and spray.

The house was old. It was designed when there were no roads in the area and the occupants arrived by boat. Doug handled the boat with care as he pulled into the dock that was protected from the weather by an extension of the first floor that stretched out over the Bosporus. He said to Sue, "Called a yali. The rich in the days of the Ottoman caliph escaped Istanbul heat to their cottages. Some on the islands in the Sea of Marmara, some on the Bosporus. This one is slightly over a hundred years old." He looked at Flash. "We've updated the plumbing."

Melissa stepped off the boat carrying her backpack. "Do we have stable power?"

Doug looked hurt. "Generators are our back up power. This time of year we run on Solar cells and batteries. Quieter."

"That will work so long as we have converters from DC to AC."

"You used to this?"

"I grew up on the Navajo reservation where we were lucky to have any power at all in our...cottages."

Dozer climbed up on the dock. "You have a cover for the boat?"

"Doors, mate. We have doors." Doug reached over and started cranking a winch that dropped a door to the water.

Later they sat in the living room of the yali. It was furnished with Art Nouveau wooden furniture and Turkish carpets. Doug had pulled out a chart covering the Western half of the Black Sea using Turkish blue plates to hold down the four corners.

Doug started the conversation. "Yesterday, we placed a limpet tracker on The Minotaur."

"You?" One of the SOF members named Nate looked at Doug.

"Who else? I have a friend who owns a fishing boat that stops at every ship anchored in the Sea of Marmara. Sells fish, fresh bread and fresh veggies to the crews - sometimes the Turks don't let any of the crews off - that was certainly the deal back in the old days of the USSR. Been doing this for 30 years and working for us for twenty. Great way to say hello. I bring his boat alongside and he goes up the gangway. Easy enough to plant a limpet and you don't need to wear a wetsuit. And, by the way, they bought supplies for five or six yesterday."

Doug continued. "The beacon is monitored by satellite so we can follow it 24/7 with our own SATCOM rig here." Doug pointed to the wall of electronics where Melissa and Flash were working as he spoke. "So, what is the plan? I got you here, I will get you up to the boat, but it wasn't clear from Headquarters what you intend to do after that."

"Pretty straightforward." Joe Geerson, the senior operator, answered. "We board her, disable the crew, and call for assistance. There is a US destroyer in the Black Sea right now with the rest of our team. They fast rope in from the destroyer's helicopter. Then the destroyer joins us and does a formal inspection. We disappear in the crowd. We have enough right now to detain them and if they should resist, well..." Joe shrugged.

"Three shooters enough?" Doug sounded unconvinced.

"Four." Sue made it clear.

"OK. I get my job is to deliver you and then get clear, right?"

"Exactly. We want to keep you clear of any blowback. Station made it clear your cover can't be compromised."

"What about Flash and me?" Melissa had turned away from the computer screens long enough to ask.

"We need you to set up the downloads as soon as I start the site exploitation." Sue was firm. "That's my part in this equation. Doug, can we get some sort of commo link between here and The Minotaur?"

"I brought two portable SATCOM rigs. Should be good enough for an initial cut of the data."

"We just downloaded the original blueprints for The Minotaur from a Navy database. I can't promise the ship looks like this inside anymore, but the bulkheads and internal walls won't have moved." Flash was happy with the data. She had already started to schmooze Nate and wanted to be sure she had a reason to bring her laptop over to the SOF team. Just by accident, she leaned against Nate when she offered the laptop. Sue looked at Doug. He shook his head and smiled.

Sue said, "So how did you get here, Doug?"

"Joined the Agency out of the Navy. Bounced around a bit in the Gulf and the Horn of Africa working various ocean-going platforms. Studied Turkish and never looked back. I've been Doug also known as Mustafa the engine repair guy for about ten years. Station named me to the Turks which works for most projects. I had to do a bit of running about today to be sure we were clear. This safe house is my own little project. It was our escape house back in the old days when we were bringing folks out of the Bloc and Russia, but it was really run down when I came here. The station and the base give me plenty of leeway and a fair bit of cash to keep a couple of boats and this house available. Not a bad life."

"So long as you don't mind smelling like dead fish." Flash smiled her most coy smile as she looked up from the couch where she was sitting between the two SOF operators.

"Anything for the cause, dear lady."

"Doug, you doing the cyber stuff as well?" Melissa looked up from the wall of electronics.

"Yup. Self-taught with some tech advice from back home. Mostly capturing cellphone traffic in the neighboring yalis. Lots of folks up here enjoying their weekends. Syrians, Iraqis, Iranians and, of course,

Russians. No telling what people will talk about when they are out in the boondocks. Another reason the station lets me putter about out here."

"I could do some modifications here if you like to make it more efficient - just some software tweets..."

"Careful. She will be accessing your bank account."

"Sue, I only did that to teach you a lesson on cyber security."

"Any help you can do will be appreciated. And you can have my bank account records if you promise to fix my overdrafts."

Sue could see this banter was going to go on for some time. "I'm going to get a nap. It is going to be a late night."

"Up the stairs. You are the first one so take any room. They are all the same."

Sue tried not to show how hard it was to climb the old, narrow and steep stairs. She wasn't sure that Dozer knew about her leg and she was sure the MACE guys didn't. If they found out, she was unlikely to be allowed on The Minotaur and that wouldn't do since she had more than one mission to accomplish.

It was 2320hrs when Doug wandered around the yali waking up the team. "They are on the move and will clear our location in about 20 minutes. Come up to the top floor if you want to see them."

There was a hatch on the top floor that lead to a rooftop patio. On the patio were multiple antennas and a night vision device on a tripod peering over the roofline and linked to a laptop. The team sat below the roofline and watched as The Minotaur passed within a hundred yards of the house. They could hear the rumble of the twin diesels and could see two of the passengers on deck. The ship was in no hurry as it cleared the Bosporus and headed into the Black Sea.

"No more than 10 knots" was Doug's only comment as they sat on the roof. They waited until the stern of the ship disappeared in the darkness before they went downstairs.

Once downstairs, Melissa was the first to speak. "We captured two cellphone calls and a large data transmission on their Thuraya. We should get a decryption and translation feed from MACE in an hour. Will that work, Doug?"

"Assuming they keep at 10 knots, we don't need to leave for at least another two hours. We can make 25 knots easily and will give us plenty of time."

Dozer said "Let's empty the picnic baskets."

Inside the first basket they had four lightweight, black climbing helmets with binocular night vision and a video camera, four light armor load bearing vests and four pistols with suppressors: three Sig Sauers for the MACE team and Dozer and a Glock 19 for Sue. In the bottom of the baskets were six sets of flex cuffs and large sand bags for securing prisoners. Doug opened a closet and pulled out two black duffels. In the first were sets of black low profile black life vests.

Doug said, "With the armor and weapons, if you go overboard you are finished. The vests won't keep you afloat but they will buy you time while you ditch the gear. The Black Sea is treacherous, so you will wear these."

"Roger, Doug. Underway raids are no foolin' hard so we get the point." Joe's comment ended any potential argument.

In the second basket, Doug pulled out four mesh vests with a small transmitter attached to the back. Flash explained, "A gift from MACE. A specialized dosimeter sensor. It will let us monitor your exposure to any gamma radiation from radiological waste."

"Allow us to find where they kept the material on the ship?" Dozer looked at the network of wires and small plates on the vests.

"And make sure you don't end up in some hot zone and microwave yourself."

"Nice image, Flash." Sue shook her head.

"Just sayin' you don't want to get too close."

An hour later, MACE sent their first take on the transmissions. "Well, this is interesting." Melissa said as she scrolled through the data on her screen.

"Sharing is a good thing, sister." Flash was sitting cross legged on the Turkish carpet.

"MACE translations on the data include a discussion from Minotaur to someone in Batumi asking for more hot sauce for shipment to Syria. The Batumi end answered with a simple statement of 20 available at a cost of 50. And before you ask, they didn't say 20 what or 50 what - could be 50 or 50 grand or 50 rubles... Anyhow, it looks like they are going back for another shipment."

"Anything else?"

"Cellphone coverage to and from The Minotaur and Istanbul numbers. They have been passed to Ankara station and Istanbul base."

"Thank you!" Doug seemed surprised that the military team at Balad was sharing the take. "How many phones?"

"Your antenna picked up four onboard. That only means there were four turned on."

"No, it means four onboard. My techs set up a capture system that picks up any unshielded phones - on or off. It should mean there are only four on board. Does that make sense?"

"No telling. How many to run the ship?"

"Three at a minimum. But probably a crew of five. The crew other than the skipper would be too poor to have phones. So maybe three passengers?"

"Excellent." Joe was obviously pleased at the odds.

They started an equipment check in the yali. Sue realized this was more of a ritual than a necessity. First you checked your own kit and then your teammate's gear. Sue looked over to Melissa who was watching the ritual. It was probably the first time she had seen the drill. Sue noticed the Agency folks were far less rigorous in redundant equipment checks.

First, everyone donned their internal comms and did a check among themselves and between themselves and Flash who would be monitoring the communications from the house. Next, they donned black nylon flight suits, the U-shaped life vests and the dosimeters. After the life vests were secured, they pulled on the load bearing vests. Joe made everyone confirm they understood the quick releases in case they needed to ditch the armor in the water. The vests had water-proof pockets for the team radios and a survival knife on one side of the vest under the right shoulder and a pistol holster under the left shoulder. They loaded their pistols and holstered and secured them. Finally, they pulled on the helmets and walked down to the boat.

Inside the boat dock in the dark, they tested the NVGs and the video uplink with the computers in the house. Melissa confirmed that the video cameras were in good working order. Waiting for them in the boat dock was Doug dressed in the same local garb he had worn all day, wool sweater, dark green trousers and a watch cap. The only change was he was now carrying an aged Browning High Power in a shoulder holster that looked like it was made sometime in the 1950s. He also had on one of the low-profile life vests. They opened the door to the Black Sea, cast off and left in the dark. Sue noticed that the boat was now much quieter.

"I put on some special mufflers on the engines. Once we get closer, I will switch to battery powered engines — this little boat has plenty of surprises." Doug smiled in the dark as he pushed the throttles and the boat jumped in response.

Twenty minutes after they left the yali, Doug spoke to Joe. "Beacon shows us to be about three miles out coming up dead on the stern. We are about an hour earlier than your schedule. What do you want to do?"

"Let's do it. I'll contact Flash." Joe walked aft and touched Nate on the shoulder.

"Contact Flash. Tell her we are in position."

"Check." Nate threw a toggle switch on the main radio set in the boat.

"Brownstone, Brownstone, this is Otter."

"Otter, go ahead."

"Boathouse, I say again boathouse."

"Roger, otter. Boathouse. I will contact Mahan. Safe passage, otter."

"Thanks, Brownstone." Nate turned to Joe and passed a thumbs up.

"Doug, can you run this last distance on batteries?"

"Joe, we can run six hours on batteries."

"Switch over, please."

Doug throttled down on the engines and then shut them off. The boat settled in the water and the night was suddenly completely quiet. He threw another switch and worked a separate set of throttles and the boat jumped forward again at nearly the same speed. The difference was there was no engine noise.

Joe walked back to Nate, Dozer, and Sue. "We are a little early, but it doesn't make any sense to wait. Switch on the NVGs and the video up link. Set commo to the full net. We should be coming up on target in a couple of minutes. Remember the plan. Nate and I board first. We handle the command deck. Sue and Dozer stand by and then we work through the cabins in buddy teams. Got it?"

The three nodded.

Doug's voice carried from the cockpit in the front. "One minute."

The Minotaur was a large grey mass in front of them. The sound of Diesel engines from inside the hull rumbled across the water. Doug was taking care to stay aft of the ship and away from the bow wave that was angling out from the inter-coastal hauler. In the NVGs, the ship looked grey green and the waves sparkled. Doug brought the boat gently up to the hull of The Minotaur next to the gangway. Joe used a boat hook to capture the bottom step of the stairs and pulled the ladder down while Doug matched the speed of the ship. Dozer held the ladder while Joe and Nate climbed up the gangway. Sue followed and Dozer climbed up last. Doug pulled away, but stayed within 20 meters of the ship.

"Brownstone, Otter."

"Roger, Brownstone. Cutlass, I say again, Cutlass. Confirm you have video."

Back at the yali, Flash turned to Melissa. Melissa gave her a thumbs up. She was looking at a computer screen split into four green images from the video cameras mounted on the four helmets. Each helmet was marked with a name. On a second screen, there were four graphical feeds from the dosimeters. So far, all were flat line.

"Roger, Otter. We confirm cutlass. You can RTB."

"Brownstone, I will wait here a bit before I return to base. You never know."

"Your call Otter." Flash switched to the second communications network. "Mahan, Mahan. This is Brownstone."

The communications link from the USS Mahan was twice as loud on the speaker.

"Brownstone, this is Mahan."

"Cutlass, I say again, Cutlass."

"Roger, Brownstone. Mahan out."

Inside the USS Mahan combat information center, the chief petty officer on duty flipped a toggle on his workstation. "Captain, Brownstone just transmitted Cutlass."

One deck up on the bridge, the Captain answered. "Roger, chief." He turned to the lieutenant on the bridge. "Prepare for flight operations. I will be down on the flight deck."

"Aye, aye, sir."

Five minutes later, the Captain was in the helicopter bay. The bay was filled with red light — allowing everyone involved enough light to work, but the red light limited the loss of night vision. The flight operations team had pushed the helicopter out of the bay and returned the helicopter blades to their normal positions. One of the Navy aviators and their two crew chiefs were walking around the helicopter conducting their initial flight check. The other aviator was starting the engines. The helicopter bay filled with the sound of turbine engines and the smell of jet fuel. The Captain walked over to the SOF lieutenant working through a final equipment check with his team.

The captain walked around the row of SOF operators. "Norris, you guys ready?" It was hardly a question that needed to be asked, but as the skipper, he felt it was necessary. It was part of what was called the Rickover rule, named after the father of the US nuclear navy: a commander never gets what he expects, he only gets what he inspects.

"Yes, sir. Six of us will link up with Joe and Nate onboard with the two MACE team members. We secure the bridge, shut down the engines and wait for you. Once the Mahan is alongside, we bring in the SOF forensics team. I expect most of the work will already be done by Joe and Nate before we fast rope down to The Minotaur."

"Let's hope it's that easy."

"Check, Sir. We will be ready if it's not."

"Aircraft will launch in 10. OK?"

"Sir, we are ready to load anytime."

The Captain returned to the bridge to watch the aircraft launch. From launch to the intercept point was approximately twenty minutes. "Lieutenant. Once the aircraft is launched, make way to the intercept point. "

"Aye, Aye, sir." The Captain looked up from the bridge to watch the silver gray helicopter angle off the deck into the wind and head toward The Minotaur. As soon as the aircraft was launched the bridge brought the ship about and headed in the same direction.

Melissa and Flash watched the screens as their four partners worked along the deck. Joe and Nate were in the lead, their cameras capturing the movement toward the bridge. Dozer and Sue's camera feeds were working in the opposite direction toward the hatch leading to the hold.

"Brownstone. Sierra 6."

"Roger, 6."

"No sign of life yet. We will be on the bridge soonest."

"Roger, 6. Jack 3 and Mike 4, you copy?"

Sue's voice came through the speaker. "Roger. We are headed down the hatch into the hold. I will do a commo check as soon as we are inside to confirm. Please advise if our video feed continues."

"Roger."

"Brownstone, 6. We are on the bridge. It is empty, I say again, empty. The ship is on autopilot. Disabling the autopilot now. We will work down to the crew cabins. "

"Roger 6."

"Mahan, Brownstone."

"Roger Brownstone."

"Cutlass has control of the bridge. Target is no longer underway."

"Roger, Brownstone. Target is no longer underway." The CIC forwarded the news to the Sea Hawk. "Blade one. Please be advised, target is no longer underway." The helicopter pilot in command acknowledged.

Joe and Nate continued down the stairs into the crew quarters. The entered the narrow passageway. Each of the cabin doors was open. Each cabin empty.

"Brownstone, 6. No one appears to be on board. 3 and 4, you copy?"

Sue responded. "Roger." Sue and Dozer were working their way along the walls of the large cargo hold. They were using the infrared lenses on their goggles and had two infrared torches. The hold was empty as well.

"Stand by, stand by. 3 and 4, do not proceed," Melissa had been watching the video feeds when the dosimeters had alarmed. "Your dosimeters are going crazy. There is a dangerous gamma source in the area. Move back toward the hatch that leads into the hold. Do it now."

"Roger." Sue and Dozer walked back from the hold and stopped at the hatch.

"Screw this." Sue shut down the NVGs, flipped them up on her helmet and flipped the IR lens off the torch. She turned on the flashlight and filled the hold with light from her Surefire torch. Dozer had backed through the hatch and was protecting her six as she scanned inside the hold. In the far corner, Sue saw something that definitely did not belong and definitely was not good.

"Standby, Standby. Mike 4."

"4 this is 6, go."

"We have an IED on board, wrapped around a 55 gallon drum of something. The IED is live. I say again, the IED is live. We also have six very dead bodies. It looks to be crew and passengers."

"Roger 4. You and Dozer get up on deck — now. We will meet you there. Otter, you still there?"

Doug's voice came through the speakers in the yali. "Ready for you."

"Roger."

Flash and Melissa watched as the video feeds showed all four operators working as fast as possible to the deck. Melissa had captured the image that Sue had taken of the IED — she was expanding it on another screen in the room.

"Shit. This is definitely NG."

"Got it that it is not good. How not good?"

"Looks like about a 100 pounds of explosives around the drum linked by det cord to what looks like a shaped charge pointing down. There appear to be a half dozen anti-tampering tripwires from the detonator. I can't tell if they triggered one. For sure, it is a scuttling charge. When this goes off, it will both fill the area with nuclear waste and break the ship in half. "

"All, this is Brownstone. Get off the ship now. I say again, get off the ship now."

"Brownstone, we are working our way back on deck and down to the gangway."

"No, I say again, no. I mean get off the ship and into the water, NOW."

"Shit" was all Joe said. He and Nate ran down the deck and slid down the gangway and jumped into the water. They went underwater and then bobbed up. Dozer and Sue followed.

Just as Sue hit the water, the initial explosion rocked the ship. The ship rolled away from the gangway side and split in half. The four operators swam away from the ship as fast as they could. Sue realized she was losing ground. Her prosthetic was not an ideal shape or size for swimming. Especially with 30 pounds of gear. She struggled to get the quick releases on the load bearing vest; every time she reached for the releases, she went under water. She had to stop, fight to the surface, take a breath and start again. It was not a winning proposition. The Black Sea water was cold and the vacuum created by the ship sinking was dragging her under. Sue was near panic. One of her childhood nightmares was of drowning. This was worse.

Dozer's hand grabbed her vest and pulled. The quick releases broke and Sue was clear of the vest. With less weight, the life vest was able to do its job. Sue bobbed to the surface and saw Dozer and, nearby, Doug, the boat and the rest of the team.

Dozer spoke to her. "Time to go unless you have some other reason to stay."

"Not at this precise moment."

"Excellent." He turned, swimming side stroke and pulling Sue along. Joe and Nate pulled him aboard. Sue made it to the boat with very little energy left. When they pulled her aboard, Joe and Nate stared at her.

"What?"

"Sue, your leg?"

"Oh, I think I lost it when the vest broke free. I can get another one."

Dozer turned to the two SOF operators. "That is one tough operator." Doug hit the throttles and pulled away from sinking Minotaur. By the time they were 100 meters away, the ship was gone.

"Mahan, this is Brownstone. "

"Brownstone, go ahead."

"Target has exploded and sunk. I say again. Target has sunk. It was an ambush and Otter's arrival triggered scuttling charges. Otter is returning to base. No need for CSAR. There was no crew on board."

"Brownstone, please send your message again. Please confirm there is no target for Blade One."

"Roger, Mahan. Blade One can return to Mahan. We will be sending video feeds to you soonest. "

A new voice, "Brownstone, this is Mahan6. Please confirm all of our people are safe."

"Mahan6. We can confirm, we have recovered all of our operators and they are on their way back to Brownstone."

"Roger, Brownstone. Mahan6 out."

On the beach on the east side of the Bosporus, the Russian team watched as The Minotaur went down and the speedboat pulled away.

"Not exactly what the special services wanted." Ivan often stated the obvious.

"Not exactly. But, we did our part, documented it with videos and reports, so if that agent doesn't like it, he can send his complaints to the commander. As far as I'm concerned we are done." He turned to Boris who was working a SATCOM rig. "Tell Skorpion we need an extraction. We can be at the beach in one hour."

"Yes, sir."

On the Turkish Airways flight to Vienna, the agent was sitting in business class half asleep. He didn't understand why the Turks put up with the landing positions and times in Europe that meant their flights always left in the middle of the night. Still, he would be on the ground and in Vienna by morning. He would engage his headquarters when he got to his apartment and then, assuming they approved, return to the USA to continue his work there. If all went well, he would be able to start a new operation as soon as he returned.

The conference room in Balad had not changed since the last time Sue visited. Folding tables and chairs in a U-shape with some additional chairs against the plywood walls that created the fiction of a "formal" conference room. The central set of chairs were for SOF commander and his staff. The two legs of the U were for key briefers. In front of the entire audience were three video screens. In this case, the briefing was a special briefing. The duct tape on the screens had changed. The first screen was labeled BRAGG. The second screen was labeled NSC. The third screen was labeled EUCOM — the US European Command.

Sue sat next to Flash on folding chairs behind Smith and Massoni who were on the first set of chairs to the right of the center seats. Smith and Massoni were sitting in front of a paper "tent card" labeled 171. Next to the 171 team was the MACE team leader for their most recent effort in the Black Sea. Behind him sat Joe and Nate. Finally, at the end of the table was the SBS contingent. Dozer and George sat behind an officer who they called "a Rupert" which didn't sound like a positive term. Across the room, Sue could see the CIA card with the COS from Baghdad sitting at the table, a senior Agency officer assigned to SOF and, behind them, Melissa and Jamie — still in his body cast holding his arm straight out from his chest. His ear seemed to be healing. From across the room, they couldn't see any stitches. Next to the CIA team was the tent card titled DOE — a team from the Department of Energy. Sue hadn't been introduced to any of them so she whispered to Flash.

"Know any of the Energy guys?"

"You kidding me? They have kept those guys in a box inside a box on Balad the whole time we have been here. Notice the pale complexions. Very secret team." Flash turned to Sue. "By the way, when were you going to tell me that you had a prosthetic?"

"When were you going to ask?"

Flash rolled her eyes. "Note to self: Always ask your team mates if they have all their parts. Useful information."

"Hey, does it matter?"

"Well, it was a little hard to cope with when I saw you get off the boat."

"By the way, why isn't Doug here?"

"Really? Can you imagine him cleaning up enough to attend this sort of meeting? I think he would rather eat ground glass."

"Too true. Here comes the boss."

Everyone stood up as the SOF commander arrived. Tall, bone thin, and intense, he was also terrifying to any briefer because he was super smart and could smell bullshit inside a briefing the way a tiger smells its prey. The good news was he also was exceptionally polite and if you knew what you were talking about, you could count on him talking to you more as a colleague than a three-star general.

"OK, folks. Let's get started. Do we have connectivity with Main?"

The first screen filled with the SOF Chief of Staff. "Yes sir."

The second screen opened and series of men and women in Washington power suits appeared. "NSC staff here, General."

"Excellent."

The final screen opened and a Navy Admiral and his staff appeared.

CG/SOF said, "Sir, thank you for taking the time today. I wanted you to be part of this because much of the MACE discussion has to do with your AOR."

"Too true. Thanks for the invitation."

The SOF commander looked around the room. He turned looked directly at Smith. "Jed, are you going to start the briefing?"

"Yes, sir."

The briefing lasted an hour, long by SOF standards. Sue was pleased that Smith handled the briefing without turning to her or Flash. Melissa and Jamie were not as lucky. The COS turned to them to explain the Syrian MACE nexus and how it morphed into a Black Sea operation. The DOE personnel explained in detail what they knew about the source of the radiological material that, for the first time, Sue found out was research reactor waste from Sochi, Russia. They also offered, as much as they could, how it entered into the black market based on their analysis and the work from the MACE team. The NSC personnel were very supportive of what MACE had accomplished in the last few weeks. The Admiral listened to the briefing and asked some questions to the DOE team.

At the end, the SOF commander summed up. "We face an ongoing threat from radiological weapons, but for now, it appears that this specific network has been disrupted. Please note. I am not saying it has been destroyed, but it definitely has been disrupted as a result of this US and UK partnership. And, I might add, at no small cost to this team. I will defer to the NSC on whether we should keep the MACE program here in Balad, but I know that SOF and CIA resources here in Iraq are needed on several other fronts. Therefore, I am going to recommend…" he looked directly into the camera at the NSC screen "that we focus our attention on other aspects of the terrorist threat here in theater. When the Community determines that there is another network of this sort that needs to be disrupted, I am confident that we will have the resources here to resolve it. In the meantime, we have other targets of importance here that need our attention. I look forward to recommendations from my Command and from Washington." He paused and looked around the table. "Thank you for your hard work and commitment to this program," he stood up and left.

On the walk back to the MACE tent, Sue asked Flash. "So, what's next?"

Smith came up behind them and answered before Flash. "We continue to run assets that will provide the sort of material that allows SOF to find, fix and finish our enemies. I thought that would be self-evident."

Flash took over. "Boss, I think what Sue meant was do we stay or do we go?"

"We pack up and return to the warehouse. O'Connell, on the other hand, has been requested by the COS in Nicosia to return to Cyprus for a short TDY to meet with an asset. Apparently you haven't done enough damage in the Eastern Med. Perhaps Dentmann has another ship that needs to be blown up." Smith was smiling as he strode past Sue and Flash.

"Does he ever quit?" Sue was shaking her head.

"Well, you have to admit that you seem to attract more than your share of drama."

"It's a gift."

"So it would appear. I don't suppose you need a field analyst in Nicosia?"

"It would mean leaving this garden spot."

"I was thinking about buying my own piece of this jewel, but…"

"You can't get the loan?"

"No, money was not the problem. I heard you lived in Akrotiri with the SBS chums. Not a bad crew to live with and then there is the entire RAF contingent to work on as well."

"Let me see what I can do. Since I don't know the mission, I can't really say what I am going to need."

THE MINOTAUR

S ue rode back to Cyprus on an RAF C130 Hercules. The aircraft was empty. She used the opportunity to get some well needed rest. The ride from Iraq was uneventful and Sue didn't suffer from her standard nightmare of discovering she was missing her leg just when she needed to either fight or run. Later, she assumed that the last few weeks working the MACE program had been frightening enough that her internal demons decided to rest. The Hercules arrived at Akrotiri an hour before dawn, so Sue made her way back to her shipping container quarters, took a shower, ditched her clothes from Iraq, and switched into what she thought of as her combat jammies which included an OD tank top and black running shorts known in the SOF community as Ranger Panties. She walked over to the bunk, pulled the camouflaged nylon poncho liner blanket over her and was asleep in minutes.

Her computer alarm went off warning her that there was an incoming secure video conference request. After the multiple time zones travel in the past month, Sue wasn't sure what time it was, where she was, or why the alarm was going off. After a minute of confusion, Sue turned on the lights in her container, looked at the 24hour clock next to the computer, wiped the sleep from her eyes, reset her watch to local time, took a swig from a long abandoned water bottle, used a wet one on her face, smashed her hair into some order and grabbed the first available outfit which was her flight suit. Once she was halfway presentable, she turned on the computer and opened the communications channel to whoever was on the other end.

The first face she saw was Massoni's. The small lens on the laptop at his end made Massoni's head look like a jack-o-latern. Normally, 171 operated a formal camera system. She wasn't quite sure why they were not using their normal technology, so her first question was, "Jim, where are you? You look like a cartoon figure and sound like you are talking from inside a garbage can."

"I love you too, Sue. We are heading home and right now, the boss and I are inside a C17 heading back to Fayetteville. The Boss wants to talk to you, but I warn you, he's a bit brumpy because he hasn't had any coffee."

Sue decided she could use some coffee as well, so she offered, "I can wait if you want to get some Air Force coffee for him."

"Are you kidding? I am a command sergeant major in the United States Army. Do you really think I go anywhere without my own thermos of perfectly brewed Army coffee?"

"Never mind."

Smith's face appeared on the screen. He looked even more distorted and sounded even more annoyed than usual. "O'Connell. I was asleep. Do you know how rarely I can get six plus hours of sleep? A flight from Ramstein to Bragg is a good eight hours. I was looking forward to my rest."

"Sorry, Boss." Sue decided that it wasn't her place to remind her boss that he was the one who called her.

"Here's the deal, O'Connell. We just got word from Marconi and some of the FBI forensics wizards. You may not remember, but there was this Mercedes that was government property that you had blown up when you first got to Cyprus."

"Boss, I didn't blow up the vehicle, it was blown in place to prevent it from being used as a car bomb with me inside." Smith's face disappeared from the screen for a moment and all Sue saw was his hand and a coffee cup.

"Whatever," was all he said. "While you have been on vacation in Iraq and Turkey, I had Marconi fly out to Akrotiri and work with the Brits to check your other vehicles. Want to guess what he found?"

Sue knew this was a rhetorical question, so she waited.

"It turns out all of your vehicles were beaconed and very good, deep implanted beacons. Marconi couldn't say how long they had been there, but it appears it was the source of the surveillance you had months ago. We matched the GSM signal to one of the ones we tracked in both your previous op in Cyprus, SLINGSHOT, and MACE."

Sue wasn't sure if her confusion was based on lack of sleep or the complex tale. "So, it could have been there for months?"

"O'Connell, we can't say for sure. It looks like it was there for at least a couple of months, but Marconi and the Brit gurus are not prepared to say whether it precedes your arrival or not. For sure, this was not a simple magnetically mounted device that you slip on in a few seconds. It was bolted to the frame."

"Owners?" Adrenaline was starting to wake Sue up and she was finally awake and in the discussion.

"That's something our techs are going ot hae to consider. Definitely looks beyond the skills of most of the targets we work against." Sue felt even more concerned that either Smith or Massoni sounded. A sophisticated beacone, possibly linked to Daniel's time in Cyprus? Russians? Chinese? Iranians? Or the Beroslavs? "O'Connell, have you ever parked any of our vehicles outside the compound since you arrived?"

"No, Boss. Just running out of the compound, doing meetings and returning. All rolling car meetings."

In the screen, Smith took a long sip of coffee. He made a face. "Can you believe my tough guy CSM puts sugar in his coffee?"

In the background, Sue heard Massoni cry out, "It's a perfect cup of coffee."

"O'Connell, I already forwarded this information to the COS in Nicosia and to the Base Commander at RAF Akrotiri. I haven't hear from him yet, but the COS' response was immediate. Unlike some people, I guess she doesn't sleep after sunrise…". Smith paused and for the first time looked carefully at Sue's sleepy face. "She said she wants to see you in Nicosia to talk this over. For some reason, she intends to give you a chance to catch up on your long abandoned 171 paperwork. She invited you to join her for Independence Day celebrations at the Embassy. She said Jack Williams volunteered to fly down to Akrotiri early in the AM and then fly back to Nicosia." Smith took another sip of coffee and made another face. "Do you think you can live in Cyprus for two weeks without blowing anything up and, if you have the time, completing some of your reporting ON YOUR 171 CASE WORK?"

Sue could see that Smith was not in a joking mood, so she simply said, "Yes, sir."

"Then do so. Also, enjoy your beach front property while you can.

We are moving all of 171 to Italy and you are going to be doing some legwork for us by the end of the year. I am transferring Ginger to Cyprus. After months in Kurdistan, I figured he could use a break. So, do the needful in Nicosia, do turnovers with Ginger when he arrives in September and be prepared to receive orders from Massoni for the move. Clear?" Smith didn't wait for a response. He continued, "And, by the way, remember to wear your class As for the trip to the Embassy. I don't know what sort of party the COS has planned for you, but the rest of the Embassy is going to be on their best behavior. You too!"

"Yes, sir."

"Out here." The screen went blank.

Sue realized she had two weeks to worry over what this new development meant to her and her operations. She would have preferred to make a run to Nicosia immediately, but it was clear that both her boss in 171 and the COS in Nicosia had other things in mind. She would need the two weeks to start a dialogue with Ginger on when he was coming to Cyprus and when they could conduct agent turnovers.

Sue got off the Defense Attaché's aircraft. Sue was in her class A uniform — short sleeve bouse, black trousers, shined jump boots, and red beret. She was wearing her nylon flight jacket and carrying a suit bag with her navy blue dress jacket inside. Williams walked out of the aircraft. He was also in uniform wearing his leather flight jacket. Sue followed Williams to his personal car parked next to the Suburban — a vintage Jaguar XJ. British Racing Green with tan leather interior. He opened the left side passenger door and let Sue in then walked over to the rear door and threw the jacket inside. His dress uniform jacket was hanging on a hanger behind his seat. He opened the driver's door and got in.

"I found this for sale when I first got here. 1973, V12. The only V12 four door sedan ever made. Former owner was the sergeant major in the Royal Marines here. He didn't take it home because he was certain it would cost a fortune to maintain in Britain. It isn't cheap here, but it is a sweet ride — better than I will ever have when I return home." He turned the ignition key and the twelve cylinder engine responded with a muffled roar. "I offered to drive down to Akrotiri so you could enjoy the ride for a couple of hours, but we all agreed that it would be a good time for a check ride in the our bird. Still, a sweet ride, no?"

"Roger, that." The car smelled of leather and a small dose of old pipe tobacco. The Royal Marine must have smoked a pipe. He probably wore a tweed coat and flat cap when he rode in this dream mobile. Williams put the car in gear and headed out of the military gate of Nicosia airport.

"OK, here's the deal. Today, we are going to focus exclusively on the ongoing angles of ELEKTRA that touch Cyprus. Before you ask, I can't tell you what those angles are. Patty likes to surprise her audience, so I suppose we all get to enjoy the show. Relax because I don't think you have a speaking role in this performance. Just sit tight, keep on her good side, and then we will join the Embassy down on the grounds for Independence Day speeches and fireworks."

"Check, sir. I am glad you said I don't have a speaking role because I haven't thought about ELEKTRA for months. Been kinda busy…"

"I heard that…"

The rest of the trip was small talk as Williams negotiated his prize automobile through the Nicosia traffic and eventually on the compound. They got a very crisp salute from the local guards and an even better salute from the Marine at the main gate — dressed in his best uniform and white gloves. Sue was certain that somewhere on some rooftop in the compound there was probably a Marine in fatigues with a sniper rifle on call, just in case. Independence Day celebrations were ideal for hostile action. The Marine Security Detachment would know that and along with their men in dress blues, there would be men in fatigues ready for action.

Sue and Williams left their flight gear in the car, put on their Class A jackets and headed into the Embassy, receiving another razor sharp salute from the Marine at Post One. Sue expected the meeting to be held in Dentmann's office, but, instead, it was held in a conference room in the basement of the embassy. As soon as she walked through the cipher locked door, she realized it was a going to be a secure video conference. The large screen opposite the doorway was split into four smaller screens labeled "FBI," "CIA," "DIA," and "SOF." Sue didn't recognize any of the faces on the screen except the SOF window. There the screen was shared by the SOF Chief of Staff and Smith. They were both in dress uniforms. It was the first time she had ever seen the SOF chief of staff in his uniform. Her first introduction to Jed Smith at the Farm had been the last time she had seen him in anything resembling a regulation uniform. Smith even had a regulation haircut and no beard. Sue said to no one in particular, "This must be serious."

Williams and Sue sat down at their assigned seats. She noticed that across from her were two seats marked FBI. The FBI legal attaché and Dentmann's Deputy came in and took their seats and about two minutes later, precisely at 1600hrs, Dentmann and Cyzneski took their seats. Patty Dentmann was at the head of the table, Cyzneski between the LEGATT and Dentmann's deputy.

There were no pleasantries.

"Thank you all for coming today. We are going to discuss the current status of the ELEKTRA operation and how it affects everyone in this room. We are under some time constraint here because of the local celebration here and because I don't want to keep you from your own celebrations there."

The heads on the screen nodded and said nothing. Sue had the feeling that she was the only one in the room who didn't know what was going to happen next. Later at the party, she realized how wrong she was about that.

Dentmann continued, "We have been working on some loose ends in ELEKTRA since Chief O'Connell first visited station and had the confrontation with the Beroslav's. It was clear that there was some sort of compromise in the operation here and that compromise almost resulted in the death of 171 case officer O'Connell." Patty nodded to Sue. Sue decided it was appropriate to nod back.

"Of course, the leads we followed through on took us to the most likely link which was another 171 case officer and former Army CI officer named Dave Daniels who went missing shortly after O'Connell arrived and turned up in Syria in a Russian mafia safe house. Daniels was recovered through a SOF operation. Unfortunately, as I told our CI officer this morning," Dentmann nodded to Stan Cyzneski, "Daniels died in Balad from a gunshot wound sustained by his captors before he could be taken into custody. More recently, we have found some additional links to Daniels when we found a hard-wired beacon in one of the 171 vehicles."

Dentmann paused and looked around the room and directly at the camera. "Any comments so far, gentlemen?"

None of the faces on the screen spoke.

"So, where do we go from here? It appears we have patched the hole in our CI defenses, but at this point, it is not clear to me, at least, that we know how much the Russian mafia compromised our operation targeting the GRU. There is certainly some evidence that the Russian government did not find acceptable the Beroslav sale of sophisticated Russian hardware to Sunni extremists. They…eliminated that threat through their own special means. Mr. Cyzneski, any thoughts?"

Stan had been looking at a small notebook while the COS spoke. Sue could see from the other side of the table that he had three bullet points that he had written in the notebook and was preparing to give. "Thanks, Chief. From my perspective as O'Connell's handler, I have a couple of things that I want to raise with the assembled team." He paused and looked up at Sue. Sue wasn't entirely certain, but she thought he might have winked at her.

"First, I think it is nearly certain that the ELEKTRA operation is compromised beyond repair. The link between the Russian Mafia and the Russian security services may be competitive and possibly even hostile at times, but not disloyal. The Mafia know better than to hold back from the SVR, FSB, or the GRU. If they crossed that line, the FSB would use the full resources of the Russian security state to shut down their operations inside Russia and the SVR and the GRU would use their very special resources to do grave harm to the mafia leadership living abroad. So, since we know the Russian Mafia knew O'Connell was a double agent, we can be certain that the Russian security services — SVR, GRU and FSB - all know it as well." He crossed off the first bullet.

"Secondly, the fact that a 171 agent here in Cyprus was already working for the Russians, most probably the SVR, meant that any operation we tried to conduct here was compromised from the start. Daniels would have seen O'Connell's file and passed details to his handlers. They would have been watching her on arrival. The beacon found on the 171 vehicles gives proof to that point. It seems to me that we need to consider a more expansive investigation into the SOF 171 program to determine if Daniels was the only penetration in this relatively new, secret intelligence outfit." Another bullet on the paper crossed off.

"Finally, I want to admit I was wrong when I gave my recommendation to the Double Agent team back at Headquarters that O'Connell was a good choice for the ELEKTRA operation. It seemed obvious given her links to the Agency and her own father's sacrifice, but it turned out that she was too much of a special operator and too little of a case officer to pull off this sensitive operation. It isn't that she didn't try. It is that she wasn't the right personality to successfully pull off what is the most delicate of operations — the double agent operation."

Williams had seen this coming and had put his hand on Sue's right wrist when it started. It was probably the only thing that prevented Sue from reaching under her shirt and launching her neck knife into Cyzneski's forehead.

Dentmann put her hand up at this point. "Stan, we talked about this in advance and I know you wanted to present your position and I have given you some time to do so. I think you have made it clear that how you feel about the case."

"Thank you, Chief," Stan looked around the room and focused his attention on the monitor with the four separate groups of faces. Sue couldn't help but feel that Stan had a smug grin on his face.

The COS looked at the screen. "SOF, I believe you have some additional data at this point?"

The four subscreens compressed and a single face showed up on the main screen. It was Smith. "Chief, while I appreciate Mr. Cyzneski's perspective, I think we have an individual here who can provide some clarity to his second bullet."

Smith backed away from the screen and Dave Daniels face appeared. "The reports of my death have been greatly exaggerated specifically for the benefit of one in the audience."

Sue looked first at Dentmann who showed no surprise and at Stan. Even in the reduced light of the secure teleconference room illuminated most by at large plasma screen, the color appeared to have drained from his face.

Daniels continued, "I have already made my report to both SOF and the FBI. They seem pretty satisfied with my side of the story. What they were most interested in was the fact that I received a European lead for MACE from an Agency CI officer named Cyzneski. I knew Stan a few years ago when I was in Army CI and he was a newly minted CI staff officer working out of Washington. I had no reason to suspect that the lead he offered over a secure call was anything other than guidance coming directly from OGA, sorry, CIA, headquarters. Turns out, it wasn't any of that. Hi, Stan!"

The screen went back to four smaller screens and Dentmann took over once again. "I asked my legal attaché to help us on the beacon that we found on the 171 car. Very home-made, very generic and very clean of finger prints. However, when you opened the beacon and checked the components, we did find some interesting data. It appears that during the wiring process the maker of the beacon stuck a wire through his gloves into his hand. He left a small drop of blood on the beacon. Now, it was old and...well, why don't I let the LEGATT continue the story..."

The LEGATT took over. He was a large man in his late 40s. The classic image of an FBI special agent. He had flat top haircut, freshly shaved face, hands the size of dinner plates. Sue suspected twenty years ago, he had been a middle linebacker in some Midwest University, most probably Notre Dame. He would not be the man you would want to see on your threshold if you were a fugitive from justice. "I'm Ben Nelson, Supervisory Special Agent here in Cyprus. Patty and the SOF team asked if we could get a forensics team on top of this beacon ASAP and luckily, we have a good team in our regional base out of Vienna. They are there mostly to track smugglers and terrorists, but they were more than up to the challenge of taking the device apart and finding whether there was anything we could find out about the person who made it. I was quite surprised when they found the blood on the electronics and even more surprised when they found a full hair follicle in the case — probably pulled out when the perpetrator mounted the device on the car. Given my previous conversations with Patty, I was not surprised when I found out that we had a DNA and blood type match." He looked at Stan. Sue suddenly realized that this was all being stage managed for Stan's benefit. She wondered when he would break.

Dentmann continued, "OK, so now we have one more piece of the puzzle to discuss. We need FBI headquarters to help on that one. " The four screens collapsed and one opened with a very senior FBI agent and a slightly younger, female agent standing behind him. "For those of you who don't know me, I am SAC Jerome Fellows. I am the Special Agent in Charge at Washington Field office. This is Supervisory Special Agent Janice Mackintosh. She runs the FCI squad here.

She has a part of the investigation based on the attack on Agent Bill O'Connell by some thugs earlier this year. "

The screen switched to Special Agent Mackintosh. Sue remembered her from when she served with her folks in Prague. She looked older and more sleep deprived that most of the other figures on the screen, but otherwise, a welcome face. "We apprehended the actual shooters of Special Agent O'Connell in short order. They gave us some additional leads to follow up, but they were mostly links to other gang related criminal enterprises. We expanded the investigation beyond the shooting of Agent O'Connell when Mr. Creeter was killed at the O'Connell residence in the Spring."

Sue heard this and felt a cold knife slide through her ribs and hit her heart. Max dead? Max couldn't die. It was like saying the sun wouldn't rise tomorrow. She tried to keep quiet but she let out a little yelp. Patty Dentmann nodded to Sue and Jack Williams grabbed her hand again.

"When we did the electronic forensics research, we found the assailants were all contacted by a single disposable phone and via email through several internet cafes. Hard to trace except, since 9/11, one of the things the Patriot Act has "encouraged" internet cafes to do is enable the webcam on all computers. Of course, it is only useful if you know a time and a place, but that's the great thing about having the dead assailants' electronics. We had times and places. The rest was just plain, hard work that the FBI is famous for accomplishing. We were eventually able to link the connection to this operator photo." The screen had a blurry but recognizable picture of Stan Cyzneski working a keyboard with a time stamp and the address. It was marked as FBI evidence.

"Thanks." Dentmann appeared to be just about done. "Now, we have one more thing to raise and then we are done. CIA, can you provide something?"

The full screen opened to show Mary Sanderson. Sue wasn't sure what this meant — the entire story was so Alice in Wonderland that this point, she didn't know what to expect. Sanderson was a traitor, so how could she help? "For those of you who don't know me, my name is Mary Sanderson. I'm a senior Agency officer who served for the past dozen years under cover as a part of a long running double-agent operation. It was called LABYRINTH run out of our Counterintelligence Center in partnership with the FBI National Security Division in Washington. There were three cases inside LABYRINTH. Peter O'Connell was AGAMMEMNON and was charged with penetrating the KGB. I was CLYTEMNESTRA, charged with penetrating the GRU, and, as we all know, Sue O'Connell was supposed to be ELEKTRA, also working as a GRU plant. Compartmentation was essential for the success of the operation, so Sue O'Connell never knew I was operating as a double-agent when I attempted to recruit her. Sorry, Sue."

Sue couldn't face the screen. She just stared at the table. Mary continued. "What none of us knew at the time was that LABYRINTH was actually a much more complicated effort on the part of the GRU to identify how the CIA would try to run Russian operations. It wasn't the first time the Russians conducted this sort of thing. In the early days of the USSR, a predecessor to the KGB known as the CHEKA conducted a complicated international operation called "The TRUST" where they created a well-funded, apparently successful anti-Soviet exile and internal resistance movement. It was designed exclusively to draw real anti-Soviet Russian exiles and foreign intelligence services hostile to the USSR, specifically the British Service, into collaboration with the Trust and then, at the right point in time, simply eliminate them or expose them for the fools that they had become."

Mary paused and looked directly at the screen. "We now know LABYRINTH was that type of operation, though it was the first GRU operation of its kind that we know. Previously, complex double-agent operations were all KGB operations. The LABYRINTH operation was started by two very different people in the CIA. One was Sue's grandfather, Peter O'Connell, who blamed the Soviets for killing his wife in Berlin and wanted revenge. He was the perfect, committed, unwitting resource for the GRU. He wanted to punish the KGB and he needed a way to do so. The other founder of LABYRINTH was a Polish exile named Cyzneski. Mikhail Anders Cyzneski. Cyzneski offered O'Connell a plan that would attack the heart of the Soviet intelligence enterprise. O'Connell grabbed the idea and ran with it, creating what appeared to be a successful and potent double agent network targeting both the KGB and the GRU."

"The only problem is that once we started to unravel some of the pieces of LABYRINTH and with the help of our Polish allies, it turned out that Mikhail Cyzneski was the name of a Polish para-trooper who died in the Battle of Arnhem in 1944. His identity was taken by a Soviet sleeper agent in 1945. Cyzneski was really Mikhail Strassman, born in Latvia with a Russian father and Polish mother. We matched the Strassman files from the recovered KGB files cap-tured when Estonia declared its independence. He was a member of the NKVD and then the KGB. The picture matches exactly with the CIA identity card issued to Michael Cyzneski in 1959. He was the Minotaur in the center of the Labyrinth, killing all who saw him," Sanderson paused. Sue wasn't sure, but she thought there was noth-ing positive in her demeanor. Only sadness.

"It was all part of a larger Soviet and now Russian plan to wrap the CIA and, most recently, SOF into knots in search of hobgoblins. Of course, it also allowed them to eliminate some of those members of the Russian Mafia that were unwilling to accept direction from the Kremlin and find members of the GRU who were susceptible to recruitment. The Beroslavs had many reasons for hating the O'Con-nells, but they were being manipulated by GRU handlers in the field as well. The GRU team involved in this effort used the Beroslavs to maintain good relationships with terrorists hostile to the West and neutral to Russia. If they needed to shut down a specific part of the LABYRINTH program, they simply pointed the Beroslavs at that target or they fed the CIA intelligence which could be used to take down the disloyal networks." Another pause, this time Sue looked around the table. Each participant was staring down at the table, except for Stan. He was staring at Sue.

"In the early days of the Cold War, CIA brought a displaced person and his family into the US on a CIA parole in 1958. They did so because this man they knew as Cyzneski helped Berlin base on sev-eral operations. They brought him into the circle of trust and he and his family did the rest. We can assume he raised his family to be the perfect choices for the national security enterprise and the enterprise accepted them with open arms. By the way, Stan's brother is a newly minted Lieutenant Commander in the US Navy and just got assigned to Fleet headquarters in Norfolk. He has been detained by a Naval Criminal Investigative Service and FBI team based, in part, on Mr. Daniel's debriefings."

The screen went back to four. Dentman took over the room and said "So, that's it. Stan, you need to go now." Both the LEGATT and the DCOS grabbed Stan's arms and hoisted him up.

He started to speak. "You were so easy to manipulate. You are in such a hurry to succeed and all we had to do was put leads in front of you. You did the rest. We were good, there is no question of that, but you were the ones who decided that you needed to handle the leads, track down the intelligence. You never really checked to see if there were any alternative solutions. For over twenty years, my family has been operating in your own back yards as resistance fighters in the long war. You will never know how much damage was done."

Stan paused and stared directly at Sue. "You should know that Mary is wrong. We never had anything to do with the Beroslavs. Of course, once they killed your father, everyone in the Russian Special Services realized they were a rogue organization operating on their own. Because of LABYRINTH, we were tasked to eliminate the Beroslavs using the resources of the US intelligence community. We used you to hunt them down. In the end, Sue, you just weren't quite good enough to finish the job. I had to kill the last of them myself with the help of Russian Navy Commandos. They were no longer of any use and that family line needed to end. It only seemed proper that they should end their time on The Minotaur."

Sue couldn't hold back. "Why? It doesn't look like you gained any intelligence at all. It was all disruption. Like some evil game." If it hadn't been for the MILATT at this point, Sue would have been over the table and choking Stan with her own hands.

Stan smiled and said, "Susan O'Connell, how sad. You still don't understand. Of course, it was disruption. And yes, it was a game. The great game between superpowers. We are in a 100 year war with the

USA. Your intelligence and military establishment had the money and the technologies, especially after the sad end of the USSR. The KGB had the power of the Kremlin behind them. Now, that power resides with the FSB. If LABYRINTH created chaos inside the CIA, it meant that there were fewer resources focused on the Russia. If we could disrupt SOF intelligence, so much the better. We were just a small part of a larger operation to disrupt and defeat the entire American Intelligence Community. We are foot soldiers in this war. We never thought about strategy — only tactics and operational art. It was an elegant operation. Now you have to wonder: how many more LABYRINTHs are out there?"

Nelson looked like he was about to use one of his enormous hands to twist Stan's head 180 degrees. Instead, he stood up and grabbed Stan's right arm with considerable vigor, put him in the classic police "come along" arm lock that forced Stan's chest into the table. "He's done, folks. No more speeches." The LEGATT put stainless steel handcuffs on Stan and started to read him his Miranda rights. When he got to one of the subordinate charges of the murder of retired Army Sergeant Major Max Creeter and the attempted murder of Special Agent William O'Connell, Stan flinched.

The LEGATT finished the Miranda statement and then said. "Oh, that's right. You aren't being charged just under the Espionage Act of 1917, we are charging you as an accessory to murder. We don't buy this story that you were not complicit in the murders in Virginia. The US attorney hasn't decided yet if you are also going to be charged under several terrorism statutes. You will be tried in Virginia. You do know that Virginia still has the death penalty, right?" The last time Sue saw Stan Cyzneski, he was being pushed him out the door. She couldn't be sure, but she thought he might have winked at her.

Patty Dentmann looked at everyone left that the table and everyone on the screen. She sighed and shook her head, "Thank you for helping bring closure to the LABYRINTH. Mary, thank you for all the years of working under cover and please accept my apologies for not believing in you. I promise you all, when Cyzneski gets back to CONUS today he will be turned over to the US Marshalls. We have an FBI G4 waiting at the airport to take him home. I hope you are still able to have a good Independence Day. Goodbye." The screen when blank, the lights went up and everyone filed out of the room. It was not a jovial departure.

Sue turned to the MILATT. "Sir, how long did you know?"

"Patty told me this morning just before I picked you up."

"How long did she know?"

"I think she suspected from the beginning. ELEKTRA just didn't feel right to her, but she couldn't figure out why it didn't feel right. The LEGATT was her only confidant. The original conflict with Beroslav on the docks a few months ago when the Russians helped take him out made her wonder about how in the world he knew about you. When she heard about the hard-wired electronic tag on your car, she began to look in Cyzneski's direction. The FBI took over at that point. It took all the pieces to fall into place before she was willing to make a case to her headquarters and ours. You have to admit, it is not an easy, straight line from start to this ending."

"It would appear that it never is with O'Connell's."

"Oh, by the way, there are some folks here who want to see you." They took the elevator up to the main entryway. Waiting in the entrance were Barb and Bill O'Connell and Beth Parsons. Next to Beth was a lean man in his sixties in a dark suit and a Special Forces Club tie. Sue was certain that on his lapel was a miniature Distinguished Service Cross ribbon.

After hugs all around and more than a few tears, Sue asked Bill, "What are you doing here?"

"I'm here because I am doing prisoner escort with the LEGATT." Sue wasn't sure if Bill was happy, dismayed or simply drained of emotion.

Beth was next. "We were brought here in case they needed more evidence. We will be witnesses for the prosecution at his trial."

"Why?"

This time, the man next to Beth spoke, "Because we went out to avenge Max and Cyzneski prevented us from doing so."

The man held out his hand, "Jake Longstreet. I knew Max longer than just about anyone in this story. I owed him that much."

"But what happened?"

"Cyzneski called the Beroslavs up when he suspected your mom was going down to meet them. They got away on their boat, the Minotaur."

This time, Sue had something to surprise them. "Well, actually, they didn't get away. They were killed and their boat destroyed in the Black Sea. Almost got me as well. It turns out that Stan just confessed to murdering them."

"Oh, that's just perfect." Bill shook his head. "I hate this cloak and dagger stuff. Give me a simple set of villains who always respond in the same way."

"Good luck," this time Beth spoke with some degree of cynicism.

"Give me a terrorist to hunt and I'll be happy," Sue was very serious. She paused, "And all along, I thought it was the Beroslavs trying to kill me."

"Well, they might have been, dear, but for more reasons than one." Barb put her arm around Sue and whispered in Sue's ear. "Welcome to the family business, daughter mine."

J.R. SEEGER is a western New York native who served as a U.S. Army paratrooper and as a CIA case officer for a total of 27 years of federal service. In October 2001, Mr. Seeger led a CIA paramilitary team into Afghanistan. He splits his time between western New York and Central New Mexico.

Made in the USA
Middletown, DE
25 April 2023

29128996R00165